No Remorse

by

Robert Crouch

(Kent Fisher Mystery #3)

Best wishes

Robert Crouch

10/07/24

Published by RWC Publishing
Copyright © Robert Crouch 2018

The right of Robert Crouch to be identified as the Author of the Work has been asserted by him in accordance with the Copyright, Designs and Patents Act 1988.

All rights reserved. No part of this publication may be reproduced, stored in or transmitted into any retrieval system, in any form, or by any means (electronic, photocopying, recording or otherwise) without the prior written permission of the publisher. Any person who does any unauthorised act in relation to this publication may be liable to criminal prosecution and civil claims for damages.

This is a work of fiction. Names, characters, businesses, places, events and incidents are either the products of the author's imagination or used in a fictitious manner. Any resemblance to actual persons, living or dead, or actual events is purely coincidental.

Cover by String Design, Eastbourne

For Tamara – friend, writer and inspiration

Acknowledgements

I couldn't have written and produced this book without the help of Dee Johnson, who gave me advice, information and guidance on residential care homes. I will never forget the afternoon we spent plotting how to kill homes' inspectors and residents (in a fictional way, of course!).

My grateful thanks to Liz Bailey, whose editing skills and suggestions helped to polish and improve the story more than I thought possible. I must also thank Kath Middleton and Joy Mutter, whose canny eyes and suggestions also lifted the story and my spirits.

My thanks and appreciation must also go to Will Hatchett, Editor of Environmental Health News, and Jim van den Bos, Communications Officer at Wealden DC, for their continued support, and for helping to spread the word.

Special thanks go to Caroline Vincent of Bits about Books, for supporting the Kent Fisher mysteries and for organising the blog tour for this novel. I'm also indebted to the bloggers who are working with Caroline to review and promote No Remorse through their blog sites and social media. These lovely people are passionate about books and work tirelessly to help authors bring their work to a wider audience.

My special thanks must also go to Jane Prior, of String Design, who produced the stunning cover for No Remorse, and to Debbie Carter, who suggested the name, Nightingales, for the care home in this story.

And finally, I must thank my lovely wife, Carol. Not only does she put up with me talking endlessly about my stories, she also reads and comments on them so the novels are the best we can produce.

One

The old man's grip tightens on my forearm. "They're killing me."

"Who is?" I ask, leaning closer.

His stale breath reeks from the rotting food trapped between his yellow teeth. His voice is weak, but his piercing blue eyes remain defiant. "They know who I am, but they'll never learn my secret."

"Your secret?"

He nods. "I won't tell them, no matter what they do to me."

My gaze drifts back across the lounge to the elderly women in their best frocks. These women spent hours in the salon upstairs, having their hair set, their nails manicured and painted. They perched in the upright armchairs, waiting their turn to meet my West Highland terrier, Columbo, as they did during my first *Pets as Therapy* visit a couple of weeks ago. But unlike the old man beside me, they didn't want my dog on their laps, leaving fur on their clothes.

"Why are they interested in your secret?" I ask.

He chuckles. "It will ruin a lot of people. Important people. People like your father."

"My father? What do you mean?"

His hand stops stroking Columbo and falls to his side. His eyes glaze over. Like a zombie, he stares at the Christmas tree, glittering in the bay window.

"Is everything all right, Mr Fisher?"

Miss Rudolf, the manager of Nightingales, has a smile that bypasses her dark eyes. Smart and precise in a black suit, trimmed with gold lapels, her smooth skin and clear complexion makes her difficult to age. She pulls back her dark hair, allowing only a curl to escape onto her forehead between her pencilled eyebrows. From the way she regards me, I suspect she prefers spreadsheets to people.

"Mr Trimble drifts in and out," she says, patting the shoulder of his velvet jacket as if it's about to disintegrate. "Don't you, Anthony? Drift in and out."

Her slow, emphasised words fail to penetrate his trance. When his head slumps forward, spittle runs down his chin. I lift my dog to safety and set him on the deep carpet, wondering if Mr Trimble should be in a home that can provide specialist care. Before I can give it any thought, Columbo pulls on his lead, straining to meet the next resident, who's managed to smear her teeth with scarlet lipstick.

"Hello, darling," she says, on her knees to greet him. "Come and say hello to Gladys. I'm eighty-four and a half, you know."

Columbo hesitates, sniffing at the halo of lavender that emanates from her bouffant blue rinse. Her floral dress, and the bracelets that slide over her bony wrists, belong to a younger, fuller bodied woman. Twisted fingers, tipped with scarlet, tilt his head to hers. When she speaks to him in a simpering tone, usually reserved for babies, he growls.

"Gladys only wants to give you a kiss."

"Gladys is going to get a bite on the nose," I say, pulling Columbo back.

She glares at me, her sharp eyes confirming there's plenty of life and fight in this resident. She struggles to her feet, ignoring my offer of help, and collapses into her chair.

"I bred champion Standard Poodles, you know."

It might explain her hairstyle, but not what she's doing in a 5-star luxury care home. With an East End voice and big toes poking through her carpet slippers, she looks out of place, like Mr Trimble.

I wonder what he meant about a secret that could destroy important people.

What secret? It's probably a figment of his failing mind, a plea for attention in a home where appearance matters more than friendship. He won't be celebrating the New Year later, if his snores are anything to go by.

Like the decorations and furniture, he looks past his best.

Everyone does. They're living off memories, clinging to a past where growing old and giving up their grand homes for rooms in a retirement home never entered their plans.

Maybe I'm being unkind, having grown up in a damp basement flat, which was almost as miserable as my mother. At school, I soon discovered how appearance and social status mattered if you wanted to belong. I didn't, which meant the attitude of others only reinforced my sense of injustice at a world that had robbed me of my father at a young age.

Except he wasn't dead. And he wasn't my father, as it

turned out.

He had plenty of secrets though, like most politicians, so Mr Trimble could have something to tell.

Columbo tugs at his lead, pulling me back to the present.

"Miss Donavon won best of breed at Crufts." Miss Rudolf straightens the white linen antimacassar, emblazoned with a gold nightingale motif. "Didn't you, Gladys?"

"I'm eighty-four and half, you know."

Miss Rudolf guides me across the lounge, past the conservatory that offers glimpses of the village of East Dean, nestled within the slopes of the South Downs. We can just make out a small corner of the village green through the tiled roofs and flint walls of the cottages below. Smoke spirals from the chimneys and flattens into a haze, trapped by the dense, cold air that creeps off the hills. The weak sun stays over the sea, unable to melt the frost that has accumulated since Boxing Day.

We pass through double doors into a wide corridor, lined with prints and photographs of Birling Gap and the Seven Sisters on the coast a couple of miles away.

She pauses to check her scarlet lipstick in a gilt-edged mirror. "I understand you used to inspect our kitchen," she says, retrieving a pink flower that's fallen from a Christmas cactus.

"I used to inspect lots of kitchens."

"Have you hung up your white coat?"

"Why do you say that?"

"You solve murders, don't you?" She turns the flower in her thin fingers as she speaks. "Environmental health must seem dull in comparison."

"It has its moments."

She crushes the flower and drops it into a black waste bin, trimmed with gold. "But moments don't last."

"Values do."

"We have strong values at Nightingales," she says, strolling on. "Our residents demand high standards of personal care, but with the freedom to make their own choices."

I'm not sure Mr Trimble can make many choices. "Wouldn't he be better off in a nursing home?"

"I'm sure Dr Puncheon, our local GP, would say if Mr Trimble needed more specialised care."

The corridor opens out into a reception area with sofas, a noticeboard, posters of forthcoming events, and a polished oak counter. An alert receptionist with sultry hazel eyes, a cute upturned nose, and short auburn hair watches me approach. Miss Rudolf weaves straight behind the counter, pausing to straighten the framed award for Best Managed Residential Facility 2012.

Like the residents, the home is living off past glories.

I rest an elbow on the counter. "What if Mr Trimble has dementia?"

"Are you playing detective, Mr Fisher?"

"No, I'm wondering why he thinks someone wants to kill him."

Miss Rudolf turns, her expression the epitome of control – unlike the receptionist, who spills her tea. Blushing, she puts the cup down and dabs the tea with a tissue.

"Mr Trimble believes the world is against him," Miss Rudolf says, heading into her office. "Now, if you'd be kind enough to sign the visitors' book before you leave, I need to make some important calls."

The door closes before I can respond.

"Last time, she offered me coffee," I tell the receptionist.

She pulls off her headset. "I can order you coffee, if you'd like to take a seat."

She rises, revealing a slim figure, snug inside the crisp Nightingales' jacket and skirt. Long, elegant fingers gesture to the black sofas, facing each other across a glass table. It's smothered in brochures for Sherlock's Homes, the company which owns Nightingales and four others in the south east.

Her black lapel badge, with her name etched in gold, makes me smile. With a name like Watson, she must have had an advantage at the interview. "Have you worked here long, Louise?"

"About six months."

Her eyes regard me a little longer than necessary. Either she likes me or she wants to tell me something. Before I can find out, Columbo whines and pulls on his lead, trying to get her attention. She drops to one knee and ruffles his fur.

"Does Mr Trimble really think someone's trying to kill him?" she asks.

"He probably watches too many episodes of Midsomer Murders."

"He doesn't have a TV. In his room, I mean."

Several residents in faux fur coats and mittens burst through the front door, chatting about someone's ever-so-young-and-flamboyant partner. They linger in reception, swapping comments about the woman's hair, makeup, jewellery and that short skirt, so inappropriate for church. When one of them beckons, Louise retreats behind the counter, my coffee long forgotten.

I zip up my fleece and head into the cold, leading Columbo across the gravel to my car, parked by the main gate. I lift him onto the back seat and remove his lead so he's free to leap up onto the parcel shelf. The moment I settle in my seat and close the door, I spot a piece of paper flapping under the windscreen wiper. Though tempted to ignore an invite to Weight Watchers or the offer of top prices for my unwanted jewellery, I'm outside a home in the countryside, not a supermarket.

The paper turns out to be a note, printed on A5 paper and folded in half with a sharp crease only a ruler or thumbnail can produce. The large, italicised black print runs across the centre of the paper.

You think you're so clever, don't you?

Two

I look around the car park, wondering who left the note. We're hardly on the beaten track, set halfway up the hill outside East Dean. Nightingales sits back from the main route used by ramblers and dog walkers on their way up to St Mary the Virgin Church, Friston. The florist's van by the main steps wasn't here when I arrived, but any number of people could have come and gone while I was inside.

Maybe a member of staff left the note. In my day job, checking hygiene in commercial kitchens, some people don't appreciate my candour. Maybe someone with a long memory recognised me and wants to make a point.

Maybe one of the residents left the note.

I scan the windows of the home, hoping to see a net curtain twitch. None do, so I slip the note into the glove box and drive off.

"What do you think Trimble meant?" I ask Columbo. *"They know who I am, but they'll never learn my secret.* Do you think he's having an affair with Miss Rudolf?"

Columbo ignores me, more interested in a man in a Barbour coat and wellingtons, striding back from the Downs with his spaniels. I stop the car and call out to him.

"Have you seen anyone suspicious, hanging around the car park?"

The man hurries past, dragging his gundogs away as Columbo barks at them.

I laugh, realising how ridiculous my question sounded. Am I looking for something that's not there, based on a sad old man who's losing his grip on reality? It wouldn't be the first time, or the last. But I'm certain Trimble belongs in a nursing home.

At the edge of the village, I turn left onto the A259, slotting in behind a Brighton bus that crawls up the steep hill, flanked with hawthorn, ash and sycamore. I glance through the weave of bare branches at the grassy slopes of the Downs, heavy with frost. Columbo stares too, imagining the walks he'll enjoy in spring, now that my stepmother, Niamh, has moved to Friston, which overlooks East Dean.

Colonel Witherington left me Belmont, and Meadow Farm in Jevington, in his will after I solved the murder of his wife. The grand house should have gone to Alice, his loyal housekeeper for over forty years, but she's happy with the settlement he left her and her flat above the garage. Niamh, who's had to live with me at my animal sanctuary for the past few months, can't wait to take her furniture out of my barn and transform the Colonel's old home.

I can't wait to wander around my flat in my underwear and not have to search every dresser and wardrobe to discover where she's put my clothes. Frances, who runs the sanctuary for me, can now sleep once more in the spare room. The draughty old caravan she occupies belongs in a scrap yard, but she's adamant about her independence. As I pay her a pittance, I don't want to upset her or lose her.

At the top of the hill, opposite the church, I turn right towards Jevington. I slow down as I approach Old Willingdon Road, where Belmont resides, wondering whether to pop in for a word with Niamh. As the loyal wife of William Fisher, MP, she took care of his personal and constituency business for nearly 40 years. She may have come across Trimble. It's hardly a common name, after all.

She also kept a personal journal in case her husband wanted to write his memoirs one day.

I smile, wondering what secrets she keeps.

"Tomorrow," I tell Columbo, speeding past the turning. I'll ring her later so she can check her records before we talk.

In Jevington, the road narrows and weaves between flint cottages rooted in the chalk. A brief glimpse of St Andrews Church sets me thinking about choirs, carols and Noel, the chef at the Eight Bells, a few hundred yards ahead.

It's only 11am, but the pub's Christmas lights are flashing their monotonous routine. Columbo heads straight for the wall, relieving himself against the blackened weeds. The smell of dead cigarettes, spilling out of ashtrays, drives me inside. I skirt around the bristling arms of a huge Christmas tree, which is bent over where it meets the ceiling, like Doug Leverett, who has to duck between the beams. Broad, bearded, and with a voice that shakes dust off the shelves, he towers over the polished wooden bar, crowded with last night's empty glasses.

"Morning, Kent. You're a bit early for tonight's party."

The poster for the party looks as tired as Doug's bloodshot eyes. Maybe he's having sleepless nights, worrying about ticket sales for the five-course dinner, followed by live music from a rock 'n' roll band called *The Delinquents*.

"They sound more punk than rock 'n' roll," I say, studying the poster of the three young rockers with glossy quiffs and pierced ears, eyebrows and noses

"They're local," he says, pushing back his tousled hair, flecked with silver.

He means cheap.

"The atmosphere will be epic, Kent. I still have a few tickets left."

The stack of tickets on the bar suggests more than a few. "Have you sold any, Doug?"

"There's always a last minute rush."

Usually for the door, if previous local band nights are anything to go by.

"Is Noel in the kitchen?" I ask.

"Where else would a chef be? Say, this isn't official, is it?"

"I thought Noel could cook for me this evening as he won't be doing much here."

"I'd book you to do stand up, Kent, but you'd fall flat on your face."

"Keep an eye on Columbo, will you?"

The sound of Pink Floyd's, *Wish You Were Here*, lulls me down the short flight of steps into the kitchen, where I find Noel singing along, his eyes shut tight. Maybe the pungent fumes from the diced onions on the green chopping board have affected him. They've certainly done nothing to improve his voice. In an effort to remedy this, I pick up the remote and mute the sound.

He opens his eyes and smiles. "All right, Kent? Long

time no see."

Noel's in his twenties, though he looks more like a Status Quo fan with his long hair, pulled into a ponytail. His pale, thin face tells me he should get out more, but he's happy with his music and his cooking.

I stroll across to the bubbling pan on the gas range. "You won't need that many potatoes tonight."

"Doug will drop the price mid-afternoon, word will spread, and people will turn up. They always do. So, what brings you here?"

"Didn't you chef at Nightingales?"

"For a few months, sure. Why, you got a problem there?"

"Why do you say that?"

"You don't do social calls. What do you want to know?"

"I take my dog there to entertain the residents. It's only our second visit, but there's something odd, something false about the place. How did you find it?"

"Apart from the penny-pinching, lack of staff and unrealistic demands, you mean?" He laughs and picks up his knife, ready to start on a second onion. "We were always short of staff, Kent, even though we had hygiene certificates on the wall for nine people. I never had more than two women helping me, and they used to chatter away in Estonian, or whatever language they spoke."

"Didn't they speak any English?"

"Not in front of me."

"So how did you train them?"

"I didn't. I supervised them. Not that they ever stayed for more than a few weeks. None of them did. I took it up with the owners, but they didn't care."

"The Sherlocks? What were they like?"

"Don't know, I never met them. We corresponded by

email. Kieran Sherlock came from an IT background, so it was all systems and spreadsheets, computerised stock control. The system could tell you how many sheets there were on a roll of kitchen paper. If you used too many, it sent you a warning email."

My head of service, Danni, would appreciate a system like that at the council. She has a thing about us using too many Post It notes.

"How did they treat the residents?" I ask.

"Why do want to know?" He sets the knife on the worktop and wipes his hands on a small, grubby towel, hanging from his belt. "You found another murder?"

People often compliment me on my subtlety and discretion, asking questions without generating rumours and a furore on social media.

"Nothing like that," I reply.

Noel doesn't look convinced. "First the guy at the amusement park, then those missing women. How do you get involved in all that?"

At least he hasn't apologised for the lack of a body in the freezer. That's becoming rather tedious and predictable during hygiene inspections.

"Noel, I'm not looking for dead bodies – just your impression of the place."

With a deep sigh, he returns to his onion. "Marina Rudolf runs Nightingales like a high security prison. She installed cameras everywhere, watching to make sure no one walked off with a stick of celery. She accused me of wasteful practices - ordering too much food, throwing too much away. That happens when you have too many choices on the menu, but she wouldn't listen."

"So you left."

"Doug needed a new chef when his wife ran off with his accountant. You must remember that. He got stung for unpaid tax, which is why I work for peanuts."

"You're all heart, Noel."

"Says the man who now owns a big house on the hill and a farm up the road."

"You've heard then."

"Everyone's heard, Kent. We're hoping you'll retire from environmental health and let your gorgeous assistant inspect our kitchens."

"Gemma won't be with us much longer," I say, surprised at how empty the prospect makes me feel. I should be pleased. If she leaves, she won't be around to remind me how stupid I was.

Noel pushes his chest out. "Sounds like you'll need a new assistant, Kent. I can help you solve murders and I know how to inspect kitchens."

"And you work for peanuts," I say, heading for the stairs.

"Let me know if you find any bodies," he calls, reaching for the remote.

Back in the bar, Columbo's making friends with the locals and a few hardy ramblers in sturdy boots. He's hoping for treats as usual, ignoring my calls until I walk over and wag a finger at him. He follows me outside and jumps onto the rear parcel shelf to watch the world go by. I sit there and wonder whether Noel will keep quiet.

The last thing I need is a flurry of rumours about Nightingales.

"When did I start believing elderly men with dementia?" I ask Columbo. "What happened to evidence and proof?"

He gives me an encouraging bark. He's right. I have enough problems already. Thankfully, none of them will be as awkward as Danni's merger of the Food Safety and Pollution Control teams.

Then Niamh rings. "I hope you haven't forgotten Gemma's engagement party tonight."

Three

I emerge from the shower, a towel wrapped around my waist. "This is exactly the kind of challenge I need."

Columbo tilts his head from side to side, watching me with those dark eyes. Only he knows the struggles I've had with my feelings for Gemma. In a moment of madness, when we were solving our first murder, I thought I might never see her again. I blurted out how I was hopelessly in love with her.

Hopeless just about sums it up. I told her seven years too late.

"Time to move on," I say, opening the wardrobe. "What do you think, Columbo – black shirt or electric blue?"

Niamh condemned the electric blue shirt to a charity bag, unaware that I was wearing it the day I met Gemma in La Floret. I called to inspect the kitchens and found her standing on a chair in the dining area, reaching up to change a lightbulb. There's something about a white blouse, stretched to transparency over a well-filled bra that gets me every time. When her dark eyes met mine, I lost the power of speech. Thought and movement weren't far behind.

"Be careful," I said finally. "You might fall."

"Then you'd better catch me."

When she jumped down and stumbled into my arms, I was lost. A passionate week later, fear found me and I ran.

On my way to the car, I place the electric blue shirt in the bin, beneath the remains of yesterday's curry. That should stop me recovering the shirt later.

"Isn't black rather sombre for a celebration?"

Niamh looks elegant in a sleeveless green cocktail dress that finishes above the knee. A silver bracelet and matching necklace complete the chic minimalism that's become her trademark. Subtle makeup allows her Irish eyes to sparkle. Her black hair simply tumbles over her shoulders in soft waves that smell of citrus. She rests a hand on my shoulder to balance as she steps into matching stilettos.

"Have you been down the gym?" I ask, aware of how toned she looks. Even her face appears younger, tighter around her mouth and along her jaw.

No one would ever know she's approaching her 50th birthday, only seven years older than me. She's more stepsister than stepmother, though technically she's neither as William Fisher wasn't my natural father. But she's such good company, I don't want to change or complicate our relationship.

"Alice has all the equipment we need in the garage," she replies. "And before you get any ideas, it's women only."

She hands me the gift-wrapped box, containing the cut glass crystal champagne flutes engraved with the names of Richard and Gemma. Niamh suggested a joint gift because I had no idea what to buy, being a stranger to marriage and engagement.

"You look amazing," I say, easing the green coat over her shoulders.

She kisses my cheek and then links her arm through mine as we walk across the drive to my Ford Fusion, cleaned this afternoon to remove Columbo's fur and muddy paw prints.

"You always look uncomfortable in a suit, as if you dress in a hurry."

She checks me over in the harsh halogen light of the security lamps and sighs. With a wink and a smile, she unknots the white tie. With a giggle, she slowly pulls and teases it from under my collar.

"You'd better undo the top button or you'll get the wrong idea," she says, handing me the tie. "And don't think I'm not flattered, Kent, but it would never do now, would it?"

"No, but I wish I could find someone like you."

"Find? Are you finally looking for someone your own age?"

I've never felt any desire to settle, happy to enjoy the company of women without complications. While I have a weakness for waitresses, who I meet during hygiene inspections, no one has ever held my interest for more than a few weeks because I can't help noticing other women out there. That's the problem. I don't look for them. They're just there, wherever I go, whatever I do. It's shallow and selfish, I know, but I'd hate to settle down with the wrong person.

"No, but I'm interested in someone I met earlier today at Nightingales."

She stares at me in horror. "You wouldn't be talking about Miss Rudolf, would you now?"

"No, I spoke to an old man called Trimble. He's convinced they're trying to kill him."

"I'm not surprised, having met Miss Rudolf. Talk about a cold fish." Niamh studies for a moment and sighs. "Tell me this isn't another of your investigations, Kent."

"No, I'm sure the man's suffering from delusions or dementia. He belongs in a specialist home, not Nightingales," I say, opening the passenger door for her. "But he said something about a secret. One that could hurt a lot of important people, including –"

"William." She takes a moment to compose herself, but she can't banish the pain in her eyes. "Is this how it's going to be – people crawling out of the woodwork to blame my husband for everything? He's hardly cold in his grave, Kent. I don't need you stirring things up that are best left forgotten."

I put a reassuring hand on her arm. "I'm only asking if you remember someone called Trimble."

She shakes her head. "You want to know what this secret is, don't you? So why didn't you ask this man, Trimble?"

"He went into a trance."

"Then you'd better ask him next time you visit, hadn't you?"

If he's still there … and alive.

Four

When we reach Alfriston, I drive up the hill to the Broadway, which runs parallel to the High Street. Richard Compton, son of local solicitor, Jeremy, lives at home with his parents in a modern, six-bedroomed house that's surrounded by tall Leylandii hedges. Cars line both sides of the road, forcing us to park around the corner, some distance away. As we walk back, I spot several familiar cars, including Danni's new BMW, bought after her promotion to HEHaW. It stands for Head of Environmental Health and Waste, but I prefer Donkey.

Congratulations Gemma and Richard.

The banner hanging over the driveway must be visible from space. It makes the gift in my hands seem insignificant.

Spotlights illuminate the paved drive and beautifully sculpted gardens filled with evergreen shrubs, statues and cutting edge topiary. Light bursts from every window in the impressive house, complete with a porch the size of a conservatory and a double garage that contains Compton Senior's Mercedes and Richard's new Audi TT.

No sign of Gemma's beat up Volvo estate though.

We tag along behind an older couple in dinner jacket and furs. They leave a wake of stale cigar smoke and expensive perfume, reminding me of dinner parties in Downland Manor when William Kenneth Fisher, MP, entertained dignitaries, nobility and the cream of British commerce. The tense, nervous feeling in my gut that accompanied such events returns when I step inside the porch, which is hot enough to bake bread.

Years of poverty in Manchester have made me nervous of the wealthy and well-heeled.

Inside the hall, a man in a sharp black suit helps Niamh out of her coat. He hands her a ticket and then ducks under another congratulatory banner and out of sight.

"Are you okay?" Niamh asks. "You're sweating."

"We perspire in places like this."

I wipe my forehead on the back of my hand and walk through the reception hall with a high ceiling, oak panelling and Regency striped wallpaper. A solid oak staircase, lined with a thick red carpet, tracks one wall to a spacious landing, lit by a modern cluster of lights with lily-shaped shades. Without the family portraits to admire as you ascend or descend the stairs, and the all-important coat of arms the Fishers displayed in Downland Manor, the room remains an ostentatious display of new money.

Says the man who loathes snobbery and envy.

Glancing around at the dinner jackets and bow ties on display, it looks like the movers and shakers from Eastbourne and the surrounding districts have turned up for the party. I recognise a few local councillors, the chairs of two chambers of commerce, and the prospective Conservative candidate for Downland, Lawrence Beauchamp, who makes a beeline for Niamh.

I wonder if Trimble knows any of his secrets.

The haunting strings of Tchaikovsky's Romeo and Juliet seep through the chatter and laughter of people who all seem to know each other. Armed with glasses of champagne, they move effortlessly across the plush carpet, oblivious to the waitress who's standing by the staircase. She must do exercises to keep smiling for so long.

Niamh places our gift at the back of a long, sturdy table, packed with numerous boxes, wrapped in expensive paper and finished with exquisite ribbons and bows. Most people have spent more on decoration than we did on the champagne flutes, as she predicted.

With a broad smile, she introduces Beauchamp to an older man with greased back grey hair and a bulbous nose. She drifts away, weaving through the people, stopping to greet and shake hands every few seconds. She knows so many people from her time as a politician's wife, even if she can't remember all their names.

Maybe I'll take her to Nightingales next time I visit. She might recognise Trimble.

I wander through a couple of reception rooms and a library, all furnished with what retailers call 'real wood'. After an unexpected encounter with a councillor whose name I don't remember, I reach the open plan kitchen dining room, which runs across the back of the house. It leads into a full-width conservatory where men in black suits, armed with an array of tongs, serving spoons and pie cutters, stand guard over tables of nibbles. I can't see any of those pizza bites you cook from frozen, so I sidle over to a slim, blonde waitress and take a glass of orange from her tray, smiling when our eyes meet.

See, there's always another woman out there.

"I may return for more," I say in my deepest voice.

"No you won't." Kelly slides her arm through mine and leads me away. "It's time you stopped flirting with teenagers, lover."

"You scrub up well," I say, surprised at how sophisticated she looks with short, ash blonde hair.

As Danni's personal assistant, Kelly disguises herself with a rugby club barmaid look, based on tight tops and short skirts. Big, Bonnie Tyler hair and bright makeup reflects her love of Dynasty, Dallas and the American soaps of the 1980s. The disguise fools most men, especially older councillors and senior managers, who let all kinds of gossip and news slip when they try to impress her.

"Corporate Personal Assistant or what?" she says, twirling to show off her pastel blue suit and cream blouse.

"I'll miss your hoop earrings and chunky bracelets."

"Grow up and I might wear them for you."

Before I can work out whether she's teasing, Kelly leads me over to Nigel and Lucy, the remaining two members of the Food and Safety Team I manage. Like me, Nigel's found a less crumpled suit for the party. Lucy's polished her Doc Marten shoes and substituted jeans for cargo pants. Her hair contains more purple streaks to show she's made an effort.

"So, boss, when were you going to tell us about the merger with the Pollution Team?"

Trust Lucy to make small talk.

"This is hardly the place," Nigel says, looking up from his glass of lager.

"Why not? We're only here for the free booze and grub."

"Gemma's a colleague."

Lucy shakes her head at him. "Are you blind as well as naïve? Take a look around. She's not coming back. From now on, it's dinner parties, charity lunches and WI meetings. Her intended won't let her rummage around in dirty kitchens, will he?"

"Has anyone seen Gemma?" I ask, keen to change the subject.

"That's right, ignore the concerns of your team."

Lucy drains her champagne and thrusts the glass into Nigel's hand before pushing her way through the guests to the garden. He places the glass on a nearby table and shrugs.

"Here's Gemma," he says.

Dressed in a simple black number that accentuates every curve, she strolls effortlessly. From the glow in her dark eyes to the beaming smile, I've never seen her so radiant or relaxed. She's the most attractive woman I know, but with her hair pulled into a chignon to show off her smooth, oval face and slender neck, she's gained the cool sophistication of Audrey Hepburn.

Even the scarring to her upper arm, tamed by cosmetics, can't dull the sparkle in her eyes. When the shotgun went off, I thought I'd lost her.

Now I know I have.

Thankfully, I spot someone familiar entering from the conservatory.

"Does Miss Rudolf know you moonlight as a waitress?" I ask, enjoying Louise Watson's blush. She looks sexy in her white shirt and short black skirt.

"I'm helping out a friend," she replies, avoiding my

eyes. "I'm needed in the hall."

She glides past, almost colliding with Gemma, who sighs. "Still chatting up waitresses, Kent?"

Richard's hand crushes mine before he surprises me with a clumsy man hug. We've only know each other a couple of months, but he treats me like an old friend.

"When I didn't see you earlier, Kent, I thought you might be uncovering another body somewhere. Some of father's old cronies are ready to drop."

"You certainly know how to throw a party," I say, putting some space between us.

"That's mother's domain. She has an incredible eye for detail. She suggested the hair and the dress for Gemma."

"Your mother has taste."

"Gemma chose her own dress. She looks amazing in black, don't you think?"

She looks even more amazing without a dress, but I don't mention that.

"Father's going to say a few words then it's time for chow." He slides a relaxed arm around Gemma's waist, steering her towards more family friends and associates.

I turn to Nigel and guide him away from the others. "You carried out the last hygiene inspection of Nightingales in East Dean. Do you think the place flatters to deceive?"

"The owners think it's the dog's whatnots." He drains his lager and leans closer. "It's good, don't get me wrong, and their written systems are some of the best I've seen, but they can't handle criticism."

"What did you find?"

"Little things like a couple of out of date yogurts, a few missing temperature records. As usual, the chef couldn't find a probe thermometer. Mind you, the chef looked like he hadn't slept for a week. I don't think he had much help."

Nigel strokes the tip of his nose, straightening the bristling hairs that protrude from his nostrils. "Have you met the manager?"

"Miss Rudolf?"

He nods. "She followed me like a hawk, answering when I asked the chef a question, always ready with an explanation. When I asked to see the training records she became evasive, saying they were on computer. When I insisted she show me, she sat there watching me, never blinking once. Thankfully, she was called away."

"What did you find?"

"Plenty of people work in the kitchen. East Europeans, judging by their names. They had Level Two food hygiene certificates, even though Chef said their English wasn't good."

"Maybe they did it in their own language."

"Miss Rudolf said that, but she couldn't provide details of the trainer. She told me to contact head office. They said they used a consultant, approved by CQC."

"Since when did the Care Quality Commission approve food hygiene trainers?"

"That's what I thought, so I rang them – four times before an officious man called Malcolm Knott rang me. He said Sherlock's Homes were one of the best managed providers he'd ever inspected. And when you look online at the reports, he's right."

"Maybe that's why Miss Rudolf was prickly," I say, not believing it for a moment.

A ripple of expectation sweeps silence in its wake. People turn and shuffle towards the lounge. We follow, urged on by Kelly, who's gained a male admirer. We stop in the doorway, leaving the admirer to push into the crowded room. I can only see the backs of heads, but Jeremy Compton's authoritative voice carries well beyond me to the conservatory and village below.

After thanking everyone for sharing in the joyous occasion, he talks about how Gemma and Richard met and the first time he brought her home. Compton Senior admits he was delighted to discover that his son had met someone so beautiful and charming.

"Gemma, beautiful Gemma, made a man of my son," he says. "He's never been happier or more decisive."

"The old man sounds rather smitten," I remark.

Kelly raises her eyebrows. "You can talk."

"He sounds like a proud father," Nigel says.

"So, without further ado, ladies and gentlemen, please raise your glasses to toast Richard and Gemma."

"Richard and Gemma," the throng echoes.

I drain the last mouthful of orange juice and turn towards the conservatory, keen to beat the stampede for food. Richard's hesitant voice tells me the speeches aren't over. He thanks his mother and father for organising the party, and for making his lovely fiancée so welcome.

"She's made me the happiest man on the planet, but I didn't realise how much I loved her until I almost lost her. Two months ago Gemma was lying in a hospital bed, her arm and shoulder in bandages after she was wounded. I know it was only a skin graze, but it could have been so much worse. That's when I knew I couldn't bear to be without her."

A murmur of approval builds into another hearty round of applause and cheers.

Nigel pats me on the shoulder. "So, you're to blame."

Richard raises his voice. "That's why I want to thank the man who saved her life and gave me the courage to tell her how much I loved her. Would you join us, Kent? Kent Fisher, ladies and gentlemen."

Nigel nudges me forward. People start looking around. Then someone calls out and the crowd parts to let me through. On my way, I spot Louise Watson and wonder whether she would talk to Trimble on my behalf. Then applause breaks out when I reach my hosts by the grand fireplace and mantelpiece.

Jeremy Compton, tall, dignified and immaculately dressed in an evening suit, studies me with critical grey eyes. Like his wife, Matilda, glittering in her best jewellery, he seems perplexed. Gemma looks down at her feet, crushed into stilettos.

Richard shakes my hand, almost wrenching my arm from its socket. After another fumbling man hug, he turns to the masses. "Raise your glasses to toast the man who's an inspiration and a dear friend. Kent Fisher."

While people applaud and cheer, I pray he doesn't want me to make a speech.

I needn't have worried. He only wants me to be his best man.

Five

By nine o'clock on Tuesday morning, 3rd January, the first working day of the New Year, I'm tempted to hand in my notice.

Officers from the Food and Safety Team sit down one side of the table in Committee Room One. Officers from the Pollution Control Team sit on the opposite side. We're waiting for Danni to chair the meeting. She announced the merger late on Christmas Eve, hoping everyone had gone home and wouldn't find out till this morning. She didn't expect Lucy to log in from home and check her emails. As the union representative for environmental health, she sent a text to everyone affected.

Kelly walks in as the town hall clock chimes nine. She places a thick folder on the table in front of me. "Danni's unwell and asked you to chair the meeting."

I raise my hands to abate the protests and groans. "What's wrong with her?"

"I don't know. She sent me a text five minutes ago.

Bernard Doolittle from Human Remains is also sick, so he won't be attending. Do you still need me to take minutes?"

I reach for my wallet. "Would you pop over the road and buy some cakes?"

Iced buns and sticky willies won't solve anything, but it silences officers for a few minutes while I go through the implications of the merger. Like me, they know increased resilience means doing more with less people. So does flexible working, channel shifting, whatever that is, and dynamic work flows. As the questions and complaints rise to a crescendo, I cast aside Danni's flow charts, pie graphs and bullet point notes, watching them scatter across the floor.

That silences the room.

"We'll drop the least important stuff," I say.

Lucy smirks and pushes the last of the cream slice into her mouth. "Like my health?"

When the meeting ends, Gemma remains, a frosty glare in her eyes. "I hope you'll be more tactful when you tell Richard you can't be his best man."

She strides out, unaware that I've no intention of going to the wedding.

Once I've collected the papers from the floor, I join Nigel in the café of the leisure centre, down the road from the Town Hall. He often spends half an hour on the treadmill at lunchtime, followed by a BLT sandwich, served by the cute blonde catering assistant. Only today, she's not working and he's sitting in the corner, shaking his head at the performance report for Pollution Control.

"What a pickle," he says when I sit opposite.

"Niamh's sweet onion chutney," I say, lifting the top slice of granary to reveal the contents of my cheese sandwiches. "Or do you mean the pollution problems?"

"Danni must have known how bad it was. Why didn't she do anything?"

"She had to rescue the joint refuse collection service," I reply. "It can't be easy, getting four councils to agree a countywide scheme."

He chuckles. "You sound more like a manager every day. During the meeting, you even put a positive spin on the merger with pollution."

"I said shit happens."

"And no one clears up shit as well as environmental health." He takes a bite of his sandwich and pulls a printout from his jacket pocket. "I did some digging."

The printout summarises the actions he took following a complaint the previous year about conditions at Nightingales.

"The Care Quality Commission weren't interested," he says, as if it's their default position. "The complainant thought the surface temperature of the radiator could scald her mother if she rolled against it while she slept."

"Did you take a look?"

He shakes his head. "CQC told me the daughter was a vexatious complainant who objected to the fees Nightingales charged. In the space of six months, she'd complained about the quality of the food, nutrition, lack of care and exercise, and a whole load of other stuff."

The notes tell me Nigel asked them several times to confirm the details in writing, but we never received anything.

"Who got the mother moved?" I ask.

"I assumed CQC sorted it out and closed the file, but you never know with that place."

"What do you mean?"

He chews on his sandwich for a moment. "Nightingales seems too good to be true."

Back in the office, I check the last inspection report on the Care Quality Commission's website. It takes a few minutes to navigate to the correct page as they inspect and regulate hospitals, GP surgeries, nursing and care homes. Nightingales was assessed in five categories to ensure their service was safe, effective, caring, responsive and well-led.

It scored 'Outstanding' in every category.

Two officers carried out an unannounced inspection over two and a half days in October. Residents received excellent care and support, living safe, fulfilled and meaningful lives. Staff knew how to protect people from abuse and what to do if they thought someone was at risk. Risks to individuals were extremely well managed and residents were kept safe without any loss of freedom. Incidents and accidents were well reported and investigated with staff learning to prevent further recurrences. The rest of the summary covered medicines, mental health, healthy eating, and how caring and supportive staff were, led by focused managers with clear values.

No mention of residents who believe they're about to be killed though.

Six

Nightingales postpone my scheduled Saturday visit with Columbo, asking me to return the following weekend. While eleven days have passed since the previous visit, Columbo remembers where we're going, barking and scurrying up and down the back seat the moment I turn off the A259 into East Dean. He strains at the lead as we enter the reception area, undaunted by the oppressive heat from the radiators. Louise Watson looks up from her computer and beckons me over.

"Please don't mention the waitressing," she says in a low voice. "They don't like us having second jobs."

"Then maybe they should pay better."

"I like working here, Mr Fisher."

I stroll over to the window while she announces my arrival. Miss Rudolf soon appears, striding over in a black trouser suit and squeaking brogues that look new.

"Christmas present from a loved one?" I ask.

"January sales," she replies, clasping her hands together.

"I cancelled your visit last Saturday because some of our residents were not happy with your prior visit. They claim your dog ignored them while you made no attempt to encourage him to be friendly with them."

"Are you saying we're no longer welcome?"

She tugs at her jacket sleeve. "With a little more experience, I'm sure you'll be as polished as the other volunteers."

Columbo stirs, sensing the tension as I speak. "You could have rung to save me a wasted journey."

"I'm not turning you away, Mr Fisher. I believe your dog deserves a chance to prove himself. I simply want you to be aware, so you can motivate him to produce his best."

"He's a rescue dog not an Olympic athlete."

"To help you, the residents who don't appreciate your efforts are not in the lounge. Dogs sense hostility, don't they?"

Right on cue, Columbo lets out a low growl. Miss Rudolf stares down at him and then strides towards the lounge.

"Did someone complain about Columbo?" I ask Louise.

"I don't think so. Would you like a tea or coffee when you're finished?"

"Sure, if you'll join me."

She turns back to her computer, her cheeks flushing delightfully. "I have work to do,"

The lounge looks tidier without the Christmas tree and decorations. While many residents remain in their chairs, others come over to fuss Columbo and chat. A foursome in the corner plays cards as if we don't exist – though one of them slides their plate of biscuits out of Columbo's reach. During his first visit, he helped himself to a biscuit on a low table. He also ran off with a lunch menu, offering a fine selection of upmarket dishes, and played 'tug the slipper' with several residents, who enjoyed the game more than him.

"Where's Mr Trimble?" I ask Gladys.

She ruffles Columbo's fur. "He's not well."

"Mr Trimble has a virus," Miss Rudolf says, straightening a nearby armchair. "He walked into the village and rather overdid things."

I can't imagine him walking to his room.

Gladys rises from her armchair. "I like walking. I'm eighty-four and a half, you know. Mr Trimble's eighty-seven."

"Which he often forgets," Miss Rudolf says.

Gladys wobbles. "He fell over in the garden, trying to escape."

Miss Rudolf guides me away. "Gladys leaves us tomorrow. She told everyone she's escaping and asked them to join her."

"Is that why Mr Trimble fell in the garden?"

"Gladys lives in a fantasy world, something she shares with Mr Trimble. She only has to read a book and she's Miss Marple or Harry Potter. She nearly took out someone's eye, waving her stick around like a wand."

Miss Rudolf leaves me to the residents, who share their experiences of the dogs and cats they weren't allowed to bring to Nightingales. Some go on to tell me their life stories, recounting them as if I was there with them. While I listen and nod, an assistant in a white coat escorts a protesting Gladys from the room.

Everyone ignores her pleas, but the uncomfortable atmosphere lingers after she's gone.

"Her son's moving her out tomorrow." Dorothy

Plummer, a former magistrate, who once granted a warrant to one of my colleagues, has no sympathy in her voice. "She's spending too much of his inheritance, I imagine."

"What about Mr Trimble?"

"Now there's a basket case," she replies, polishing the lens of her spectacles with a silk handkerchief. "He's far too old and unstable for a place like this, but he has more money than sense. It's all he ever talks about. When he's coherent, I mean."

On my way out a little over an hour later, I stop to chat to Louise. "Do you know what happened to Mr Trimble? I heard he had a fall."

"He has a chest infection."

"Miss Rudolf said he caught it when he walked to the village."

"He can just about walk to his room." Louise looks around to make sure we're alone and leans closer. "I haven't seen him for over a week."

"Where's his room?"

She nibbles her lower lip. Then in a quiet voice she says, "Walk around the back of the building past the oil tank and his room's straight after the fire exit."

"I'll report back," I say with a grin.

She lowers her head and returns to her work as if I'm not there.

Outside, I follow the flagged path around the back of the building. Columbo, nose to the ground, stops every few feet to pee on the many evergreen shrubs that line the boundary.

As we walk towards the modern extension at the rear of the property, the garden opens out into lawns with flower borders, filled with winter-flowering pansies, elephant's ears and Christmas Roses in full bloom. Dogwood stems thrust out of the ground like coloured bristles, filling the gaps between the French doors and windows of each room.

"Must be the cheaper rooms," I tell Columbo when we reach the extension. He scurries about, excited by the scent of a fox or a rabbit. I'd let him off the lead, but if he disappears into the trees, it could take me the rest of the day to find him.

We walk past the fire escape and stop outside Trimble's room. The drapes on the window and French doors obscure the inside. The window sills look dusty, while the flowers in a small glass vase have wilted. After looking around to make sure no one will disturb us, I reach for the handle. As I do, the French door swings open, almost hitting me in the face.

Columbo barks, his tail and ears erect. Anthony Trimble, pale and stooped, stares at me with glazed eyes.

"Walter?" he asks in a low, cracked voice. "Is that you, Walter?"

A stout woman in a white coat appears by his side. She has arctic eyes and grey hair scraped into a bun. She hauls him back into the tiny room, dominated by the bed and a wardrobe with matching dresser. She chides him in broken English as if he's a misbehaving puppy.

"Naughty boy," she says over and over. "You fall, you die. You understand?"

She closes the lid of a laptop on the dresser as she passes. Then she sits him on the bed, wagging a finger in his face. He doesn't move, flinch or blink. He simply stares at the floor, his eyes dull and glazed, the only part of him not trembling.

When I step into the room, the carer blocks my way "You go or I report you."

She slams the door after me and locks it. Then she wrenches the drape across, leaving me with an image of a sad, lonely old man, foiled in his bid for freedom.

Back at the car, I find another note, folded beneath the windscreen wiper.

But you're not very smart.

I rummage in the glove box to retrieve the first note.

You think you're so clever, don't you?

Someone in Nightingales doesn't like my interest in Trimble.

At home, my Google search for Anthony Trimble leads me on a fruitless journey across social media and beyond. Anthony Trimble and Walter nets me Walter Trimble on one of the ancestry sites. Thirty minutes later I know why I never became a research assistant.

At work on Monday, I want to check the database for information on Nightingales, but I'm distracted by the register of out-of-hours calls received over the weekend. Noisy neighbours, barking dogs and parties make up the bulk, along with a smoky bonfire and antisocial behaviour in the communal refuse area at a block of flats. I pass the last one to Pollution Control Officer, Sylvie Redmond, who's just arrived, and tell her to keep a lid on it.

She thuds the out-of-hours flight case on the floor and drops into her chair. "Sorry, I'm late. I got a call as I was leaving the house. An old boy's passed away in a residential home. No next of kin or relatives, so it looks like we'll have to bury him."

"Welfare burial?"

She nods. "I'll pop down to East Dean and collect his possessions, get things moving."

"East Dean?"

"Yeah, Nightingales, the posh place on the hill. He must be loaded to live there, so we'll get our costs back in full, no problem."

"What's his name?" I ask, certain I already know the answer.

Sylvie flicks open her notebook. "Anthony Nolan Lawrence Trimble."

Seven

I watch Sylvie push her long dark hair behind her ears before leaning forward to check Trimble's possessions. Short, thin and in her 40s, she has cynical eyes and a sardonic smile. Happiest in leathers on the back of a Harley Davidson, she's a practical woman who has no time for fashion, gossip or subtlety. The only time she wears makeup is when she plays bass guitar in a female heavy metal band called *Emasculate*.

They tried a similar name when they first formed, but it turned out to be premature.

"Not much for 87 years on this earth," she says in her East Anglian drawl.

Miss Rudolf has organised Trimble's possessions on the low table in front of the black leather sofa we're sitting on. A small collection of paperbacks, mainly Dick Francis, stack up in one corner. A wristwatch and wallet spend time in the second, while a bulging toiletry bag has been dumped in the third. A box of electrical items, including a radio, an electric shaver and a toothbrush, plus chargers, occupies the remaining space.

No laptop though.

Miss Rudolf sits on an armchair, her back straight, her head upright. She clutches a thin wallet folder, labelled *ANL Trimble,* and stares at the beige walls and ceiling. Her tidy desk, polished to a high sheen, moves more than she does.

"We've laundered his clothes, of course." Her detached voice makes it sound like an afterthought. Trimble's nothing to her now. The dead don't pay rent. "He wanted them to go to a charity shop."

Sylvie picks up the radio, turning it in her hands to check every side. She switches it on and extends the aerial, listening to the sound of an orchestra for a few seconds before turning the radio off. I'm the same with hip hop and rap music.

"Did Mr Trimble have a mobile phone?" I ask. "Or a laptop?"

"This is everything from his room," Miss Rudolf replies.

Either she's lying or one of her staff has taken the laptop.

Maybe someone intends to produce more notes for my windscreen.

"He was going to email me some photographs," I say, nonchalantly leafing through one of the cryptic crossword puzzle books. "He had some of my old house, Downland Manor."

"He would have used our internet café," Miss Rudolf says. Not once does her gaze drift from mine. Not once does she blink. "Mr Trimble wasn't a regular silver surfer."

"He turned the corners down," Sylvie says, showing me one of the paperbacks. "Why do people do that?"

Miss Rudolf wrinkles her nose. "Mr Trimble had a

number of disagreeable habits. That's why we laundered his clothes."

"Good choice," I say, spotting a copy of *Nemesis*, my favourite Miss Marple story. "Do you like crime, Miss Rudolf?"

"I'm more of a closet romantic."

I can't quite conjure up an image of her bonking one of the staff in the linen cupboard. She wouldn't want to disturb all those neatly folded towels and sheets.

A polite knock on the door precedes the arrival of Louise Watson with a tray of tea and biscuits. The crockery rattles as she passes the tray to Miss Rudolf, who places it on a second table beside her chair.

"Hobnobs!" Sylvie leans across to slide a biscuit off the plate before offering them to me.

I decline, preferring plain chocolate digestives and the sight of Louise scurrying out of the office. I flick through the other five volumes of cryptic crosswords. Trimble's shaky writing fills four of them. He makes notes beside the clues and in the margins, crossing out those that don't work. Beneath the grid, he attempts to work out anagrams. Despite the well-thumbed pages, he never started the most recent volume.

While Miss Rudolf dispenses pale tea from a stainless steel pot, Sylvie showers biscuit crumbs over Trimble's folder. She passes me a letter from Compton and Bergman Solicitors, confirming power of attorney granted to Marina Rudolf, Kieran and Georgina Sherlock. The attached legal documents date back eight months to last May.

Sylvie hands me the folder so she can take her tea. "Did Mr Trimble have a will?" she asks. "Or any specific wishes for his funeral?"

Miss Rudolf shakes her head. "I don't think he'd considered dying."

"How about a birth certificate? Driving licence? Address book? Diary?"

"You have everything we recovered, Miss Redmond. Naturally, we'll check again beneath the mattress and inside the pillow cases before we clean them." Her brittle smile does nothing to hide her irritation. "Please, have another biscuit."

Inside the folder I find takeaway menus, and junk mail for life insurance, prepayment funeral plans, cordless vacuum cleaners and several broadband providers. From a clear plastic wallet, I pull out Trimble's RAF Service Book and a squadron of black and white photographs, featuring a dashing man who looks the archetypal pilot with his combed back hair and bomber jacket. His service record tells me he left in December 1963 as a Trade Assistant General.

"Doesn't sound like it involves flying," I say, showing Sylvie.

"In charge of paperclips," she says.

Miss Rudolf twitches, watching the biscuit crumbs tumble onto the beige carpet. Her hand hovers close to the plate, ready to seize it before Sylvie takes any more Hobnobs.

"Did Mr Trimble have a bank account?" I ask.

"It was closed a few weeks ago." Miss Rudolf straightens the sleeves of her black jacket before placing her hands in her lap. "We offer an equity exchange service. Some of our residents have savings, others rely on their property to generate the income needed to enjoy our many comforts."

"He sold his house to you."

"He released his assets, yes."

Sylvie drains her tea and licks her lips. "We'll need to see the records. Any remaining money will be part of his estate."

"There is no residue, Miss Redmond."

"Then how could he afford to live here?"

"His funds ran out a few weeks ago, which is why we closed his account." Once again, Miss Rudolf adjusts her sleeves. "I approached the local authority to fund a place in another home. It was upsetting for him, of course, but he didn't leave us any choice."

Interesting how she blames Trimble for the problem.

"If you ran his affairs, you must have known he was short of money," I say.

Her back stiffens. "He had several endowment policies, which turned out to be false."

"As in bogus?"

"They didn't exist." A flash of anger darkens her eyes before she regains control. "We accepted him as a resident based on the security offered by his property and those endowments. I wanted to report the matter to the police, but Mr Sherlock didn't see any point as Mr Trimble was leaving. He didn't want to leave, of course, which is why he became agitated. Dr Puncheon believes the anxiety and stress hastened his death."

"When did you break the news to him?" I ask.

Miss Rudolf rises and straightens her jacket. "We left it as long as possible. We could hardly throw him out on the street before Christmas, could we?"

Sylvie pulls a bin liner from her pocket. "We'll need all the details."

"I'll ask head office to forward the relevant documents."

"All documents," I say, rising.

We put Trimble's possessions into the bin liner and leave. While Sylvie places it in the boot, I check the front windscreen. No note this time.

Inside the car, she laughs. "Sounds like a bit of a rogue, doesn't he?"

"Trimble?"

"Yeah, pretending he had money."

"What makes you think he got a fair price for his house?"

Back in the office, Sylvie makes an itinerary of Trimble's possessions and places them in the fireproof safe. As soon as she's registered the death and liaised with the undertaker, we can arrange the burial. After that, we send all relevant details to the Treasury Solicitors in London and close the case.

When she returns, she stops at my desk. "What was that about a laptop?"

"I spotted a laptop in his room when I visited a week ago."

Her eyebrows dip. "Why didn't you tell me you knew him?"

"He never tells us anything," Gemma calls from her desk.

"I take Columbo every fortnight to entertain the residents. *Pets as Therapy*."

"You take him into their rooms?" Sylvie chuckles. "I'd love to see Marina Rudolf's face when she finds all those dog hairs."

"Marina Rudolf?" Gemma strolls over to join us. "Nightingales Residential Retreat?"

"You know her?"

"Richard handles Nightingales' legal affairs. He was rather taken with Marina Rudolf."

I have a feeling my friendship with Richard might prove more fruitful than expected.

"What are you up to?" Gemma asks. "You've got that look in your eyes."

"What look?"

Gemma raises a finger, her expression stern. "Leave Richard out of it, okay? I can cope with him reading Agatha Christie and telling me who the murderer is after every chapter, but I don't need you filling his head with ideas."

As if I would.

Eight

While I don't believe in serendipity, fate or karma, the chance to meet Richard in Eastbourne the following lunchtime is too good to miss. On the downside, I have to attend the quarterly meeting of the Sussex Pollution Group, where officers from each local authority share information and discuss topical issues. With an agenda that covers air quality, contaminated land, radiation monitoring, noise mapping and technical references that might as well be written in hieroglyphics, I need to send a Pollution Control Officer to these meetings.

My resolve doubles by the time I escape from the rarefied atmosphere of scientific jargon to the pavement outside the council offices in Grove Road. While I have a much better idea of the exhaust pollutants I'm breathing in, they can't damage my health as much as a meeting where I was clearly out of my depth.

At least the sun tries its best to lift the chill from a crisp January morning. It flashes through the spaces between the

Victorian terraces and occasional concrete monolith as I cut through to Gildredge Road and the offices of Compton Bergman Solicitors. Set back from the road, the modern glass façade, topped with a fashionable purple sign, banishes any thought of a stuffy legal practice, occupied by aging solicitors.

The purple theme continues into a sleek reception area. The white walls, brightened by uplighters, host a series of large posters. There's a smiling old lady clutching her will, a young couple with perfect teeth outside their first home, and various scenes to cover litigation, industrial injury claims and compensation. The poster covering divorce adds an alternative meaning to the Compton Bergman strapline – 'Let us manage your affairs'.

My shoes sink into the plush purple carpet that leads me to the curved, silver-coloured reception desk. It's occupied by a young man with short hair, manicured nails and a suit that makes mine look like it came from a recycling depot. His impressive purple nameplate, almost as wide as his flat screen monitor, tells me Devlin Carter-Bergman didn't come from the Job Centre.

His expression remains friendly but neutral. "Good afternoon, sir. How can I help?"

I'm tempted to ask him how he can afford an expensive suit on the wages they pay him, but his surname suggests he's related to one of the partners.

"I have an appointment with Richard Compton at 12.30."

"Mr Fisher," he says, checking his screen. "I'll let Mr Compton know you're here. If you'd like to take a seat, I'm sure he won't be long."

I wander over to the L-shaped silver sofa and cast an indifferent eye over the magazines on the glass table. After a plastic beaker of chilled spring water, I wander over to the window to watch the cars rush past. Like the pedestrians who hurry along the pavements, heads bowed to study their smart phones, the drivers are in a world of their own, almost unaware of the world around them. I take a gentle stroll around the reception area, hands in pockets, wondering if client confidentiality will allow Richard to tell me anything about Trimble.

Asking him not to tell Gemma about my interest could prove a bigger challenge.

He joins me within a couple of minutes, his cheerful, grinning disposition accentuating the whiteness of his teeth and the strong square jaw that makes him look like a young Robert Redford or Brad Pitt. He sweeps his tousled blond hair back from his forehead and greets me with twinkling blue eyes and an eager handshake.

"I can't believe you're consulting me," he says, his voice purring with nervous energy. "Is it linked to a case you're working on?"

Before I can answer, he's guiding me through the smoked glass door into what feels like a sauna. A narrow corridor cuts between offices, divided by opaque glass walls. Purple signs on each door tell me who or what is behind. Some of the signs are shaped to give me a further clue in case I'm in any doubt that kettles are often found in a kitchen.

"I thought you'd gravitate to the kitchen," he says, pushing open the door. "I don't suppose you can help it in your line of work. Mind you, Gemms said you're running the Pollution Team now."

Gemms? Is that his pet name for Gemma?

"Does that mean you'll be tackling smoky bonfires and

noisy generators?" he asks, approaching the coffee machine. "You prefer decaff, don't you? Latte, okay?"

I nod, aware this kitchen makes mine look like a display reject, which it was. Alongside the coffee machine, there's a combination microwave oven, toaster, and one of those taps that can dispense chilled or boiling water at the push of a button.

"I was delighted when you phoned," he says, sliding a purple Compton Bergman mug under the dispenser. "You made it sound quite intriguing. But everything you do is intriguing. Environmental health covers so many disciplines. You need to know so much."

"You have the same challenge with the law."

"Contracts, conveyancing, wills and codicils are dull by comparison. Sometimes we get a dispute over a covenant, but it's not like closing down a restaurant, is it?"

"Maybe you should specialise in criminal law."

"We leave that to the bigger practices. We don't do company law either."

"Why not specialise in environmental law?"

He gasps, his face a picture of surprise and excitement. "That's a great idea, Kent. When Gemms leaves the council, she can …"

His voice dries up. His expression creases into a grimace. "Bother," he mutters, handing me the mug of coffee. "You're not supposed to know about that. Keep it under your hat, will you?"

I'm not surprised. Things were bound to change when she married Richard. But I'm surprised by how disappointed I feel. "I'll be sorry to lose her," I say, putting on my professional face.

Richard looks guilty. "Sorry, I didn't mean to spring it on

you. I know how much she means to you. But if it's any consolation, you mean a great deal to her."

"I do?"

"You're like a father to her. You look out for her. You make sure she's included. You show her how to do the job, how to make a difference."

Like a father? As reality checks go, this one's difficult to beat.

I run a finger under my collar, wondering what else Gemma's told her fiancé.

I want to get out of this stuffy, windowless room, but Richard's blocking the way, looking awkward and worried. I should be pleased for him. I should tell him so he doesn't feel bad.

"When did she decide to leave?" I ask.

"After your last case." He looks up, his brows heavy over his eyes. "You're so clever, solving those murders, facing up to killers, but I want to start a family. I can't bear the thought of what might happen to Gemms. I don't want her getting shot again."

I nod, aware of the nightmares Niamh's suffered since the last case. She denies it, of course, but she freezes every time she hears the shots from a clay pigeon shoot or a farmer hunting rabbits. Occasionally, I wake up sweating, my heart pounding.

"I never thought I'd meet someone like Gemms," Richard says, his voice warm and contented.

Neither did I.

If only I'd realised at the time. "You're a lucky man, Richard."

He slides another mug under the coffee machine. "When I first saw Gemms I couldn't speak. When we looked into each other's eyes, it was like my whole future was settled. I knew what I wanted. I had purpose and meaning. Does that make sense?"

While I don't want the details, part of me wants to hear how he felt about Gemma. Maybe it will help me understand why I felt so scared, why I ran.

"I wasn't the shy, awkward boy anymore," he says. "It never occurred to me for a moment that she would turn me down. And she didn't. I know that sounds trite, but since that day I've only wanted to make her happy and give her everything she deserves."

"You will," I say, realising that's not how I felt about Gemma. I wanted her, but that's where it started and stopped. I never had any plans or dreams for us.

I shake his hand, feeling a curious sense of relief.

"I'm so pleased you agreed to be my best man. I expected you to turn me down as we haven't known each other long, but it seemed right, you being so close to Gemms."

I should tell him I can't be his best man, but he looks so happy and excited, I let the moment pass.

We walk to his office with its steel and glass furniture. So much for the towering bookcases filled with musty tomes and a creaking oak desk, covered in dusty bundles of papers. Everything's on computer and the internet now, allowing Richard to fill his walls with wildlife photos of the South Downs and atmospheric shots of villages like Alfriston, Wilmington and West Dean. He even has a photograph of my old home, Downland Manor. On his desk, family photos of his mother and father compete with cute shots of their Labradors and a stunning portrait photo of Gemma, looking like a young Carrie Fisher.

Once settled, I ask him what he can tell me about Nightingales.

"I represented Anthony Trimble," he replies. "Not the home. He needed to grant power of attorney as he was becoming forgetful and disorientated."

"You had nothing to do with the release of equity he used to pay for his stay there?"

"I was aware of it, but Mr Trimble never consulted me about it."

"Did he make a will?"

Richard takes a sip of coffee. "He said he had no assets or anyone to bequeath them to."

"He had some endowment policies."

"Did he? He never mentioned them to me."

I lean forward. "They were bogus, according to Miss Rudolf."

"I knew it," he says, sinking into his chair. "You're investigating another of your mysteries. Do you think Nightingales cashed the insurance policies?"

"It's a thought," I reply.

"I wish I could help, Kent, but Anthony Trimble didn't confide in me."

"Out of interest, do you know if Nightingales regularly use equity release?"

He rises from his chair and looks out of the window. "I've advised clients on releasing equity from their property, but not to fund a room in a residential home. If I did, I would want my clients to appreciate the risks."

"Like outliving the amount of money released?"

"Or the converse," he replies, turning. "Anthony Trimble had a portfolio of properties, I believe. He cashed in the equity on a substantial property. That's all I can tell you."

"No problem," I say, getting to my feet. "I appreciate your help."

He accompanies me to the door and stops to shake my hand. "Please don't breathe a word to Gemms. She told me not to get involved with your investigations."

"So, why did you?"

"I want to help if I can."

"You did, and without breaching any confidences."

He seems relieved. "Talking of confidences, please don't say anything about her leaving the council. She wants to tell you herself."

"I'll act suitably shocked when she does."

Outside, I breathe in the cool air, letting it fill my lungs and clear my mind. On the surface, Nightingales is a luxury home with an excellent reputation, solid management and healthy residents. Yet they took Trimble. Did they take advantage of his poor mental health to make him sign over his house?

Did he die before his equity was spent, netting Nightingales a healthy windfall?

I can't help thinking it's in Sherlock's interest if residents die early.

Nine

While Sylvie makes good progress over the next couple of days, registering Trimble's death and arranging the funeral, I feel frustrated. No matter how many times I study the certificate, Dr Puncheon still states Coronary Heart Disease as the cause of death. It appears that high blood cholesterol, diabetes, and cigarette smoking all contributed to the heart failure that killed him in his sleep.

No mention of murder or foul play. Nothing suspicious about Trimble's death.

No inquest. Nothing more to say.

Nothing much to say about his life, considering he spent 87 years on the planet.

I flick through his RAF Certificate of Service, which gives his date of birth, previous occupation as a farm labourer, date of enlistment (and discharge), his rank, and a few physical details about height. During his twelve years in the RAF, he didn't excel at anything, had no commendations, and worked mainly on grounds maintenance, where he could be relied on to carry out unskilled tasks without supervision.

Trimble made a bigger impression in death than he made during his life.

"You're working late," Gemma says, strolling into the office at five forty.

"I'm waiting for you to ring to say you're safe."

She shrugs off her overcoat and tosses it on the desk that faces mine in the reconfigured office. Now a hot desk, it may help to warm her pale fingers. It won't make any impact on her frosty expression. With a deep sigh, she flops into the chair and texts me to say she's safe.

"I'm glad you're still here," she says, unwrapping the long scarf from her slender neck

I slide the Certificate of Service back into the clear plastic wallet. "Something you want to talk about?"

She takes her time, pulling out a comb to tease the waves of thick brown hair into place. The tip of her nose, red against her pale complexion, makes me think of Miss Rudolf, who's also withholding information from me.

"Would you be upset if I left the food team?" Gemma asks.

I've already perfected my look of surprise, tinged with hurt and disappointment. I've worked on what I can say to see if she'll reconsider her decision. And as I'm now in charge of a bigger team, with a bigger budget, I can tempt her with an additional increment or two.

But when I open my mouth, I say, "If you want to waste the skills you've developed, don't let me stop you."

That jolts her.

"Come on, Kent, you know I appreciate the help and training you've given me. I love inspecting kitchens and –"

"But your future's elsewhere, now you're going up in the world."

She's on her feet, grabbing her scarf as if she wants to wrap it around my neck. "I knew you'd react like this."

"Like what?"

"Like I don't know what I'm doing." She slings her coat over her arm and marches past, brushing papers from my desk. "Danni's happy for me to become a Pollution Control Officer."

I'm out of my chair and after her. "I thought you wanted to leave the council."

In the corridor I almost collide with Danni, who blocks my path. "Something tells me you need a crash course in diplomacy and not jumping to conclusions, Kent."

"I thought she was going to leave," I say, watching Gemma disappear around the corner.

"Perhaps it would be better if she did."

My best friend, Mike, detects my mood when he calls around at seven. We have to deliver some microwave ovens and a commercial washing machine to Summer Breeze, a care home on the outskirts of Herstmonceux. We buy second hand catering equipment from failing and closed businesses and store it in the barn beneath my flat. It's his business really, but the profits help to run my animal sanctuary.

"What's eating you?" he asks during the drive.

"I'm more concerned with what you're eating," I reply.

He's devouring his second Chunky Kit Kat, unconcerned about his girth or his teeth. His New Year resolution to eat healthy food and take more exercise took a hit when he discovered the fees for joining the gym at Tollingdon

Leisure Centre. When I told him he spent more on cigarettes each month, he told me health was a state of mind.

"I have a healthy mind," he says, stopping at a junction to allow two women in hi-vis running tops and leggings to cross. "It's just filled with unhealthy thoughts."

"You can see the benefits of running, Mike."

"Sure," he says, waving to the women, "but I'd always be chasing, wouldn't I? You know me, pal. If I fell into a barrel of boobs I'd come up sucking my thumb."

His sense of humour and ability to laugh at himself broke down barriers when he was the only black police officer in the division during the early 1970s. Many years later, when he became a Scenes of Crime Officer, humour helped him deal with the tragic and often gruesome aftermath of rape, suicide and murder. Now divorced and retired, he runs Mike's Mighty Munch, a mobile café converted out of an old ambulance. It's ideal for rushing people to hospital if they suffer a heart attack after eating his huge portions.

"You could reduce your expectations to increase your successes," I say, quoting from Danni's Motivational Pinboard.

"Says the man who only has eyes for the woman he can't have." Mike play punches my shoulder, enjoying his moment. "How can all that frustration be healthy?"

"Frustrated, moi? I've agreed to be Richard's best man."

"So that's why you've got a face like a smacked arse."

"No, it's the merger between my team and Pollution Control," I say, wondering who I'm trying to convince. "We've lost two officers, there's a backlog of unresolved complaints, three ombudsman cases, and what do you think everyone's steamed up about?"

He swings the van to dodge a pothole. "Knowing your

lot, I'd say hot desking."

"No, we can't agree on a name for the new team. Never mind the fact we're expected to do more with less. Honestly, Mike, I spend all my time fighting battles I can't win."

"Why bother?" he asks, slowing as we reach Summer Breeze. He eases the van down the bumpy, narrow track that leads to the rear. "How much is your house in Friston worth – a million plus?"

"The sanctuary will soon gobble that up – after the tax man takes his wedge."

Mike drives beyond the tradesman's entrance, stops, and reverses into the yard, narrowly avoiding the bins. "What about Birchill's millions? Doesn't he want to build a visitor centre at the sanctuary?"

Birchill wants to be my father. He might be biologically, but in terms of values we're light years apart. Any investment he makes is conditional on extending the access road to the woodland beyond, where he plans to build a holiday park. He's asked me to help make it sustainable with a neutral carbon footprint, but I want the woods to remain untouched.

"I'm an environmental health officer," I say, unbuckling the seatbelt. "It's what I do, what I enjoy. You always wanted to be a copper, didn't you?"

"I never had a rich daddy and property to sell." He jumps from the cab and we meet at the rear of the van. "Anyway, you're a manager now. You've joined the dark side."

Is that the cause of my frustration?

"You must want to spend more time and develop the sanctuary," he says. "We can still sell catering equipment. And you'll have more time to investigate conspiracies and murders."

"Funny you should say that, Mike."

Before I can tell him about Trimble, the rear door to the home opens, flooding the yard with light. It takes me a moment to focus on a familiar, if unexpected, face.

I met Yvonne Parris a couple of months ago during my last investigation. She had blonde hair and worked in reception for a funeral director. Now, she's a redhead in chef's whites and cap.

"Well, if it isn't Kent Fisher, entering by the rear as usual."

Her grin's as sassy as her words. Tall, slim and in her late thirties, she has the effortless confidence I've noticed in most Americans and a wit to match.

"At least I'm up front about it," I say. "I didn't realise you cooked as well."

"Stick around and you might see me wash dishes."

"Maybe you need a dishwasher," Mike says, his voice a little deeper than usual. "I might have something that will interest you."

"That's what Kent said." She pushes her glasses up the bridge of her small nose and walks over to peer into the van. "Are you allowed to sell equipment to places you inspect?"

"It's Mike's business," I reply. "And I don't inspect you."

"I'm not stopping you."

Mike clears his throat and gestures to the washing machine we've brought. "Just tell me where you want it. The washing machine," he adds, realising he's drifted into innuendo.

"In the laundry room. And while you work up a sweat, I'll make coffee."

"You never mentioned her," Mike says once she's gone. "Afraid of the competition?"

"She's not my type."

"What, too old or too smart?"

"Too keen."

His eyebrows reach his hairline. "And that's an issue?"

We lower the washing machine onto a trolley, which Mike hauls into the laundry room inside the first door on the left. The flickering light from the strip bulbs reveals whitewashed breeze block walls, streaked with condensation. Black mould creeps out of the corners and along the junction with the unpainted plasterboard ceiling. The rattle of the trolley wheels echoes off the quarry tiles as we push past the sluice sink beneath the window and line up beside a second washing machine. Mike examines the hose and waste fittings fixed to the wall and nods.

"Shall I fetch the microwaves while you connect up?" I ask.

"Why not? It's warm in the kitchen. I know where I'd like to warm my hands," he says, cupping them in front of him.

"I'll fetch you some mittens," Yvonne calls from the doorway.

The blast of heat from Mike's face warms me more than his cursing and grunting as he stretches to retrieve the hose he dropped.

I load two microwaves onto a trolley and make for the kitchen on the opposite side to the laundry room. Small and fitted with domestic cupboards and units, the kitchen has a homely feel, thanks to the Aga within the chimney breast. The old fashioned scales, food mixers and storage pots add a touch of nostalgia that matches the worn Formica worktops. The old wall tiles, alternately decorated with motifs of wheat and other cereals, gleam in the space adjacent to the chimney breast, reserved for the microwave ovens.

I heave the first one into position. "I thought you'd returned to America."

"I needed cash after I lost my job. We don't all have rich benefactors." Yvonne retrieves a carton of skimmed milk from the fridge. "You must be relieved to have the apartment to yourself."

"I didn't realise you were keeping tabs on me."

She laughs. "You should be so privileged. Gemma popped by before Christmas. We need to upgrade the facilities, as you can see. Homely, but it's not up to modern hygiene standards, as your Care Quality Commission inspector pointed out. He sure gave us a long list of works."

I haul the second microwave into place. "The kitchen's not that bad," I say.

"No, a long list for the property. Hey, I know they got to be thorough because there are some unscrupulous types, you know? But we're a small home. We'd make zip from ripping off the residents. Your council pays for most of them and it's not top rates, right?"

"How would you rip off the residents?" I ask, taking the mug she holds out.

She shrugs. "I work the kitchen, Kent. Why, you want to buy in now you're rich?"

"Just curious, that's all."

"You're never just curious," she says, moving alongside me. "You found something?"

"If I knew what to look for, I might."

"I can do this." She takes the plug for the second

microwave and pushes it into the wall socket. The microwave lights up when she switches on. "So, what about Gemma? She couldn't wait to show off her engagement ring and fill me in on the news. News about you, Kent, not Richard."

"So that's why you moved into catering, Yvonne. You like stirring."

"Says the master," Mike remarks, joining us. "Everything's hooked up. I can run a quick wash cycle, show you how to programme the machine."

"I'll learn," she says, handing him a coffee.

Thanks to a quirk of nature that lined his mouth and throat with asbestos, he takes a sip straight away. "You know Kent's best man," he says.

She looks at me for a moment and then laughs, as if I'm pathetic. "Geez, you really don't want to let go, do you?"

I slam my mug on the worktop and walk out. Outside, I stare into the black that consumes the countryside, wondering why I can't take to Yvonne. She's smart, attractive, witty … but she gets under my skin, reminding me what an idiot I can be. Is that what people think – that I'm fixated with Gemma?

"You okay, pal?"

I turn to Mike. "She thinks I'm not interested in her because I'm hung up on Gemma. Why can't she accept I'm not interested?"

He pats me on the shoulder. "I don't think you know what you want, pal. That's your trouble."

No, I can't have what I want. That's my trouble.

I'm not sure Anthony Trimble got what he wanted either.

On Friday morning, the following week, a bitter wind

rakes through the cemetery, numbing my face. Opposite me, Louise Watson and Miss Rudolf stand with their backs to the wind, coats pulled up tight to their pale faces. Louise stamps her feet, probably wishing she could wear trousers, thick socks and boots instead of the black skirt, tights and shoes demanded by Sherlock's Homes. She removes the brightly-coloured mitten from her hand, and pulls the hood of her parka tight.

When our eyes meet, she manages a glimpse of a smile and then looks away. Miss Rudolf holds my gaze and nods.

The rector completes his austere speech, muttering the last couple of sentences before stepping back from the grave, his vestments swirling like drapes around his legs. The pallbearers step forward and lower Trimble to his final resting place in a corner of the cemetery. While I could have let Sylvie represent the council, Louise rang the day before, asking if she could attend.

Now, as Miss Rudolf adjusts her black leather gloves, I walk over.

"Thank you for attending," I say, pushing my cold hands into my trouser pockets.

She pulls back her coat sleeve to check her watch. "Thank you for organising a simple, but respectful service. Now I need to tend to the living."

"I still haven't received details of the equity release on Mr Trimble's house."

"I referred the matter to head office, Mr Fisher. I'm sure it's being dealt with."

"Maybe I should talk to Mr and Mrs Sherlock."

A nerve twitches in her jaw. "They're in the Caribbean at the moment."

"They must check their emails," I say, enjoying her

discomfort. "We'll have the address on our database."

Miss Rudolf manages a short nod. "Come on, Louise, let's get back to work."

Louise looks at me for a moment and then follows.

"Miss Rudolf, I'd like a quick word with Louise. There's no need to wait in the cold."

"I'm used to the cold, Mr Fisher."

I lead Louise a few yards from the grave, stopping beside the trunk of a mighty yew tree. Though tempted to move out of sight, I don't want to make things more difficult for her, in case Miss Rudolf interrogates her later.

"Is there something you want to tell me?" I ask.

Louise shakes her head, unable to stop her teeth chattering.

"Then why did you want to come to the service?"

"To pay my respects. I didn't like Mr Trimble, but he didn't deserve to die like that."

"Like what?"

She glances over her shoulder at Miss Rudolf, who's motionless, impervious to the wind, it seems. Louise removes a mitten, thrusting it into her coat pocket. From her clutch bag, she pulls out a piece of faded paper, folded into a two inch square, secured by a paperclip. Her shivering fingers pass it to me.

"He told me to give you this," she says.

I slide the paper into my jacket pocket. "What is it?"

"He said you'd work it out."

"Work what out?"

She pushes her shivering hand back into the mitten. "I'd better go."

"Tell Miss Rudolf I was sounding you out about a job on my team."

"I didn't know you needed a receptionist."

With Gemma transferring to pollution I need a new sidekick.

Ten

Back in the car, I unfold the paper and flatten it on my notebook to study a list of numbers written in shaky handwriting.

17	9	7
2	26	4
26	15	6
26	15	6
9	13	6
11	14	7

My first thought involves letters of the alphabet, represented by the numbers, but that leads me nowhere. I can't find any words or acronyms that make sense. They could be anagrams – three words of seven letters, except the third column would have five Fs. Even allowing for a stammer, it doesn't spell anything.

Reversing the letters of the alphabet gives me the same problem. The third column makes no sense, whatever I try.

Half an hour later, cold, frustrated and no closer to a solution, I photograph the paper and email the image home. If Trimble asked Louise to give the numbers to me, he wrote them down in the last three weeks. He also trusted her to keep them safe until after his death.

He didn't trust Miss Rudolf or the other staff at Nightingales.

With the paper safe inside my wallet, I walk back to the village green, desperate for a cup of tea. I stop outside the Tiger Inn, which stretches along the gentle incline beside the green. In summer, people fill the tables in front of the pub. They spill out onto the green, where they recline with their pints of local beer and glasses of wine. Their laughter and excited chatter roll across the grass to the sleepy flint cottages beyond.

On a raw Friday morning in February, the bare wooden tables look as grey and dull as the leaden sky. The spiteful wind tugs at the naked branches of the climbing roses, determined to wrench them from the sturdy flint walls, now painted white. Like the rusty brown roof, they've resisted the elements for centuries, offering shelter and comfort to walkers, strangers and locals.

Unfortunately, the pub doesn't open until eleven, so I keep walking, considering Trimble's coded message.

Does it contain a secret he couldn't reveal while he was alive?

Do the numbers relate to dishes on a takeaway menu?

I recall the menus we found among his belongings and wonder if Trimble's watching from the other side, tucking into Chow Mein while we run around like headless chickens.

I stop outside the cottage at the top of the green as I always do, seeking inspiration from the blue plaque on the flint wall,.

'Sherlock Holmes, consulting detective & beekeeper, retired here 1903-1917.'

How would Holmes tackle the mystery of the code? Where would he start? He'd want to know more about Trimble, I'm sure. Well, I already have my Watson in Nightingales. But my appearance there could arouse Miss Rudolf's suspicions.

On the walk back to the car, I wonder if anything could arouse Miss Rudolf.

Back in the office at eleven, Kelly intercepts me. I miss her blousy barmaid, big hair look. While she still wears spike heels and short skirts, the pastel jacket looks too conventional, despite the scarlet tie with its huge knot, nestled inside. She glances at Danni's door.

"Someone's not happy with your unhealthy interest in funerals, lover. She wants to know why you're doing your team's work for them."

"I need to find out how the pollution guys spend their time."

"No," she says, straightening my tie, "you need to gain a greater understanding of the nature and complexities of pollution control work. Remember that when we get to the relevant agenda item during this afternoon's Team Talk."

"Who told her where I was? It wasn't in my diary."

Kelly shrugs. "Your team's doubled in size, so you have twice as many people to criticise you. You can put that top of your Motivational Pinboard when it arrives. Managers are getting their own pinboards. It's on the agenda."

"Where am I going to stick it?"

"I'll avoid the obvious answer and simply say office restructure. It's –"

"On the agenda. I know."

She laughs and struts back to her desk, leaving me to a stack of green folders on mine.

"Danni asked me to identify all pollution complaints that weren't completed within target times," Gemma says, peering around her monitor. "Those are the ones that have received standard responses or some input by officers. The ones that haven't had a response yet are listed in a separate email."

Kelly breezes over to Lucy's desk. "Unresolved complaints are also on the agenda."

If I work through lunch, I have about three hours to prepare for Team Talk.

"Danni's moved the meeting forward to one o'clock," she says on her way back, "to allow more time for the long agenda."

Sylvie grins as she pulls on her duffel coat. "That'll teach you to go to the funeral."

Gemma frowns. "Who's died?"

"The old bloke from Nightingales. Kent has the hots for the receptionist there. When she asked if she could attend the funeral, he pulled rank."

She gives Gemma a conspiratorial wink and heads out of the office.

Gemma turns back to her computer and continues working for a few minutes. "What's her name – this receptionist?"

"What do you care?"

"There are seven receptionists on the Nightingales' group

photo."

"Haven't you got anything better to do?" I click on the email for Team Talk and open the attachment, which contains the agenda.

"I'll text Sylvie then."

On the way to the printer, I stop to look at the photo on her monitor. Seven smiling women in matching suits pose in front of the reception desk. Two look bored, Louise looks embarrassed, and the others want to impress. Their names are listed beneath.

"Third from the left," I say.

"Louise Watson." Gemma double clicks the name to bring up a portrait photo. "She's pretty in an understated, self-conscious sort of way."

"And damned by faint praise, it seems."

"She's got kind eyes. Not your type at all."

"Like Yvonne Parris, you mean?"

"She's perfect for you, Kent. Why didn't you bring her to the party?"

"Why didn't you tell me you'd visited Summer Breeze?"

"She wanted advice about updating the place." Gemma pauses and smiles. "She didn't tell you she was buying Summer Breeze, did she?"

Why would Yvonne tell me when she knows I'm not interested in her?

Maybe I should change that. As a fellow care home owner, she could prove useful to my investigation.

Danni's Team Talk fills every Friday afternoon with gossip, chocolate muffins and an occasional foray into work issues. Fiona Wick, the appropriately-named Waste Manager, trashes the reputation of two telephonists, several restaurants in Eastbourne, and her ex-husband, who won't take time off work to look after the children while she attends a four-day project planning course in Leeds.

"You think he'd want to spend time with his children," she says, shaking her head in frustration. "Mind you, it only took him minutes to conceive them."

It takes another two hours and more chocolate muffins before we reach the item on outstanding pollution complaints.

"Gemma's going to clear the backlog," Danni announces, avoiding any need for discussion. "Sylvie and Terry will support her, of course."

"How did the backlog get so big?" I ask, flipping through the printout. "Some of the complaints go back over eighteen months. How many standard letters do we send out before someone actually visits to witness the problem?"

"Challenge," Fiona says. "Effective managers don't deal in problems, only challenges."

It turns out her husband refused to look after the children when she attended a two day course on Effective Management in Newcastle.

"You won't believe the problems he created," she says.

"Kent, you're going to introduce new systems and procedures to ensure pollution control operates to the same high standards as the rest of the department," Danni says, folding the muffin case into a quadrant. "We'll need comprehensive update training, so we all sing off the same hymn sheet. Note that as an action on the minutes, Kelly, with regular feedback each Friday until completion in four weeks' time."

"Four weeks?"

"Do you have a problem with that?" Danni asks,

frowning at my outburst. "You'll have plenty of time now I've dismissed two of the ombudsman cases with one phone call. Make a note of that in the minutes, Kelly. It's another example of efficiency and cost saving for the vultures in Whitehall."

"When you say you've dismissed two of the ombudsman cases, what do you mean?" I ask, sensing she's made the challenges worse.

"I told her I had better things to do than justify my actions to some government lackey who's never set foot in the real world. I told her I'd make a formal complaint if she continued to waste my officers' time."

"Bravo," Fiona says, reaching for her third muffin.

"I was too late with the third case," Danni says, handing me a letter. "As you can see, the ombudsman has instructed us to carry out a new investigation, using noise monitoring equipment and surveillance visits by officers to witness any nuisance arising from the premises, including the overgrown garden."

"Do we know anything about Anderida Villas?" I ask.

"It's divided into flats or bedsits," Kelly says, reading from the file.

"Do we know which tenants are causing the problems?"

She shakes her head. "We only have details of the owner, Mr Anthony Trimble."

Eleven

On Monday morning, the temperature inside my car matches the one outside. We're at Stone Cross, waiting for the traffic lights to change. While the cars belch out their exhaust fumes into the cold morning air, Gemma poisons the atmosphere inside with her grievances.

"Why am I a Pollution Control Assistant?" she demands. "I've taken over a Pollution Control Officer's post."

"You have no pollution experience."

"Then why am I on the weekend callout rota?"

"You volunteered."

"I showed willing, Kent. And how do they repay me?"

Modern houses block the view to the South Downs, where the winter sun lifts the white veils of frost from the brittle grass. I wish I was running on the Downs, my trainers bouncing off soil as hard as iron, weary muscles protesting to the top of the slope. Then the thrill of those majestic views across a rolling green landscape that dips and rises along the coast as far as the eye can see.

"I could have given Anderida Villas to Sylvie," I say, knowing it's an empty threat.

"After the mess she made of the original investigation?"

"That's harsh, considering she and the team had no management support."

"Sylvie screwed up, Kent, and you're asking an inexperienced officer on the bottom grade to sort out the mess. That's unfair."

"Think of the valuable experience you'll gain."

"Like keeping property details up to date? How difficult is that?"

It took me five minutes with Housing Benefits and Business Rates to discover Anthony Trimble sold Anderida Villas to Kieran and Georgina Sherlock nine months ago. But what happened to the proceeds of the sale? Even with tenants in the property, its value exceeded the cost of staying at Nightingales for nine months. Yet Miss Rudolf claims Trimble ran out of money.

That's why I'm on my way to Pevensey, hoping to find someone who knew Trimble.

"We have to rebuild our reputation," I say, relieved the lights have changed. "That's why I wanted you on the case. You'll show the side of environmental health that gets things done."

"Even though I don't have any pollution experience?"

"You'll be fact-finding, talking to locals, building relationships, gathering evidence. Stuff you can do in your sleep, Gemma."

"Then why are you holding my hand? Can't you bear to let me go?"

We drive on in silence, dipping into Westham past red brick Victorian terraces that face modern estates of bungalows and houses across the road. When we reach the main High Street, peppered with a few local businesses and a pub, we pass Tudor cottages with uneven roofs that stagger over leaning, timber-framed walls. We move further back in time when we exit the village and pass St Mary the Virgin, the first church built by the Normans after they invaded in 1066. When they landed at Pevensey Bay, they headed inland and set up in the remains of Anderida, an old Roman fort. After defeating King Harold, they returned to the fort and built Pevensey Castle. Though a ruin, the site's flanked by a substantial perimeter wall of stone that stretches alongside the road.

And like Elton John, the wall's still standing.

I've run through the grounds and past the moated keep many times, tingling with excitement when I realise I'm treading on land once walked by William the Conqueror.

Once through the chicane outside the eastern gate, we drive down Pevensey High Street where flint houses rise above narrow pavements. The mixture of flint and half-tiled houses then gives way to larger properties, set back from the road. Anderida Villas lurks somewhere behind, surrounded by residents who don't like bedsits occupied by families on benefits.

It takes a few minutes to weave through the lanes and find a parking space adjacent to a crumbling brick wall, overrun with brambles and elderflower bushes. Ivy races up the bare trees that fill a large, overgrown garden. Beyond, the three-storey Victorian house looks dark and neglected, stained by leaking gutters and downpipes, scarred by part-boarded windows.

"Why did Trimble fill the place with bedsits when he could have created flats to sell to the upwardly mobile?" I ask, taking photographs for the file.

Gemma joins me by the wall. "The rats must like it here."

So do the tenants, I imagine, zooming in on the collection of empty beer and wine bottles next to the recycling bin. "Come on, let's get on with it."

Gemma steps in front of me, folding her arms. "About Anderida Villas or Anthony Trimble? You attended his funeral instead of Sylvie, and now you're here on a routine complaint because he once owned this dump."

"Which he sold to the Sherlocks to pay for his time at Nightingales, where he died, owing them money, they say."

"What's that got to do with us unless …" A smile warms her face. "Unless you think his death was suspicious. That's why you wanted my help, Holmes."

"Trimble left a puzzle."

Gemma removes her gloves and unfolds the paper. While she studies the numbers, I peer into the garden, reminded of Boo Radley and how the locals misunderstood him.

Have I misjudged Trimble, dismissing his dementia because I want to solve a mystery?

"What do the numbers mean?" she asks, handing back the paper.

"I wish I knew. That's why I want to find out more about Trimble."

At the front of the house, we pause at the end of an uneven driveway, blotched with oil stains and weeds. Brick steps lead to a faded front door, recessed inside an arch. Two rows of symmetrical sash windows, all rotting, delineate the first and second floors, with dormer windows in the attic rooms below the slate roof. With more bedsits at the rear, I estimate ten, maybe twelve tenants, sharing one or two bathrooms and a communal kitchen.

Next to the refuse bins, I spot a rusty engine, several mouldy mattresses, and various plastic bin liners, ripped open by the local foxes and gulls. Waste food packaging and old clothes lie strewn across the grass and among the bushes that spill over the boundary wall.

"What's this?" Gemma asks, stretching a hand into the bushes. She pulls out a narrow, saturated board with faded letters that spell out *No Vacancies*. "Was it a hotel?"

"Let's ask," I reply, spotting an elderly woman in the bay window of a bungalow opposite. "Who lives there?"

Gemma opens the file. "Miss Olivia Williams, one of our more vocal complainants."

We stroll across the road and up the narrow brick path, squeezed between borders of regimented snowdrops and crocus, bulked out with marauding winter pansies. Miss Williams opens the door before my finger reaches the bell. A stout woman with a severe expression and haircut, she studies me with eyes that once intimidated schoolchildren, I suspect.

"I know who you are," she says, waving away my ID card. "And you won't find any bodies over there, Mr Fisher, more's the pity. A corpse might just get you people off your backsides. Have you any idea what they get up to over there?"

"Let's go inside and you can tell us."

She doesn't move. "You have records of the antisocial behaviour of these people. Drugs and alcohol, parties till dawn, music blaring at all hours, cars coming and going, ladies of the night. But what do you do about it?"

"The police deal with those issues," Gemma replies.

"But you have the power to close the place down." The

woman sighs as if she's wasting her time. "But you'd rather send me those infernal diary sheets that you never take any notice of. I could write a bloody novel with the number I've completed."

"Our records show you've never returned any diary sheets," Gemma says, looking up from the file. "That's why no one followed up on your complaints, Miss Williams."

The woman's chest swells inside her cardigan. "How dare you blame me for your incompetence, young lady? Every day in the Daily Mail I read stories about council workers like you, wasting taxpayers' money."

Stories being the appropriate word, I suspect.

"If we're to make any progress," I say, "we need to talk to the owner, Miss Williams. Can you tell me anything about Mr Anthony Trimble?"

She stares across the road and wrinkles her nose. "Violet Hughes, next door but one, might. She's deaf as a post, mind, so knock hard. And don't accept any Victoria sponge," she adds in a weary tone. "The last one she made was raw in the middle."

Miss Williams shuts the door with a thud.

Gemma sighs. "Helpful woman, wasn't she?"

Like many complainants, Miss Williams believes she's done her duty by passing the matter to us.

Violet Hughes turns out to be one of those maternal types who know everyone and everything. She invites us in, chattering away about all the lovely neighbours she has as she makes tea in a clean and precise kitchen, disinfected to within an inch of its life. The rest of the house looks spotless, with furniture and décor from decades ago, including a hostess trolley, though I'm not sure why I recognise one.

"What goes around comes around," Violet says for the fourth time. "You'd better take the tea as I'm not so steady without a stick."

Age has reduced her to a stoop that forces her to look up at people. The rest of her seems to have shrunk, leaving her bones and joints to protrude through skin that's faded and wrinkled. Her bright eyes struggle to see past eyelids that sag and droop like the rest of her face as it collects beneath a pointed chin.

She points to the cake on the table. "Have some Victoria sponge. I made it yesterday and burned my arm on the oven." She pulls up the sleeve of her loose-fitting floral dress to reveal an inflamed area of skin. "Mind you, I spilled a pan of carrots over my leg last month."

"You should see a doctor," Gemma says, raising a hand as Violet bends to lift her dress.

"He has enough to do, looking after the children across the road, poor mites. They're awfully cramped in there, you know. That's why I always give them money to buy sweets. My Bert left me well provided," she adds, picking up a black and white photo of a man in military uniform, medals proudly pinned to his chest. "Handsome sod, wasn't he?"

I nod and take the tea tray into the living room, which is filled with ornaments and photographs. They cover every flat surface from the top of an old TV to the electric fire surround. Dolls in national costumes fill a full height glass cabinet beside her bulky armchair.

"Got this for a thousand pounds," she says, patting the armrest. "It tilts and tips me out, reclines, and rises at the push of a button. The man said everyone has them. As a special offer, he let me have an adjustable double bed at half price. Wasn't that kind of him?"

I sip my milky tea, wondering whether to contact Age UK. Maybe they can help her before she gives all her money away.

She picks up another framed photo of her husband. "Bert fell down a manhole. He went out for his Sunday newspaper as usual and never came back. I heard an ambulance and saw some people gather round, but I didn't realise it was him."

Violet sips her tea, thoughtful for a few moments. "Still, mustn't grumble. We had a good life. Never had children, but the ones over the road always come here for sweets and toys. They need to get out. It's no life living in one room, is it?"

"Have you seen the rooms?" I ask.

"Me, love? No, I can't go anywhere without my stick. It'll turn up," she says, looking around. "Things always do when you stop looking for them, don't they? Are you sure you don't want any cake? I burned my arm making it."

I should arrange for someone to visit, but she'll refuse. Proud and independent, she sees the good in people. Or maybe she enjoys the company her generosity brings.

"Do you remember Mr Trimble?" I ask. "He owned the house across the road."

"Did he?" She pauses to sip more tea and frowns at the taste. "I thought he ran a hotel. That's right, the Anderida Hotel. Mind you," she says, lowering her voice, "I get easily confused these days. I mistook the window cleaner for the gardener the other day. He said he was happy to hose down my lawn, bless him."

She laughs, almost spilling tea over her lap.

"Now where was I? That's right, the hotel. It closed in the 1990s like so many of the guest houses around here. It was sad to see it empty but someone turned it into a care home. Or was it a hostel for homeless people? Whatever it was, people round here didn't like it. Not that Tony Trimble cared. He lived in a big house somewhere near Alfriston. Do you know it, love?"

I shake my head, wondering how much to believe.

"He must be in his 80s now," she says, clicking her lower set of false teeth. "Give him my regards if you see him."

"He died a couple of weeks ago, Violet."

"Tony's dead?" She looks lost, frozen in time, staring into memories that bring tears to her eyes. "What about those poor children?"

"What children?"

"He loved children," she replies in a faraway voice. "Always gave them chocolates and presents to make them feel special. He came from a home just like them, see. He knew what it was like to have no one. His parents abandoned him when he was a child, poor love."

She looks at me with sad eyes. "So why did people want to harm him?"

Twelve

Violet drifts in and out of memories, making little sense as she repeats the same details, asking us several times if we want any cake. When one of her neighbours arrives for tea and a chat, we retreat to the car.

"That was a waste of time," Gemma remarks, making a note on the file.

"Not entirely. She's unlikely to complain about Anderida Villas. You can cross her off the list and concentrate on the rest."

"She wasn't on the list. And I'd rather talk to the rest without you asking about Trimble," she says, pulling out her phone. "I'll get Richard to collect me later."

I could check with Social Services at East Sussex County Council to see if Trimble ran a home for children near Alfriston. I have no recollection of one on my inspection list, which means Trimble could have fostered or adopted children, or Violet imagined it. Then again, it might be the house he used to pay for his time at Nightingales.

If only Miss Rudolf would send me the rest of his details. Maybe Louise Watson can help.

While Gemma talks to Richard on the phone, I call Nightingales to arrange an impromptu visit to East Dean. Unfortunately, Louise isn't available.

"Don't worry," Gemma's saying, sounding a little too animated. "What can a bunch of old ladies do? Yes, Kent's still here. Okay, I'll pass you over."

I take the phone, wondering what Richard wants. "Sorry to drag you out," I say.

"Nothing's too much trouble where Gemms is concerned." He pauses for a moment and then reverts to his official tone. "Would you be interested in selling Belmont? I know it's a bit out of left field, but I know at least two clients who'd bite your hand off."

Selling Belmont to buy my sanctuary and the adjoining land would solve most of my problems. But would Niamh give up her new home? Would Alice agree to the sale? Will Birchill sell me the land? Would he insist on a new road to serve the holiday village he wants to build on the adjoining woodland?

"I'll think about it," I say.

"Don't leave it too long," Richard says. "Once Niamh gets settled, she won't want to move."

"I'll let you know."

I end the call and return the phone to Gemma.

"I hope that was nothing to do with Trimble," she says.

"No," I say, unable to resist temptation, "we're planning a stag night."

The following morning, I'm forced to confront bad news. Disbelief echoes around the offices and corridors of the town hall as the news spreads faster than a computer virus.

"How did that creep become Leader of the Council?" Gemma asks, no doubt recalling the clashes we've had with Councillor Gregory Rathbone and his many food businesses.

"He offered his fellow councillors cut price meals and weddings," Lucy replies, examining her long, lank hair. "Say, Kent, would you inspect his pub for me? It's not due until April, but I'll be clearing this year's backlog until June unless we get some help."

Gemma's move to pollution means Nigel and Lucy are the only officers inspecting food businesses as we approach the end of the financial year. I requested an urgent one-to-one with Danni to deal with the issue last week, but she demanded detailed costings, along with statistics and projections to justify employing contract environmental health officers. Now, she's sent me an agenda that makes it clear I'm responsible for resolving the challenges.

Kelly cancels the 10.30 meeting when Gregory Rathbone summons Danni.

"I've no idea when she'll be back, lover, but she won't be in a good mood."

Danni looks harassed when I enter her office at 12.18. The papers for our meeting are strewn across the table. She beckons me to sit opposite with one hand while the other flicks through the papers.

"Our new leader wants next year's Food Safety Service Plan," she says, looking up. "And the Health and Safety Service Plan. Where are they?"

"I haven't written them yet."

"Too busy attending funerals, were you?"

"I can't finalise the plans until the end of this financial

year, when I know how many inspections are still outstanding."

"There wouldn't be any outstanding inspections if you stopped going to funerals."

"There won't be any outstanding inspections if we employ contract EHOs to blitz the backlog."

"So you can waste another morning with Gemma, looking at overgrown gardens?"

Danni's clearly attended a management course in denial, though she'll never admit it.

"The ombudsman instructed us to carry out a full and proper investigation," I remind her. "I had to assess the nature and scale of the complaints so I could dedicate adequate resources."

"If you'd checked the worksheets on the database, you'd know most of the complaints are unproven and unfounded." She reaches for her bottle of water, flavoured with a blend of fruits to increase the price. "You'd also know that only three complainants returned any diary sheets. Most of them were useless."

"Only because we don't explain what we need them to record."

"Like the different species of weeds in the garden?" She gulps down some water, raising a finger to cut off my objections. "Priorities," she says, thudding the bottle onto the table. "Priorities, Kent. Put them at the top of your list."

Where else would I put them?

"Now, before I have to explain to Councillor Rathbone why you're so interested in Anthony Trimble," she says, mopping spilt water with a tissue, "perhaps you could tell me. First you bury him. Then you make enquiries about his ownership of Anderida Villas. Now you're knocking on doors. Is this another of your nefarious investigations?"

"He doesn't own Anderida Villas," I reply.

"Then there's nothing to stop you reducing your backlog of food inspections." She slides a sheet of paper across the desk. "You're the worst offender, Kent. Doesn't say much for your leadership, does it?"

"I don't have the time to manage a new team and keep up with my inspections. I'm not Superman."

"No, you're not that kind of Kent," she says.

"Then let me bring in contract environmental health officers and clear the backlog. I can then produce the service plans and reports you want while you recruit an officer to replace Gemma's post in food. Kelly would make an excellent food officer."

"So you can corrupt her as well? I don't think so," Danni adds with a mocking laugh. "Gemma's post is frozen. Councillor Rathbone's reinstated the moratorium on recruitment."

I'm not sure how the council or the government expect us to carry out our statutory duties without sufficient staff, but arguing won't change anything.

"Then let's use the salary savings from the post to pay for contractors."

"She starts on Monday." Danni slides a manila folder across the table. "I believe you already know her."

Cecile Montgomery upset almost every food business operator in the district when she spent three months with us as a trainee. She went on to qualify as an environmental health officer about a year and a half ago and set up her own company, performing third party audits for retailers and national chains and inspections for understaffed councils.

"Yes, she made quite an impression last time," I say.

Back in the office, Lucy shows her support with a few well-chosen expletives. Even Nigel, who's more forgiving, looks shell shocked. Sylvie simply laughs.

"Have you got the equity agreement for Mr Trimble yet?" I ask her.

"That's one for the Treasury Solicitor," she replies.

"Have you rung Miss Rudolf to chase it up?"

"Danni said it wasn't a priority."

"You went to Danni?"

"Of course I didn't. I'm not stupid."

"You might just have proved the opposite," Danni says, appearing at the worst moment as usual. "Don't make the same mistake, Kent. Discretion isn't something to shout about."

Once she's gone, I ring Nightingales, but Louise Watson's not back until Thursday. With a sigh, I print off a list of outstanding inspections. It won't be easy, finding businesses where Cecile Montgomery won't antagonise the owners.

Then I spot a familiar name.

"I need to swap one of your inspections," I tell Nigel over a cup of tea. "I'll allocate you a care home of equal rating in return."

"Is this something to do with the guy you buried?"

"Of course not," I reply. "If I leave Nightingales on your list, I'll have to pass it to Cecile. Then you'll have to deal with the complaints from Miss Rudolf."

He sighs and nods. "Okay, but why did you pick Cecile Montgomery?"

"She can start next week."

"Yeah, because no one else will employ her."

Back at my desk I transfer Nightingales to my inspection

list. I also update the database and spreadsheets in case Danni takes a look.

Mind you, if she's already checked the outstanding inspection list, I'm sunk.

Thirteen

On Thursday, I arrive at the Tiger Inn a few minutes before one o'clock. The log fire spits and crackles in the brick fireplace beneath a posse of horse brasses. It's the centrepiece of a room built centuries ago from sturdy oak beams that stretch across the ceiling and down to frame the solid bar. Polished by the elbows and sleeves of patrons, the bar shines through the knocks and dents of the years, reflecting the gleaming parade of modern pumps and dispensers above it. I glance around the empty tables, wondering if the bitter wind and cold have deterred the ramblers and hikers who usually pass through the pub.

After twenty minutes, looking out across the green, I suspect the weather has deterred Louise, though it's more likely to be me.

When I rang her at midday, she didn't sound enthusiastic about meeting me for lunch. Miss Rudolf was nearby, which led to a stilted conversation where Louise responded mainly in monosyllables, as if I was a customer. In the end,

I said I would wait in the Tiger for her and ended the call.

"She won't be long," the homely waitress says, taking my empty glass. "It must be a woman or you wouldn't be looking outside every few seconds and fiddling with your tie."

She makes me sound like a teenager on a first date. That went badly too, like most of my teenage experiences. For almost an hour and a half, I stood in the halo of a shop door, watching bus after bus arrive, spilling passengers onto the damp pavements. I searched the sea of faces for Barbara Booth, the most gorgeous girl at school, knowing deep down that she was too classy for me. But I couldn't leave in case she was late.

As it was the last day of term, I never saw her again.

The waitress gives me an encouraging smile. "I'll bring you another mineral water," she says. "Ten more minutes won't hurt now, will it?"

My phone vibrates, announcing another marketing email that offers training and courses I can't manage without. Somehow, I manage to resist the offers, aware that my training budget would disappear within a couple of months at the prices demanded. No wonder so many of my environmental health colleagues set up their own companies. One or two have offered me a position, but I like my job, even though it becomes more difficult with every passing week.

If Danni tells me *less is more* another time, my two word response will prove her right.

I look out of the window once more. A woman in a blue scarf and coat battles the wind, clinging onto her bag as it flaps about like a windsock. She pushes open the door of the café opposite and tumbles inside. With a wry smile, I turn back to my vibrating phone.

That's when I notice the blue mittens on the table.

Louise Watson looks snug inside her black parka. Surrounded by faux fur, her face seems small and delicate, blushed by the cold wind. She eases back the hood and shakes her short hair into place, giving me a smile that warms me far more than the fire.

"Is there a secret passage?" I ask, almost knocking over the table as I get to my feet. "Only I didn't see you walking across the green."

"There's a smugglers' tunnel that comes out in the cellar," she replies, grabbing her mittens. "But it's full of cobwebs so I came via the church."

"To pray for strength?"

She places her parka on the back of a chair and sits to my right, facing the fire. "I always go that way."

Before she can explain, the waitress arrives with two bottles of mineral water and two glasses. "You look perished, love," she says. "Why don't you move closer to the fire?"

"I'll soon warm up, Cynthia. Do you know Mr Fisher?"

"Everyone knows the Fishers round here, love. Mrs Fisher's moved into Colonel Witherington's old house at the top of the hill, I heard, so you might be bringing her in sometime," Cynthia says, giving me a hopeful look. "Oh, she's so elegant, Louise. Tall and slim, hair as black as the night sky. All natural too."

She wouldn't say that if she took a peek in my stepmother's bathroom cabinet.

"I met her at a party on New Year's Eve," Louise says.

"How lovely," Cynthia says, as if my stepmother's royalty.

"She's quite a character," Louise says, prolonging Cynthia's stay. With no one else to serve, she has plenty of time, despite saying she must leave us in peace at least three times. When she finally withdraws, Louise looks warm and relaxed, though she can't help fiddling with her hair.

"I met Cynthia in the graveyard," she says, pouring water into her glass. "I was reading the dedication on her mother's gravestone. We started chatting and ..." She bites her lower lip. "You want to know why I was looking at her mother's gravestone, don't you?"

I want to know what it's like to kiss her lips.

"I'm interested in names," she says. "Cynthia's a Boniface, which kind of describes her, don't you think?"

As a youngster, I invented personalities to go with the names of the authors I read. This extended to the various officials who wrote letters to my mother. Then one day Ambrose Merriweather from the local council visited. He turned out to be the antithesis of his name, perking up only when he refused my mother's application for additional benefits.

"What does Louise mean?"

"Renowned warrior or fighter." She giggles. "I know, it's hardly me, but I like it."

I like the way she unbuttons her black jacket to reveal the white blouse beneath.

"We lived next door to a cemetery," she says. "I would sit at my bedroom window, watching the hearses come and go, wondering who they were burying, what they were like."

"So, you checked the headstones."

She nods. "I found it comforting because everyone was loved and missed."

Not everyone, I'm tempted to tell her. "Does that include Trimble?"

She takes a sip of water and leans closer, her eyes widening with excitement. "You've solved the puzzle, haven't you? That's why you wanted to meet."

"I was hoping you could help me with the puzzle."

"Now? I don't have time," she says, checking her watch.

"How about this evening?"

She sighs, looking disappointed. "Tracey warned me about you."

"Who's Tracey?"

"She said you wouldn't remember her. She remembers you."

"I've never met anyone called Tracey. Who is she?"

"We job share at Nightingales. She lives in the flat below mine in Hampden Park behind Sainsbury's. You must remember it."

I've known many women over the years, but I rarely forget their names, where I met them or where they live. "Tracey's confused me with someone else," I say, keen to move on.

Louise shakes her head. "No, she had to find someone to take her son, Ben, so you could be alone together."

That definitely rules Tracey out. I'd remember a son.

"Louise, I'm not planning to seduce you, if that's what you're thinking."

"Shame," she says, looking hurt. Then she giggles. "You could pop down and visit Tracey afterwards."

I draw a breath. "Look, I could really use your help with Trimble."

She puts on her serious face. "Why me?"

"Trimble trusted you with the numbers."

"I thought Gemma Dean helped you solve the murders."

"She's planning her wedding."

"So I'm second choice?"

"Richard doesn't want her getting shot again."

"But you don't mind if I get shot?"

When I sigh in frustration, Louise giggles once more.

"Of course I'll help," she says, "but the numbers might as well be hieroglyphics. That's why Mr Trimble wanted you to have them. He read about you in the Tollingdon Tribune. Say, it could be something biblical, couldn't it?"

"The Tollingdon Tribune?" I can't think of anyone less Christian than its editor, Thomas Hardy Logan, the cynical hack who claims he's the conscience of the people.

"No, the numbers. What if they're chapters and paragraphs from the bible? Remorse sounds biblical. Guilt, repentance, that kind of thing."

"Remorse? What are you talking about?"

"My mouth doesn't always communicate with my brain, especially when I'm nervous."

"Why are you nervous?"

"Excited then." She places her hands on her chest and takes a deep breath, holding it for ten seconds, before exhaling. "Sorry, I don't normally get asked to solve murders."

"You were talking about remorse."

She nods. "I had this flash of inspiration about the numbers. Mr Trimble grabbed my arm once and muttered something about having no remorse for what he'd done. It had to be done, he kept saying. It had to be done."

"What did?"

She shrugs. "He had a mad, crazy look in his eyes, so I hurried away and told Miss Rudolf. She said it was his medication. Then they confined him to his room so he wouldn't frighten anyone else."

"Did this happen before or after he gave you the numbers?"

"After. He gave me the numbers two days after your visit on New Year's Eve."

"When he told me someone was killing him."

"That's right." She glances at her watch and sighs. "I have to get back. Miss Rudolf wasn't best pleased when I said I was going out to lunch."

"You're entitled to a proper break."

"She's the only manager at the moment and she has to prepare for an audit next week. Head office sprang it on her yesterday, so she's not a happy bunny. Then the boiler went wrong this morning. The engineer can't fix it until tomorrow when the parts arrive."

"You're still entitled to a break."

"I missed lunch altogether yesterday. And I had to stay late, which meant Tracey had to look after George. I'll probably have to work late again today," she says, getting to her feet.

"Who's George?"

She pulls on her parka, taking her time. "He's my deeply serious, incredibly protective, football mad, twelve year old son."

"Then you should be with him, not working late," I say, rising.

"It's not that simple. I've thought about getting another job, but they've got me, Mr Fisher. They own the flat I live in. It comes with the job."

I'm no property expert, but she can't possibly afford a two bedroom flat, plus utility bills, shopping, clothes and travel to work on a part time salary. I place a fiver on the table to cover the drinks and guide her towards the door.

"Do you pay rent?" I ask.

"They deduct a contribution from my salary each month. The rest comes from housing benefit, paid by Eastbourne council direct to the Sherlocks. They filled out the forms and handled everything for me."

Outside, the wind continues to whip across the green. Louise turns and pulls on her hood, disappearing beneath the faux fur for a moment. Then her face emerges once more, still anxious.

"One day, while I was in Miss Rudolf's office, I couldn't help noticing a file on her computer with my name on it. She never locks her computer when she leaves the office," Louise adds, in case I think she hacked into the network. "I found a letter from Eastbourne council, increasing my housing benefit as the rent for my flat had increased."

She pulls on her mittens as she talks. "The benefit covers the full rental, but they still take money from my salary for my contribution to the rent. If the council find out, I could be in trouble. It's my name on the claim forms, not theirs."

After learning about the equity release scheme the Sherlocks run, I'm not surprised they're fiddling the rent. They must be pulling the same trick at Anderida Villas. I wonder if they learned it from Trimble.

We walk along the rough path at the side of the green towards Lower Street opposite, heads bowed against the wind.

"I think they ripped off Trimble," I say. "He owned properties the Sherlocks now own, including a house near Alfriston. Did he ever say anything about it?"

She shrugs. "I hardly spoke to him. He was asleep most

of the time."

"I need to find out about the house near Alfriston," I say, stopping by the gate. "Miss Rudolf promised to give us all the details after his death, but she's withholding information."

"Can't you make her tell you?"

"If I could, I wouldn't be here now." I look into her hazel eyes, wondering if she'll agree. "No, it's not fair. It's too risky."

She leans closer, her face inches from mine. "What is?"

"Tomorrow morning, I'm making an unannounced hygiene inspection. While Miss Rudolf accompanies me, Gemma's going to sneak into her office and see what she can find on the computer. I know it sounds crazy," I say, when Louise looks at me in disbelief, "but I can't think of any other way. Would you keep watch so no one disturbs her?"

"It won't work, Kent."

"I know computers log everything, but Miss Rudolf must access hundreds of files each week. She won't remember what she looked at on any particular day. And if she doesn't lock her computer when she leaves the office, I can't see her spending hours checking logs."

Louise shakes her head. "She checks the security cameras though. That's why it won't work."

"Damn! I'll have to find another way, I guess. I was hoping to treat you to lunch tomorrow after my inspection, but some other time maybe."

"I'd like to see you in a white coat," she says, a wicked gleam in her eyes. "You'll make Miss Rudolf nervous."

"Next week then. Maybe I'll come up with another plan by then."

"We're being audited next week. The auditors will use Miss Rudolf's office."

We cross Lower Street and find some shelter against the buildings. We hurry along, propelled by the wind behind us. Outside the delicatessen, Louise grabs my arm and stops me. "You have to do the inspection tomorrow."

"But …"

She places her mitten against my lips. Her eyes grow wide with excitement as she leans closer. "I'll do it. I know where she keeps the personal files on the computer."

I shake my head. "If Miss Rudolf catches you … if she finds out."

"Only I can go into her office without suspicion. See you tomorrow morning."

She kisses my cheek and scurries away. I shouldn't smile, but my plan worked better than I'd anticipated.

Fourteen

At nine thirty the following morning, I arrive at Nightingales with a clean and pressed white coat, happy to leave team meetings and performance reports in the office. Though I enjoy having some control and influence as a manager, my heart and soul belong on the district, where I meet new and interesting people. When you work with businesses to improve standards, you can see the benefits of a food hygiene inspection almost immediately.

Unlike the office, where I spend most of my time justifying the actions I take.

No wonder so many managers keep their heads down in local government.

No chance of that since I began to solve murders.

Had I known the fatal work accident at Tombstone Adventure Park last September would turn out to be a murder in disguise, I would have passed the case to the police. It would have saved me a lot of grief and some unpleasant surprises.

The publicity prompted Colonel Witherington, a family friend and Leader of Downland District Council, to ask me to find his missing wife. She'd eloped with a dubious caterer, it seemed. But it wasn't a dodgy burger that killed her.

Now, Anthony Trimble's death intrigues me. He was a paranoid old man with dementia until he left me some cryptic numbers. While they could be items on a takeaway menu, they could also hold the answer to questions raised by his past. With Louise's help this morning, we may uncover a little more of the trail that could lead to murder.

Or Chicken Chow Mein.

Either way, it beats writing service plans.

Nightingales has the top National Food Hygiene rating of 5 and an excellent score from the Care Quality Commission. The past history shows a well-run business with good systems and practices. While Nigel had a few niggles and concerns during the last inspection, seventeen months ago, I can't imagine Miss Rudolf letting standards drop.

Neither will she let me roam around the kitchen unaccompanied, even if she's the only manager on duty.

It's much cooler than normal in reception. Louise, wearing a sweater under her jacket, greets me with a courteous, professional smile and announces my arrival. Miss Rudolf, who's not wearing an extra layer, summons me into her office, where she's sifting through stacks of magazines on her desk and the floor. She has a fan heater to keep her warm.

"Isn't there a conflict of interests?" she asks after we've covered the preliminaries. "You bring your dog here on therapy visits."

"Don't worry, I'll keep Columbo away from the

kitchen."

Her deadpan eyes tell me frivolity's off the menu. "I've had to review the pet visits," she says. "A flea infestation has created ill-feeling and tension in some quarters."

"Columbo isn't the only dog who comes here."

"It's a review, not a judgement," she says, leading me out of the office. "I'm taking Mr Fisher to the kitchens, Louise. Can you remove the magazines from my office and dispose of any over three months old?"

"Are you cancelling the pet visits?" I ask as we walk along the corridor.

"You'll be notified of my conclusions at the same time as the other owners." Miss Rudolf stops at the doors to the dining area. "What happened to our last inspector, Mr Long? I didn't realise his association with Nightingales would be so short."

A brief glint in her eyes tells me she enjoyed her joke.

"The boss likes to swap us around so we stay fresh."

"So fresh, you're here a month before our inspection's due."

"Well spotted, Miss Rudolf. That's why I enjoy your company."

"I don't think it's me you want to impress," she says with a smirk.

The neutral beiges and soft lighting of the spacious dining area can't disguise its functional feel. Round tables, served by two or four chairs, are laid out in a grid across a pale grey carpet that looks more industrial than residential. The windows down one side offer views across the gardens towards the wooded hills of the Downs. They also allow the sun to bring a little warmth into the room. On the opposite wall, the notice boards offer all manner of outings and clubs to fill in the time between meals. Residents can go to Eastbourne's theatres or play ping pong in the Games Room, unless they'd prefer to discuss literature in the library or discover creative cake decoration with Chloe on Wednesday afternoons.

As we walk towards the servery, I brush my fingers over the expensive-looking table cloths, emblazoned with the gold Nightingales crest. To my surprise, the cloths feel like plastic. A quick glance at the underside confirms this. Miss Rudolf prefers to straighten a rebellious cloth on one of the dressers that lines the wall. A quick look inside reveals plates and bowls, with cutlery in the drawers above.

Miss Rudolf waits by the servery, eyeing the piles of dirty bowls and plates on top of the dresser nearest the door into the kitchen. I'm sure she wants to remove the cutlery so the crockery stacks neatly.

"These will be taken into wash up shortly," she says. "I imagine the kitchen porter's on a cigarette break, or puffing on one of those ghastly electronic alternatives. He uses alpine berry flavour because it sounds healthy. It beggars belief."

No more than fruit flavoured teas, I'm tempted to suggest.

She leads me past the servery, which offers a window into the spotless and well-fitted kitchen, gleaming with stainless steel within a cocoon of plastic-clad walls. A young woman in whites and chequered trousers raises a hand to us before spraying antibacterial cleaner on a worktop in the central preparation island. Many chefs think cleaning's a job for minions. Others have little choice when their kitchen porters go vaping. This one feeds music into her ears, blotting out the noisy fans that draw the cooking odours of a full English breakfast into the gargantuan cooker hood. If only the fans could suck the grease from the cookers, deep fat fryers and worktops.

Miss Rudolf waits in the doorway while I put on my white coat and trilby.

"All our appliances are serviced annually and certificated to demonstrate due diligence," she says, as if conducting a guided tour. "Three times a year, hygiene specialists carry out a thorough deep clean, which is checked and verified by Montgomery Health. Miss Montgomery audits the kitchen and food areas twice yearly."

While I'm curious to know how an auditor can verify three deep cleans with only two audits, I'm pleased Montgomery Health has the contract.

"We've employed Cecile Montgomery to help us with some of our inspections," I say. "As I need to verify her competence, I can use her last audit here as an example."

And Danni can't challenge my decision to inspect Nightingales. I could hardly send a contractor, who already worked for the home, could I?

"As well as her last audit report, I'd like to check your documented management systems and records," I say, opening my clipboard to reveal my inspection forms. "We can do that after we've finished here, Miss Rudolf."

"While I'm sure I would find your inspection fascinating, Mr Fisher, Kylie's up to speed with our systems and procedures. I'll leave you in her capable hands while I retrieve our documentation from the computer for your scrutiny."

"In your office?" I ask, certain she'll walk in on Louise, searching for information on Trimble's file. "I was hoping to talk to you about a healthy eating award we offer."

"Let's do that later," she says, turning to leave.

I slide an *Eat Out Eat Well* leaflet from the clipboard and hand it to her. "Do you offer residents healthy food choices Miss Rudolf?"

"We are a high quality residential provider, Mr Fisher. We offer healthy choices, vegetarian and vegan alternatives, and wheat free products. We can cope with any allergy or food intolerance, having trained all our catering and waiting staff."

"You have waiters?"

"You don't expect residents to queue with trays, do you?"

"Do you inspect the kitchen as part of your management duties?" I ask, following her to the servery.

"Every afternoon, when the kitchen's closed, I come in and help myself to a cream doughnut. If anything's out of place or unsatisfactory, I notice."

"Does that include the external bin area?"

She masks her frustration with a polite smile. "Is there something you want to tell me, Mr Fisher?"

"During my last visit with Columbo, he ran into the garden. He went straight for the bins and chased something into the bushes."

"Why didn't you report it at the time?"

"I thought it was a squirrel rather than a rat," I reply, realising how feeble I sound. "That's why I brought the inspection forward. I thought we could take a closer look."

She takes in a deep breath. "We employ a pest control contractor who visits regularly. He has not reported any rodent activity, either inside the building or out."

"How often does he visit?"

"His last visit was two days ago." Her mobile phone

interrupts her with the opening strains of Beethoven's Fifth. "But I'll ask Fridrik, our maintenance operative, to show you around the bin area. He must be psychic," she says, glancing at her phone.

She strides through the door and into the dining area to take the call. Though she has her back to me, she becomes animated. Her voice rises until she snatches the phone away from her ear and ends the call.

When she turns, her face is composed once more, unlike her voice. "Fridrik will not be available. We have a situation that requires my prompt attention."

Did Fridrik stray into the office and catch Louise snooping?

Fifteen

When Miss Rudolf heads in the opposite direction to her office, I sigh with relief.

"She don't miss nuffink," Kylie says in street Cockney. "Miss Rudolf, like. She checks them bins every day. Rats wouldn't dare go near them."

Kylie talks with a rhythm, her voice rising at the end of each phrase or sentence. She has swagger and confidence, even though her rounded face and traces of acne suggest she's about sixteen, though she must be older. Her tight-fitting tabard and chunky arms betray a love of food, which she supplements with a regular helping of fingernails. When she realises I'm studying her, she gives me a cocky sneer, revealing uneven teeth and glints of many fillings.

"What's it like, solving a murder?" she asks, wiping her hands on a tea towel.

"It beats writing management reports," I reply, heading for the walk in chillers.

"Be careful, I might have a few bodies in there." She

grins, thinking she's the first person to say this. "I could easily kill the numpties that work here. Not that anyone would miss them. They're not here for long. Some of the waiters help out, but they're only interested in my tits. Still, it's less for me to do, innit?"

It sounds like Nigel was right about the staffing.

Kylie opens the left hand chiller door and steps aside so I can enter. The lower shelves are half-filled with large plastic bags of chicken breasts, cuts of beef, and fish fillets, many in breadcrumbs. Polythene bags of chips, peas and other vegetables lie scattered along the higher shelves. A few tubs of ice cream, and frozen desserts dot the rear shelves.

"Plenty of room to hide a body," she says with a wink. "All from Europe," she adds as I examine a box of vacuum-packed beef. "Don't ask me where cos the drivers don't speak much English. It's all date coded and labelled."

The food in the freezer and chiller looks fine. It's all within date, properly protected from contamination, with raw and cooked kept in separate areas. There's nothing outstanding or top quality, as I would have expected, but Kylie has an answer for that.

"With margins tight, I have to be creative, right? I jazz things up. The residents think Jamie Oliver cooked for them."

"Then I'll make sure everything's pukka," I say, moving on.

While everything complies with the minimum legal requirements of the law, the stainless steel worktops and units look tired, especially underneath. The same goes for the cookers, which look worse for wear inside the ovens.

"Are they second hand?" I ask.

"Reconditioned. Most of them come from Eastern Europe, but they're sound."

The digital readouts for the under-counter fridges show good internal temperatures, as a quick check with my hand confirms.

"They're well cool," she says with a wink. "Send the temperatures to the computer by Wi-Fi."

"You should double check with a probe thermometer."

"What for?"

"In case the readout's faulty."

"If the temperature's wrong, an alarm goes off in Miss Rudolf's office."

"So, you won't know there's a problem until she tells you," I say.

She holds up her hands and wiggles her fingers. "Got me own digit thermometers. But nuffink goes wrong. Check the temperature logs. You'll see."

Having examined next week's fridge temperatures in a few kitchens I've visited, I prefer to believe what I touch.

The remainder of the inspection passes without incident. The external bin area's spotless and smells of disinfectant, courtesy of Fridrik, I imagine. Inside, all the waste is bagged. Back in the kitchen, Kylie waits by the servery with two mugs of tea.

"Do I keep my top rating?" she asks.

While Nightingales takes a few shortcuts and dresses up average food to make it seem like cordon bleu, they exceed legal hygiene requirements, which provide a minimum standard. I should feel pleased, but it feels like a veneer.

Veneers chip and crack when pressure's applied.

"I'm concerned about the lack of staff," I say. "In the hour and half since I arrived, no one's come in to help you.

Where's the Kitchen Porter?"

"We had a problem with the boiler. Water everywhere. They'll be helping to clear that so the engineer can do his stuff. I prepped food last night so I could cope."

I nod, realising I haven't complimented her on her planning. "You're doing a good job, Kylie. I'm sure they don't appreciate how much you do."

She buffs her fingers against her lapel and grins. "I get free haircuts in the salon, facial and massage when it's quiet. I can use the gym. If I need help, Miss Rudolf always finds someone – even if it's from one of the other homes."

Right on cue, a sullen-looking man with Slavic grey eyes and thick black hair, combed back over his protruding ears, enters through the delivery doors. He pulls off a thick coat and unwinds his scarf to reveal a black tabard over a jaded white shirt and jeans. He wipes his nose on the back of his hand and heads into the kitchen.

"Grumpy Gregor does veg prep and puddings," Kylie says. "He doesn't talk much, unless you're from Slovakia, or wherever he comes from, but he's solid."

While he washes his hands at the basin, Gregor stares at me as if memorising my appearance in case I appear in an identity parade.

"What food hygiene training has he had?" I ask.

"Miss Rudolf has the certificates," she replies. "Everyone does our online course. Once you pass the exam, you get your certificate. It's cool cos you can't move on to the next question until you've answered the last one correctly."

As most foundation food hygiene courses have multiple choice questions with four possible answers, it shouldn't take candidates too long to click on the right answer.

"Is the course available in foreign languages?"

"Sure. And there's an app for your phone or tablet. How cool is that?"

Cooler than my cup of tea, which I take into the dining area. I sit at a table by the window to check my notes and add details where needed. Though concerned about the minimal staff and the quality of training, Kylie knows her job and tackles it with pride, unlike Noel at the Eight Bells, who resented the penny pinching when he worked here.

When I reach reception, Louise is not behind the counter. Her headset lies next to the keyboard and her pad contains no messages. I tap the spacebar on the keyboard to discover the screen's locked by password.

"You won't find our management systems there, Mr Fisher."

Miss Rudolf strolls out of her office, the self-satisfied look in her eyes as sharp as lipstick on her lips. "Louise will take you to our internet café on the first floor where you can work in private."

"And if I have any questions?"

"Most inspectors find our systems easy to follow. It's imperative when you employ people whose native language isn't English. Malcolm Knott of the Care Quality Commission says our documented systems are the best he's seen."

"I know, I've seen his reports," I say, wondering if Knott moonlights for Nightingales.

Maybe I should arrange to meet the elusive care homes inspector.

Louise emerges from the office, her expression neutral. She raises a finger to her lips and leads me upstairs to a small landing that needs only a log fire to complement the bookcases, armchairs and coffee tables. A door between the bookcases leads into a small room that's cold and smells of lavender. Two small tables with old computers butt up against a radiator below a long window that overlooks the entrance to Nightingales. A vending machine rests on top of a small fridge in the corner, generating the only heat in the room.

"The boiler's fixed," she says, taking a seat. "Everything should warm up soon."

She boots the computer, logging in when required. She declines a cup of pale vending tea and then opens the folder with the management systems, expanding it so I can see the various parts.

"Did you have any problems?" I ask.

Her eyes direct me to a small CCTV camera in the corner of the room. Outside on the landing, she stands at the window, her voice a whisper. "Miss Rudolf knows we met for lunch yesterday."

In a village like East Dean it's hardly surprising.

"She told me you wanted information about the home," Louise says. "That's why you brought the food inspection forward a month. How did she know that?"

"You can work out when an inspection's due from the date of the last one. But you won't know which day or week we'll call."

"She knew you were coming today, I swear it."

I shake my head. "We only decided yesterday."

"What if someone in your office warned her?"

"It's in my Outlook calendar." I pause, realising my calendar can be viewed by anyone in the council. "Did someone catch you at Miss Rudolf's computer? Only she had a heated call with someone before marching off."

"No, I was in and out in a couple of minutes." Louise

slips a folded piece of paper into my hand. "I hope that's the address you wanted. Don't look until you leave. There are cameras everywhere."

"I could come over this evening and tell you."

She shakes her head, and hurries back down the stairs.

Disappointed, I slip the paper into my pocket, wondering if Miss Rudolf's warned Louise to keep away from me. If so, it means Nightingales has something to hide, but it's not in their management systems. The documentation and records are flawless, probably copied from one of Cecile Montgomery's more prestigious clients. Maybe not, I decide. As a manager, I shouldn't let my prejudices influence my objectivity.

Why didn't Louise want to see me later?

It's not like she's my type. She has a twelve year old son and I'm not interested in playing happy families.

I switch off the computer and return to reception. There's no sign of Louise, but Miss Rudolf invites me into her office. After a polite, but formal discussion, I return to my car, half expecting to find a note beneath the wiper.

Inside the car, I open Louise's note and read the address for Barten Mill in Litlington. The small village nestles below the South Downs and overlooks the Cuckmere River as it winds its way to the coast. Hopefully, Colin Comer still frequents the Plough and Harrow public house. As one of the village's oldest residents, he'll remember Trimble.

Louise would have liked Colin, and the ploughman's lunches at the pub.

When I fold her note in half, I notice something written on the back. Eleven numbers in three columns, similar to Trimble's code.

Only his isn't a mobile phone number.

Sixteen

George, a slouching string of a boy, looks up from his smartphone and stares at Frances when she descends the steps from her draughty old caravan. His wide, surprised eyes take in her beaded dreadlocks, combat jacket and trousers and Doc Marten boots as she strides across the yard to join us beside the main barn of my animal sanctuary. For a twelve year-old, who seems incapable of speech or movement beyond a sullen shrug of the shoulders, he bursts into life, peeling off the wall that keeps him upright.

Though she's annoyed with me for foisting him on her on a busy Saturday, she gives him a big smile. "Hi, George. You like animals, I hear."

He nods, his mouth open, frozen by the hormones pulsing through his veins.

"Would you like to help me this afternoon?"

He nods again.

"If you come with me, I'll take you on a short tour and explain what we do and then we can get our hands dirty.

What do you say?"

He nods eagerly.

Trainers that dragged across the concrete a few minutes ago now move at speed. His low-hung jeans look ready to drop, but somehow cling to his hips. He brushes a hand over his dark hair to raise the gelled spikes and disappears around the corner.

Louise and I melt into laughter. Her worried frown lifts and we walk across the yard to my car. She removes her parka to reveal a pale blue sweater that accentuates her slender figure. Skinny jeans have a similar effect on her legs, making her look taller and more confident than her demeanour suggests.

She puts her parka on the back seat. "You wouldn't believe how chatty he was in the taxi on the way over. He bombarded me with questions, having read about you on the internet. Then, the moment we arrive, he reverts to moody teenager."

"And now he's in love with Frances."

"That's what worries me," she says with a frown. "He won't be able to keep quiet about Frances. He's bound to tell Ben, Tracey's son. I told her we were off to Brighton for the day."

"Are you still worried Tracey will say something to Miss Rudolf?"

She gives me her *'I know I'm being silly'* look. "I'd rather not take any chances."

"Apart from giving me your mobile number, you mean."

"I thought it was time I made up my own mind." Her smile makes the back of my neck tingle. "Tracey talks to me like I'm her trainee, telling me what to do, who to watch out for. I'm sure she means well, but I'm not a kid."

"What if I hadn't rung you yesterday?" I ask, turning the key in the ignition.

Before she can answer, Gemma's Volvo estate screeches through the gate and lurches to a halt, inches from my bumper. She's out of the seatbelt and door in one sinuous movement. A quick flick of her fingers settles her glossy hair as she saunters over in her tight jeans and heels. She pulls on the hem of her red sweater to accentuate her curves.

I switch off the engine and wind down the window. "We're on our way out," I say.

She bends so her face is level with mine, though she's looking at Louise.

"You were at my engagement party," Gemma says. "Do you work for Richard?"

"I'm Louise Watson. I was waitressing, Miss Dean."

Gemma picks a pinch of fluff from the collar of my fleece. "Seven, nearly eight years ago, I was a waitress at La Floret in the High Street when Kent walked in. You were more interested in inspecting me than the kitchen, weren't you?"

"Is there something you wanted?" I ask. "Only, we're in a hurry."

"He's so modest," she says to Louise. "I mean, look at this place. It's hard to believe that a few years ago it was a couple of derelict barns. Has he shown you the flat he created on the first floor? The views of the Downs from the bedroom are simply stunning."

"I haven't seen them," Louise says. "We never opened the curtains."

I manage to keep a straight face as I open the door and guide Gemma away from the car. "Serves you right," I say. "What brings you here?"

"You didn't waste your time," she says, her tone disparaging. "She's the receptionist from Nightingales, isn't she? Well, she may be a Watson, Holmes, but she's not your type."

"She put you in your place."

Gemma folds her arms. "You mean, I'm surplus to requirements. You've roped her into the Trimble investigation, haven't you? Like Richard."

"Is that why you're here?"

"I told you not to involve Richard. It's bad enough having you as best man without you taking advantage."

"Then make him see sense. He must have other friends."

She rolls her eyes. "But none are as exciting as you."

"And none of them slept with his fiancée."

She sighs. "Seven years ago, Kent. Isn't it time you got over it?"

"You mentioned La Floret, not me."

"Okay, it was petty," she says, looking contrite. "Richard may not be you, but he's kind and thoughtful and he won't let me down. So, stop playing games or I'll tell him I want you to walk me down the aisle and give me away. You're old enough to be my father, after all."

"Not quite," I say, surprised at how hurt I feel.

She puts a hand on my arm. "Sorry. You know what a bitch I can be."

As she walks to her car, Frances rounds the corner with her shadow, George. She hurries past with a brief nod, but he almost crashes into Gemma, stepping around her at the last moment.

"Your volunteers are getting younger," she says, watching him wave to Louise.

"George is Louise's son."

Gemma looks at me in surprise before climbing into her car and driving away.

"Gemma often pops round," I say, taking a left at the crossroads and driving into Wilmington. "We've been through a lot together. I thought we were going to die at Tombstone Adventure Park. It makes you realise what's important."

When Louise says nothing, I drive on, not sure if she's annoyed, angry or disinterested.

"The Giant's Rest was named after the Long Man of Wilmington," I say as we pass the pub that's more of a restaurant. We lose sight of the hill, where the chalk outline of a giant man holds two staffs. "No one knows who first carved the figure or when. It's a mystery."

"Like you," she says, taking in the mixture of thatched cottages, Victorian terraces and grander houses that line the long, narrow road through the village.

"What do you mean?"

"You're like Superman. You're an environmental health officer during the week. You own an animal sanctuary and run it with Frances."

"Volunteers help us during the busy seasons."

"And you still find time to solve murders as if it's all in a day's work. How come you're not exhausted?"

I pull over and wait behind some parked cars as a tractor approaches. "I never set out to solve murders. It just happened."

"Nothing happens by accident, you said. That's how the papers quoted you."

She's been checking on me. That's good, though I sense another meaning in her words. "What are you saying?"

She shrugs and stares out of the window at the red brick houses with their small front gardens. "I don't understand why you want me to help you with Mr Trimble when you already have Gemma. That's pretty much what she said."

The tractor rumbles past, leaving clods of mud in its wake. "She is helping me," I reply, pulling away. "She's checking out leads in Pevensey where he owned another property."

"But I'm sitting here, not her."

"You found Barten Mill. You left me your mobile number."

"I didn't know it would put Gemma's nose out of joint."

"She'll get over it," I say, heading over the rise and past Wilmington Priory on the right. The Long Man comes into view on the left, looking calm and peaceful on the gentle slopes of the Downs. "She's got a wedding to organise."

"I'm not sure," Louise says, twirling the strap of her bag around her finger. "You didn't see the way she glared at Richard when he asked you to be best man. If looks could kill ..."

"He took everyone by surprise, didn't he?"

"You don't understand, Kent. Gemma gave me the same look before she drove off."

Seventeen

St Michael's church with its flint walls and short, white boarded steeple, signals the start of Litlington village. It nestles on the slopes at the eastern edge of the Cuckmere Valley, looking out across flat pastures to the river. On the left hand side of the road, the Downs rise with brutal slopes that have sapped the strength from my legs on many a run. With houses on both sides and cars parked against the kerb, I ease off the accelerator and take a left when we reach the car park of my favourite tearoom.

The low sun filters through the bare branches of the trees, but can't take the edge off the chill. A couple of Range Rovers and a truck wait for their owners to return from the garden centre, but otherwise the car park's deserted. Wrapped in her parka, Louise weaves through the puddles.

"I'm glad I didn't wear my Ugg boots," she says.

"Me too," I say, pleased when she smiles. For most of the journey down, she remained silent, troubled by Gemma, I suspect.

We stop at the main road. The wind whips around the hedgerow and blusters up the valley as we cross the road. "Barten Mill," I say pointing. "I thought we'd take a look on the way to the pub."

We walk along the narrow pavement past a white rendered Victorian house and stop by the flint wall of its neighbour. Shrubs and trees rise up, obscuring the house. I walk up to the tall wooden gates, looking for a latch. There's no bell, nameplate or letterbox either. A push on the gates tells me what I already know. I peer through the slit between them.

Beyond the unkempt drive and garden, wild with rambling roses and ivy, stands a red brick Victorian house with a steep roof, punctured by chimneys. Though tall and proud, blistered and flaking paint peels away from the window frames and wooden garage doors. Filthy net curtains obscure the sash windows, but not enough to hide the vertical bars.

Were they meant to keep burglars out or residents in?

"No one lives here," I say, stepping back.

Louise shuffles forward to take a look, shifting her head to get the best view. After a few seconds, she shudders and pulls back. The colour drains from her cheeks. She stares at me with wide, frightened eyes.

"Someone just stepped on my grave," she says.

My mother used that expression, usually on the few occasions when she took me out as a child. I was much older before I realised what she meant. She used the expression about places she'd visited before, though she never told me why they made her nervous.

"I've been here before," Louise says, stepping back. "These gates weren't here."

She brushes past me and reaches over the flint wall to my left, plunging her hands into the laurel behind, determined to separate the tangle of branches. "It had a different name too."

I step up beside her and peer into the foliage, my head inches from hers. "What are we looking for?"

She pushes a branch to one side, giving me a glimpse of a faded white board, smothered with mould and algae. "I've got some wet wipes in my bag. If we can clear the dirt away…"

"You know what it says, don't you?"

She retrieves a small pack of wet wipes. She hands me one and then takes hold of the branch while I clean the board. It takes three wipes and numerous abrasions to my hand and forearms before I make out a few faded letters.

"St Cloud's," she says in a hollow voice. She pulls back and wipes her hands. "St Cloud's is the orphanage where Homer Wells spends his childhood in the *Cider House Rules*. Have you read it?"

Violet said Trimble looked after children. Did he run an orphanage here?

"Tell me about the book," I say as we walk towards the Plough and Harrow.

"It belonged to my mother. I found it among her possessions when she died."

I remain silent, never sure about expressing sympathy for people I don't know.

"Her liver failed, but she clung on for months," Louise says. "She wanted to see me pass my exams, but I never went back to school. Why go to university when you can marry a wealthy man?"

"What stopped you?" I ask.

"George."

I wait for her to say more, but she remains thoughtful until we're inside the Plough and Harrow. The sound of merriment and laughter adds to the warmth from the heating and the glow of the many lamps and lights around the room, which stretches from front to rear. It has the low ceiling, oak beams and rustic charm you'd expect from a country pub, coupled with the earthy smell of wooden floors and walking boots.

They also welcome dogs. Maybe next time, I'll bring Columbo along as well.

We grab the only empty table, tucked into a corner beside an older couple on their second bottle of red wine. They nod and smile as we shuffle into the seats, used to the unfamiliar faces of hikers and tourists.

"It's lovely," Louise says, admiring the old cider jugs, miniature cannons, gilt picture frames, steins and candlesticks that fill the windowsills. Her gaze drifts to horse brasses that hang from the oak beam adjacent to a bar lined with hand pumps that dispense local ales, charity boxes and more eclectic trinkets.

I'm delighted when Louise wants to share a fiery chilli cheddar ploughman's lunch, which I order at the bar, along with two mineral waters. The young barman, with greased back hair and two days of stubble, hasn't heard of Anthony Trimble or Colin Comer.

"Fred Bailey would know." The barmaid with tattoos on her forearms weaves past with a tray of drinks. On her return to the bar, she detours to our table. "Colin died last year. Fred says pop over to the snug if you want a word. Take a pint of best if you do."

"Who's Colin?" Louise asks.

"He lived in the village all his life. He would have known Trimble."

"If you mean Anthony Trimble, everyone's heard of him."

The woman at the adjoining table leans across. Blonde hair, fading to grey, held in place with gravity-defying hairspray, crowns a proud, heavily made up face that's unable to defeat the wrinkles of time, or a love of Merlot.

"Didn't he own St Cloud's?" I ask.

After a quick glance at her husband, she shakes her head. "Never heard of it."

"I meant Barten Mill. We heard the owners wanted to sell. It looks like a great place to settle down and raise a family."

The woman twists in her chair to look us over. With me in a sweatshirt and chinos and Louise in sweater and jeans, we don't look like we could afford a house in Litlington.

"The place looks empty," I say.

"The Sherlocks like their privacy," she adds as if it's a disease.

"They're in the Caribbean, Matilda." Her portly, silver-haired husband raises his glass of wine to his large nose and sniffs in the aroma. "Why are you interested in Anthony Trimble? He sold the property years ago."

"Three years at the most, Henry." She turns back to us and lowers her voice. "I don't want to discourage you, but the builders said he lived in one room and the rest of the place was a tip. Upstairs, the rooms were piled high with old beds and mattresses."

"We heard it was an orphanage," I say. "We like the idea of children living there."

"I wouldn't know," she says, giving her husband a

warning glance. "It's time we were going, isn't it, Henry?"

Though he looks surprised, he drains his wine and rises to help Matilda into her fur coat. As she heads for the exit, he walks back and in a hushed voice, says, "Might be prudent to let sleeping dogs lie."

Eighteen

"Deceptions start rumours," Louise says, giving me a frosty look. "Why did you say we were a couple?"

"People don't talk to officials," I reply, "especially ones from the council."

"What if Mr and Mrs Sherlock find out we've been asking about their house?"

As the Sherlocks don't appear to have moved into St Cloud's, I can't see how they would find out. "No one knows who we are," I say. "Don't worry."

"You won't be the one looking for another job."

It looks like St Cloud's has scared off Warrior Louise, but I say nothing. Though she volunteered to snoop through Miss Rudolf's computer, I can understand Louise worrying someone will find out. William Kenneth Fisher, MP, offered me no end of protection while he was alive. No councillor or director at Downland wanted to upset him, so I could do as I pleased, which explains why Danni wants to get rid of me.

The barman arrives with our chilli cheddar ploughman's, which threatens to tumble off the edge of the large, oval plate. Once satisfied there's nothing further he can get for us, he returns to the bar. When I hand Louise a knife and fork, she shakes her head.

"Everyone's looking at us, Kent. I want to leave."

I want to eat, but what can I do?

"Let's go. I'll settle up at the bar and see you outside."

I wrap the cheddar in a napkin and slide it into my pocket before heading to the bar. A rush of cold air whips through the room as Louise exits, wrestling with her parka. It takes me several attempts to placate the barman, who seems convinced he's to blame for us not eating. His agitation only draws more attention to the situation, so I'm relieved to be on my way a few moments later. Fred Bailey gives me a nod as I pass and raises his empty glass.

Outside, I find Louise with her back to the wind, staring up the road towards St Cloud's. "I thought I'd feel safe with you," she says.

It sounds like a criticism though I'm sure it's not.

"Tell me what spooked you."

"I wish I knew," she says, walking beside me. "My mother grew up in a children's home. Not St Cloud's. When she was twelve, she was fostered. She never stayed anywhere for long. Too restless, she said."

Louise pulls the hood tight around her face. "I lost count of how many schools I went to. As soon I settled, we moved. She said a moving target was harder to hit."

"Did she ever tell you what she meant by that?"

Louise shakes her head. "That's why I took a look in her personal drawer while she was out on a date. I found her birth certificate and discovered she'd changed her surname from Johnson to Watson. When I asked her why, she said she needed to be someone else. She wouldn't let me bring friends home or go on sleepovers because she was scared someone would recognise her."

"Did she say who?"

She shakes her head and becomes thoughtful once more. When we settle into the car, she turns to me. "When I found *Cider House Rules,* there was a photograph of an older man in a smart suit inside the front cover. I wondered if he was my father, but Johnny said he wasn't."

"Who's Johnny?"

"She told me to ring Johnny if anything happened to her. He dealt with everything and took me to the cremation. He found me a job in a café."

"And you didn't go back to school."

"I was already pregnant by then. Some boy at school told me you were safe if you did it standing up," she says, blushing. "Johnny told me to get rid of the baby, but I couldn't. When George was born, I knew I'd do anything to protect him, as my mother had protected me."

Did my mother take me to Manchester to protect me?

It couldn't have been easy for a German immigrant to marry into the English gentry, having others look down on her because she wasn't from the right stock. Maybe she wanted to spare me that. Though she treated me like a burden most of the time, there was always food on the table and clothes in the wardrobe, even if they came from a charity shop.

So why did she tell me my father was dead when he wasn't? Poverty, and being at school with the middle classes, had already made me resentful and bitter. When I discovered she'd cashed his maintenance cheque every month while pleading poverty, I confronted her.

"It costs money, being invisible," was all she said.

"Did you identify the man in the photo?" I ask Louise, aware of the silence in the car.

She shakes her head. "Do you believe in fate?"

I don't believe in anything I can't touch.

She turns to face me, nibbling at her lower lip. "If you hadn't brought Columbo into Nightingales, we wouldn't be here."

"Is Trimble the man in the photo? Was your mother trying to escape him?"

She shakes her head. "If she was, why would she bring me here?"

"When was this?"

She closes her eyes. "I was four or five. It wasn't called St Cloud's. The house was empty because there were sheets everywhere, draped over the furniture. It was so quiet, I felt scared." She opens her eyes. "I ran out and hid in the bushes. Maybe that's when I found the sign."

"If your mother met Trimble that day, he might have recognised you at Nightingales. That would explain why he gave you the numbers."

She shakes her head, looking lost in thought. "He gave her the book."

"*The Cider House Rules?*"

"She had it in her hand when she came out of the house. I'm sure she did. I never saw it again until she died." She looks up, her eyes wide with realisation. "There was an inscription. *To Little Lisa, my favourite*. My mother's name was Elisabeth," she says, spelling it out.

While I'm not sure how this fits in with Trimble's death, it's a lead.

"If we compare the inscription to the writing in the crossword puzzle books, we can confirm that it's Trimble," I say, pulling on my seatbelt. "Let's take a closer look."

"We can't. The book's disappeared." She sighs and gives me a helpless look. "I only noticed this morning when I was looking for something in the wardrobe."

"Why didn't you say earlier?" I ask.

She turns the handbag strap around her finger like a tourniquet. "It wasn't important until I realised we were visiting St Cloud's."

"But you could have said you no longer had the book."

"I didn't realise it was important, Kent."

"It must be if someone took it. That's what you meant, right?"

"No one knows I have it."

"That's not true, is it?"

Her head jerks up, anger flashing across her eyes. "You mean George."

"Kids like to snoop. I was always snooping to see what I could find. Hang on," I say, thinking of something else. "When did you find out the book was missing?"

"George asked about his grandmother on Thursday. They were doing family trees at school. I said I had a few bits and pieces in the wardrobe. I offered to get them, but he said we could look at the weekend as he wanted to play with Ben on the Xbox. Tracey arrived a few minutes later with a bottle of wine."

"Were you expecting her?"

"Are you suggesting she took the book?"

"Does she have a key to your flat?"

"Tracey doesn't know about the book."

"Miss Rudolf might," I say, trying to catch up with my

thoughts. "She has Trimble's laptop. If he kept a journal ..."

She shakes her head, looking confused more than anything. "You don't know that."

"If it's not George, it has to be someone who has a key to your flat. Your landlords, the Sherlocks, will have a key. Miss Rudolf too. If Trimble kept a diary on the laptop, she'd know about the book."

When I see the look of horror in her eyes, I say, "Of course, George could have it in his room, using it for homework."

"I want to get away from here."

Her hand trembles as she tugs at the seatbelt, which keeps locking. As she grows angry and frustrated, she pulls harder and harder. The belt locks each time until she lets go and slumps back in the seat. She looks at me with frightened eyes, filling with tears.

"What have you got me into, Kent?"

Nineteen

Sometimes I forget how my cases might look to others. When I investigated Syd Collins' death, I had no idea his work accident would turn out to be murder. My instincts told me something wasn't right, and I kept digging. I was used to battling those who thought they could do as they pleased.

My years protesting against fox hunting involved covert and often dangerous activities. We broke into kennels, we filmed secretly, we laid false trails and we did what we could to disrupt and spoil the sick pleasure the hunters derived from the suffering of innocent animals.

My battles against developers, companies growing genetically modified crops, and those who inflicted cruelty on animals, involved dogged investigation, breaking into private property to obtain evidence and direct action where there was no other way. I suffered the occasional beating and got to know many police officers.

I never questioned what I was doing.

Neither did anyone else.

Until now.

Gemma challenged my gung-ho attitude when she helped me investigate Syd Collins' accident, but she wasn't fazed when it became a murder. She even risked her life to help me. And when Colonel Witherington claimed his wife had been murdered, she was the one who urged me to investigate, supporting me all the way.

Maybe I assumed Louise would take things in her stride after she volunteered to find Trimble's old address.

"Do you want me to take you home?" I ask.

She dabs the corners of her eyes with a tissue. "You must think I'm a right wuss. I mean, people have always let me down, pretending to be my friend."

"We don't know if Tracey had anything to do with the theft of your book."

"You haven't heard what she says about you." Louise lets out a deep sigh of disappointment. "We need each other for childcare. We live in the same block, but we'll never be friends."

"You've had a shock, Louise. You're frightened and upset because you don't know what's happened."

"No, I'm angry," she says. "Someone's broken into my home and stolen one of the few valuable things I have. I know the book isn't worth much, but it was my mother's. It was my link to her."

"Don't forget your memories."

Her hazel eyes look into mine and she smiles. "What do I do, Kent?"

"You find out the truth before you do anything you'll regret," I reply, wondering when I'll follow my own advice. "So, what do you want to do? Do you want to go home?"

She grins. "I want to check the bulge in your pocket."

I follow her gaze and laugh. "The chilli cheddar?"

"You said it was amazing. And I'm starving."

"What if I could offer you something better?"

"You've got a double chocolate Magnum in your pocket?"

I shake my head, struggling to stifle the laughter. "How about a cream tea?"

"With two scones?"

"And thick, luscious cream."

"Wow, you must have huge pockets, Mr Fisher. Where can we get a cream tea in the middle of winter?"

I tap the side of my nose, hoping Niamh won't mind us calling at Belmont.

We talk about the South Downs as we follow the narrow road out of Litlington and through the woodland until we're alongside the Cuckmere River. The valley opens out, rising into the hills opposite, where a giant white horse, cut into the chalk, looks towards the coast.

"Do you think it watched the smugglers, coming up the river?" she asks.

"Probably," I reply, my knowledge as scant as the leaves on the trees in Friston Forest.

In a month or so, the buds will burst into leaves to fill the spaces between the holly bushes, ivy and evergreens. During April, we'll have orphaned fox and badger cubs coming into the sanctuary after their parents perished on the roads. No doubt we'll take in more horses, abandoned on roadside verges with barely enough grass to support a lamb.

"I thought you'd know about the smugglers," she says. "Your family probably ran the operations, didn't they?"

William Fisher ran Downland Manor into the ground

rather than a smuggler's tunnel, but that's a story for another day. I smile, hoping there will be more days with Louise.

I draw to a halt at the junction with the A259 coast road, waiting for a gap in the traffic before turning left. Once we've weaved past the visitor centre, I accelerate up the hill, watching the land fall away to the Cuckmere as it snakes towards the sea. Columbo loves it here, racing through the long grass, occasionally dipping his paws in the water. I prefer the walk along the hills, photographing the views to the coastguard cottages at Seaford Head, opposite the Seven Sisters.

Louise sighs. "George and I sit in the front seats on the top deck of the bus. It's like a roller coaster when it comes down the hill."

"Do you wave your hands in the air?"

"No," she says, blushing a little. "They've got cameras."

"Next time we go to Litlington, we'll come this way and you can put your hands in the air as we descend."

"You think there'll be a next time?"

"If you'd rather not go to Litlington, I understand."

"We have to return to find out more about St Cloud's, don't we?"

I like the way she says we. "Are you sure you want to be seen with me?"

"It won't be easy, but I'll force myself. Now, where are you taking me?"

"Belmont," I reply, letting the car speed away as we reach the crest of the hill. "Niamh makes wonderful scones. And you should see her buns, as she often remarks."

Though hungry, I'm interested in Niamh's knowledge of local affairs. Thirty plus years as wife and confidant to

William Fisher, MP, have given her a unique insight into local affairs. She may not remember anything about St Cloud's, but she can consult the extensive personal records she kept. Originally intended to help William write his memoirs, she didn't declare her records to the civil servants who retrieved his official files after his death.

"Shouldn't you ring first?" Louise asks.

"Niamh likes surprises."

"She might be surprised to see me."

"Of course, you were waitressing at Gemma's party when you met Niamh. I'm sure she won't ask you to serve tea in the conservatory."

"Don't tease. I'll be nervous enough without you making jokes. But I can't wait to see the house. You must have felt like you'd won the lottery."

I did until Richard mentioned how much inheritance tax I could be liable for.

At the top of East Dean hill, I swing left towards Jevington. Moments later, I turn right into Old Willingdon Road, slowing so Louise can enjoy the view across Friston Forest to the coast. My thoughts return to the night Gemma and I drove along here to meet the Colonel. She was convinced we should investigate his wife's disappearance. Now I'm here with Louise, investigating another case that could become a murder.

No, it's murder. The theft of Louise's book confirms it.

I'll need a government codebreaker to make sense of Trimble's numbers.

I should also talk to East Sussex County Council. It had its own care homes inspectors before the Care Quality Commission took over. I met several of them, often on joint visits to investigate complaints or to share information and intelligence. Most of them retired some time ago, but I only need to find one who remembers St Cloud's.

I turn into the gravel drive at Belmont and pull up behind a red, second hand Mazda MX-5 convertible. No need to ask what was top of Niamh's shopping list.

Louise gasps, wide eyes taking in the huge house with its timber beams, enormous tiled roof, and porch the size of a studio flat. We pass between the miniature cannons on either side of the porch and ring the bell. Moments later, Niamh opens the sturdy oak door. With more flour in her hair than on her RSPB apron, she looks harassed, though she retains the presence and confidence of someone used to entertaining world leaders.

"What an unexpected surprise." After kissing me on the cheek, she offers her hand to Louise. "I'm Niamh, Kent's stepmother."

"I'm Louise. We met at Gemma and Richard's engagement party."

"Are you a friend of Gemma's or one of the Compton clan?"

"I served you champagne, Mrs Fisher."

"You're a waitress?" Niamh sounds interested while casting me a despairing look.

"I'm also a receptionist at Nightingales in East Dean. I'm sure you've heard of it."

"They sent me a brochure after William passed away. I hope you're both hungry because I'm knee deep in savoury slices."

She leads us through the porch into the grand hall with its high ceiling and crystal chandeliers, casting their light over the gallery that runs along all four walls on the first floor. With most of the Colonel's robust oak furniture and belongings still in place, the hall looks the same as my first visit five months ago.

Louise stops to take it in. "I've never seen anything this grand."

"You should have seen the main hall at Downland Manor," Niamh says, her eyes twinkling. "We had oak panels and family portraits going back over 500 years. You could smell the history in the beams and inglenooks. You could spit roast an elephant in the fireplace. Not that we ever did," she says, snapping out of her reverie. "Now come along to the kitchen. It's far more interesting than this mausoleum."

The smell of bread, pastry, onion and spices emanates from the Aga. Various bowls, utensils and plastic containers of flour cover the main wooden table in the centre, forcing Niamh to cool her experiments on wire racks on the worktops and draining board.

"Blame Paul Hollywood," she says, removing baking trays from the stone sink so the kettle will fit beneath the tap. "Imagine those blue eyes, reading your thoughts."

She shudders with pleasure and almost overfills the kettle. Once it's plugged in, she wipes the flour from the cover of the recipe book. "I asked William to see if Paul would bake something for our wedding anniversary and he sent me this book."

She opens it to show off the autograph before placing the book on the shelf.

"Where's Alice?" I ask, surprised the Colonel's former housekeeper has left Niamh in the kitchen without supervision.

"Surfing the internet, I imagine." Niamh tests the temperature of some savoury slices with the tip of her finger and nods. "Goats cheese with sweet onion chutney?"

Though a little overbaked, the slices taste divine. The pastry melts onto my tongue a split second before the cheese announces its arrival. The rest of the slice disappears into my mouth while I reach for a second.

By the time Niamh's finished describing the various slices and their ingredients, I've cleared the plate. Louise has eaten at least three, declining more. After making three mugs of tea, Niamh cuts several slices of fruit cake.

"Would you like to stay for supper?" she asks. "Or do you have plans?"

"I need to collect my son, George," Louise says. "He's with Frances at the sanctuary."

"You don't look old enough to have a son," Niamh says. "Is it just you and George?"

Louise nods. "This fruit cake is heavenly, Mrs Fisher. Is it another Paul Hollywood?"

"No, my father was a master confectioner in Moy near Dungannon. He only had a shop in the village, but he supplied most of Northern Ireland. Well, that's what he was always telling us. Alice and I thought we might follow in his footsteps."

"You want to open a bakery?" I ask.

"Now don't you sound so surprised," Niamh says, wagging a finger at me. "We're going to sell savouries and homemade cakes at the farmers' markets. And before you shout food hygiene regulations, I've already enlisted Gemma's help."

"You intend to make them here?"

She pops the cake into her mouth and smiles. "No, we have plans."

"For Meadow Farm," Alice says, entering the kitchen.

She looks more relaxed now she's no longer a housekeeper, letting her grey hair fall over her shoulders. "The smaller barn will make an excellent catering unit, perfect for supplying the visitor centre with cakes."

"What visitor centre?" I ask.

"The one at your new sanctuary …" Alice pauses, glancing at Niamh. "You said you'd discussed it with Kent."

"It's only details," Niamh says with a dismissive waft of her hand. "This is Louise. She and Kent met at the engagement party."

"Don't change the subject," I say.

"Louise isn't interested in our plans," Niamh says. "So, what have you been up to?"

I raise a warning finger. "Either you tell me what you're planning or you find somewhere else to make your cakes."

"You want us to run a business from a substandard kitchen?"

Alice gives her a glare and turns to me. "You need to relocate to Meadow Farm."

"We can convert one of the barns into a flat for both of us," Niamh says.

"With a catering unit on the ground floor," Alice adds.

"We've discussed our proposals with Planning at Downland," Niamh says, "and there's no reason why we shouldn't get permission."

"Subject to the usual consultation," Alice adds.

Louise smiles, enjoying the double act, no doubt relieved she's no longer the centre of attention.

"Have you any idea how much work and time it will take to set up a new sanctuary?" I ask. "What about the stress to the animals? Most of them are old and too settled to move. I appreciate what you've done, but I've made plans of my own."

"With Miles Birchill?" Niamh speaks his name with enough venom to floor an army.

I can hardly blame her as Birchill took Downland Manor in lieu of William Fisher's gambling debts. None of us knew anything about it until he told us he was selling the ancestral home one morning. I never questioned the decision because he excluded 50 acres of land, which he gave me for the animal sanctuary I'd always wanted.

Five years later, during my first investigation last September, I discovered he'd practically given the land to Birchill. When it turned out that Birchill also owned the house the Fisher's moved to, she came to live with me at the sanctuary.

"Birchill's aware of my plans."

"Then why has he submitted plans to replace your sanctuary with a housing estate?"

Twenty

I should never have stormed out of Belmont. I shouldn't have turned on Niamh. I shouldn't have lost my temper.

It's easy to backtrack after the event.

"I'm angry with Birchill," I say, my arms resting on the gate outside Meadow Farm. I'm trying to imagine how it will look as a sanctuary with proper signs, not the homemade ones Frances and I put together. "But Niamh should have told me sooner."

Louise sighs, maybe tired of my voice. During the short drive to Jevington from Friston, I haven't stopped complaining.

"She thought you were part of the plans, Kent. I've no idea what's going on, but it sounded like you were working with Miles Birchill. I can understand why she hates him for turning your family home into a hotel, but I thought you owned the sanctuary."

So did I when it was given to me, but it was forfeited along with the rest of Downland Manor. William Kenneth

Fisher lied about everything. Niamh doesn't want anyone to know her husband was sterile and I don't blame her, but Miles Birchill believes he's my father. He wants the world to know he has a son – or rather he wants the world to know he got the better of William Fisher.

"It's complicated," I say.

Meadow Farm has enough land, usable buildings, and reasonable access. The farmhouse needs some cosmetic work and a few repairs to the roof. The smaller barn could work as a catering unit for Niamh and Alice with accommodation above, but it will take months to carry out the work. But time shouldn't be an issue. I own the place. No one can evict me or hold me to ransom. Once I've convinced the locals to welcome an animal sanctuary with a visitor centre that will bring in more people and cars, everything will be fine.

Yeah, right, as Gemma would say.

"Do you fancy a look round?" I ask.

"We should rescue Frances," she replies. "I said we'd be back by four."

"There's no rush. I'll drive you home."

"The train station will be fine. I bought return tickets."

Ten minutes later, we're back at the sanctuary. Columbo barks and races over to greet us, followed by a breathless George, who goes on to describe his amazing day in a flurry of words that tumble over each other. He talks all the way up the stairs to the kitchen, pausing only to draw in more air before praising Frances. He looks so alive, so full of energy, his mother beams with pleasure and pride.

They share the same gentle eyes and softly curving nose, but his features are more pronounced, his jaw determined, his hair thicker and darker, barely tamed by gel. He's carefree and confident, not afraid to show his feelings.

He grabs his mother's hand. "Can I show her the dogs, Frances?"

Frances, who looks exhausted, nods.

"We walked them right up the hill and they ran around, sniffing for rabbits," he says, pulling Louise along. "When I called, they came back for treats. It was epic, mum. And the spaniel really likes me, doesn't she, Frances?"

Columbo follows them through the door and Frances yawns, relaxing in relief. "He's a lovely kid," she says, heading for the kettle, "but he wants to know everything. He's a natural with dogs. The spaniel rarely left his side. He wants to take her home, but he knows his mum won't let him."

"You like him, don't you?"

"And you like his mother," she says with a grin. "She's lovely, Kent, but don't expect me to babysit too often. I'm pooped."

"I haven't made any plans."

"George wants to come over tomorrow afternoon and see how you do things."

"I'd only teach him bad habits."

"I doubt that," she says, filling the kettle.

What did I do to deserve Frances? She works for almost nothing, lives in a caravan for most of the year, and never complains.

"How would you feel if we relocated to Meadow Farm?" I ask, taking the empty diet cola cans to the sink. "It would take away the uncertainty."

She takes her time, hunting down some fresh mugs from a cupboard that's seen better days. "We need modern facilities and a visitor centre with a café to generate additional revenue and ..."

Her voice trails off as she looks at me. "I sound like Birchill, don't I?" she says, busying herself with the tea bags. "He said you'd discussed plans for a fresh start so you could create a sanctuary fit for the 21st Century."

How generous of Birchill to smooth the way for the housing estate he intends to build.

"What about you?" I ask. "What do you think?"

"You know I'll be with you whatever you decide."

Sensing her anxiety, I pull her into a reassuring hug. "Whatever *we* decide," I say, feeling a rush of air as George thunders through the door, still talking. "It's you and me. Remember that."

Louise stops at the door, watching Frances pull away.

"If we moved to a flat with a garden," George says, "we could have a dog. Couldn't we, Frances?"

"You need to talk to your mother about that."

"We're going to miss our train," Louise says, beckoning him over. "Thank you for putting up with him, Frances."

"You're welcome." Frances spots Columbo outside the door and walks over, encouraging him inside. "Lovely to meet you," she tells Louise before hugging her. George then hugs Frances before rushing away down the stairs.

"You made quite an impression," I tell Louise as we follow.

"I didn't realise you were showing me off," she says, her tone a little sharp. "First you take me to meet stepmother. Not that she was impressed when she thought I was a waitress."

"I didn't take you there to get her blessing."

"And you didn't take me to Meadow Farm to show me how much property you own?"

"What's brought this on?" I ask, puzzled by her change of mood.

Before she can answer, George comes around the barn, clutching a pair of old wellies. "Frances says I can have these for when I visit next time."

"You'd better leave them here," she says, striding towards the car.

He chatters all the way to Tollingdon Station, telling us more about his day. Louise says nothing, staring out of the side window, barely aware of his chatter. I answer his occasional questions and tell him he can visit when he wants as long as he agrees it in advance.

"Can I come tomorrow after football?"

"I think Frances has had more than enough of you for one weekend," Louise replies. "We're busy tomorrow afternoon."

"But you said I –"

Her cold stare silences him until we're parked in the station. He's out of the car in seconds, trudging the short distance to the ticket office with his hands in his pockets and his head bowed. Louise isn't far behind.

"Hang on," I call, setting off after them. "What's the problem?"

"I think we've had enough for one weekend, don't you?" She carries on inside and feeds her ticket into the turnstile, joining George on the platform.

"I know you were upset earlier," I say, halted by the turnstile, "but I thought you were fine to return to Litlington."

"You only took me because of Mr Trimble."

"I know. That's why we went there."

"Exactly," she says, with a sad shake of the head. "If I

hadn't worked at Nightingales, you wouldn't have given me a second look."

Twenty-One

Louise grabs George's arm and marches off down the platform.

The attendant offers to let me through the wheelchair gate, but I decline.

Outside, I walk, breathing in the cool air, trying to understand her mood shifts. What went wrong? Gemma's arrival at the sanctuary didn't help, obviously. Then St Cloud's spooked Louise, but not as much as the theft of her book. Niamh didn't help. Neither did the argument we had over Birchill. Then Louise accuses me of showing off.

"You asked to see Meadow Farm," I say, thinking aloud.

We returned to the sanctuary in good spirits. George was excited and took you to see the dogs. When you returned … I stop and sigh, remembering how they walked in while I was hugging Frances, who shares the flat with me during the winter.

No wonder people make assumptions.

They made assumptions at school because I preferred the

company of girls to boys.

People judge when they should try to understand.

Columbo never judges me. He lets me explain and work out my problems, encouraging me with a bark or a wag of the tail, often a lick or two on the cheek.

And people wonder why I prefer animals?

I stop walking, surprised to see Gemma's front door facing me. What brought me here when I could have gone anywhere?

When she opens the door, her bleary eyes focus on me. She runs a hand over her tousled hair before pulling down her tight sweater over her even tighter leggings. Her bare feet seem impervious to the chill from the stone threshold.

"What brings you here?" she asks.

I pick out the chorus of 'White Flag' from within. "Isn't Dido a bit maudlin?"

She pulls the door behind her. "What do you want, Kent?"

I glance down the road and spot the red Audi TT. "You're not alone, are you?"

"Neither were you." She glances up and down the road. "What have you done with her, Holmes? Has the new Watson tired of you already?"

"I dropped Louise and George at the station."

"And you pop over to update me, even though you brushed me aside earlier?"

"I did nothing of the sort."

"You both did," she says, her voice rising. "I saw the way she glared at me."

"You asked for it with all that talk about seeing the sun set from my bedroom."

"I couldn't help myself," she says with a shrug. "I

remembered the times we were in your bedroom, working at the computer. You never tried to make love to me. Why?"

Before I can answer the door opens.

"Who are you talking to, Gemms?" Richard, dressed in a crumpled shirt, jeans and multi-coloured, striped socks, steps out. "Oh, it's you, Kent. Come on in."

"I was only passing," I say, wondering how much he heard before opening the door.

"Nonsense," he says, beckoning me inside. "Come and have a glass of wine."

"Kent doesn't drink, darling,"

"Everyone drinks. It's not going to be much of wedding if we're raising glasses of Evian, is it? Now come inside and let me talk to my best man."

Gemma presses a hand against my chest. "I'll deal with it."

"And convince him to dump me as best man?"

She grins. "That's a good idea. I hadn't thought of that."

"Hadn't thought of what, darling?" He appears with a bottle of Merlot and takes her hand, leading her inside.

I close the door behind me and follow them down the narrow hall. Only the chunky red coat hooks and a large printed photo of Audrey Hepburn from *Breakfast at Tiffany's* break up the white walls. I pass the doors on the right that lead to two bedrooms and the bathroom and step into the lounge area, which stretches across the back of the building. It opens into a dining area and kitchen at the front of the building. Richard pads across the white laminate floor, hoisting up his jeans before slumping onto the white leather sofa.

"We've got orange," Gemma calls from the kitchen. "Freshly squeezed by Waitrose."

Apart from the stainless steel kitchen appliances, the huge flat screen TV and the photographs of the South Downs, everything's as white as the Antarctic, including the tables and chairs, the modular bookcase that stretches across one wall, and even the curtain poles and drapes. Thankfully, they're not drinking white wine or they might struggle to spot the bottle.

"That's enough dreary music," Richard says, pointing the remote at the mini hi fi stack. "I'm an Elgar man myself."

He must prefer the pomp and circumstance of chunky oak furniture, parquet floors, and a roaring log fire, tended by a housekeeper, if his parents' house is anything to go by. There's no way he and Gemma will live here when they're married.

I sit in the armchair at right angles to him and make some inane remark about how cosy the place looks and feels.

He looks surprised. "Haven't you been here before? I would have thought you'd have popped round, working so closely with Gemms and all that."

"I was passing when I spotted your car," I say. "I know it's putting you on the spot, but I would really appreciate your advice."

He beams at Gemma as she approaches with my orange. "Kent wants my advice. And I thought the two of you were conspiring."

"Conspiring, darling?"

"About my stag party. I thought that's why you didn't invite Kent in."

She puts a hand to her mouth. "Oh dear. Now you know what we're planning."

"I only heard your voices, Gemms. Still had my plugs in," he says, picking up two foam ear plugs, stiffened by wax. "So your secrets are safe – unless you want to tell me what you're planning."

He watches me take a sip of orange. "Are you sure you want to drink that? Oh, you're driving," he says as she mimics holding a steering wheel. "I knew there had to be a reason."

I've never understood why people struggle to accept that I don't drink, making excuses for my behaviour. I could tell them about the ten years I spent trapped with an alcoholic mother, who liked to beat me with a broom handle, but it's a conversation killer.

Gemma bundles up the magazines and newspapers on the sofa and takes them to an empty cubicle in the modular bookcase, which contains more plants than books.

"I didn't know you liked bonsai, Gemma. I thought you preferred cacti."

Richard makes the mistake of laughing, drawing a glare from his fiancée that's as sharp as the leaves on the mother-in-law's tongue. "They're mine," he says, raising an apologetic hand. "Caught the bug from Pops. He chairs the local bonsai club."

"Is it a small group?" I ask.

"No, we have over a hundred members." Then he laughs and wags a finger at me. "Good one, Kent. You could use that in your best man's speech."

"Talking about the duties of a best man," Gemma says, sauntering over, "Kent has some news about that, don't you?"

He glances at me, looking confused. "I thought you came for some advice."

"I want to talk about selling Belmont."

"I knew he would," he says, raising his glass to her.

"You'll need Alice's approval, Kent, and some form of remuneration to compensate her. Have you broached the subject with her?"

"She and Niamh want to move to Meadow Farm to start up a catering business."

He swallows a large mouthful of wine. "Yikes, it must be a pretty serious venture to need a place that size."

"They only need a small, purpose made unit," Gemma says, missing the humour in his eyes. "They asked me for advice and we agreed the kitchen at Belmont didn't comply with the law."

"You never mentioned this," he says.

"You don't tell me about your work."

"It's confidential, Gemms. You know that."

"And my work isn't?"

"That's all I needed to know," I say, rising.

"You must tell Richard about your decision," Gemma says, getting to her feet. "You know it's only going to get more difficult if you put things off."

"What decision?" he asks, looking at each of us in turn. "What are you talking about?"

"Kent's having doubts," she replies. "Aren't you?"

She looks so sweet and innocent I could almost forgive her for putting me on the spot. But I have a better idea.

"I think you'd prefer a murder mystery weekend in a country hotel," I tell him, "but Gemma thinks you'd prefer something wilder, like bungee jumping, for your stag party."

The look of surprise on his face is a picture.

And so is hers.

The grin reaches his ears. "A murder mystery weekend would be excellent," he says, almost shaking my hand off my wrist. "Isn't it a wonderful idea, Gemms?"

"As long as you're not the victim, darling."

She follows me down the hall and out onto the doorstep before she lets rip. "What the hell do you think you're doing?"

"I could ask you the same. Why shouldn't I be best man?"

Before she can answer my phone rings. It's Louise. She speaks the moment I pick up. "You're not going to believe this, Kent, but it's back."

"What's back?" I ask, turning away from Gemma.

"My book, *The Cider House Rules*. I was putting my shoes in the wardrobe and there it was, as if it had never been missing. Who's doing this, Kent? What's going on?"

Twenty-Two

"Ring the police to report the break in," I tell Louise. "I have a spare mortice lock and key in the barn. I'll be straight over."

"I don't need a new lock. No one broke in."

"Someone entered your flat without your permission or knowledge. You have to contact the police."

"Do you want me to call them?" Gemma asks. "Is Louise all right?"

"Who's that?" Louise asks.

"Gemma."

Louise ends the call.

I glance at Gemma and shrug. "It's been a funny old day. I'll see you Monday in the office."

I stride down the street, calling Louise once more, surprised when she answers.

"There's no need to come over. George has gone to fetch Tracey."

I want to argue, but she won't listen at the moment. "I'd

like to look at the book sometime," I say. "The photograph too."

"The photograph's still missing."

The culprit works at Nightingales, I'm sure of that. He leaves notes on my windscreen, like the one I can see beneath the wiper blade the moment I enter the car park.

Unfortunately, every car has the same flyer, offering a Winter Special, half price entry to Tombstone Adventure Park, which promises to *bring out the cowboy in you*. Business must be bad if Birchill's halving the entry price to his theme park.

That's why he wants to build a housing estate on my land.

Fifteen minutes later, after a terse phone call, I'm outside Downland Manor Hotel, staring at its Georgian grandeur illuminated blue and gold against the night sky. While its fabric contained the echoes and memories of Fishers past, highlighted by the portraits in the hall and in the stairwells, the manor never felt like home.

So why do I cling to my sanctuary?

Birchill, dressed in a sharp black suit, strides across the vast foyer, his shoes squeaking on the marble floor, emblazoned with the Downland Manor Hotel crest. He guides me outside, across the patio and down the steps into the formal gardens. As we walk, I'm aware of the similarity in height and build, in hair and eye colour. He reeks of cigarette smoke, of course, and his silk shirt costs more than my three suits put together. When we stop by the fountain, illuminated from beneath, he loosens his tie and undoes the top button of his shirt, releasing the loose skin of his neck from its tourniquet. The rest of his face, transfixed by plastic surgery, barely moves until a wry smile reveals a new set of lines he needs to erase.

"We could have had dinner," he says, extracting the gold cigarette case from his pocket.

"You know I don't like poncy food."

"Chef would have deep fried the foie gras and cooked you some chips," he says, tamping a cigarette on the back of his hand, "but you don't like fat or oil."

"I don't like new housing developments on my land either."

"My land, Kent, not my application." He takes a long draw on the cigarette and exhales the smoke into the air. "You haven't done your homework as usual. Anyone can make an application, as you know. I'm surprised you didn't object to the previous application by Downsview Developments."

"What application?"

"Downsview Developments have outline permission to build houses between the sanctuary and the outskirts of Tollingdon."

"When? I never received a notification from Planning. I didn't see any notices posted."

"William persuaded the Planning Committee to refuse the application so there was no need to involve you. But he had his heart attack and died, as you know. It was three days before the Planning meeting. Neville Priddy produced a new report, supporting the application. It was approved on the casting vote of the chairman, Gregory Rathbone."

I was suspended at the time, charged with gross misconduct while I recovered from injuries sustained when I tried to rescue William Fisher from a burning barn. I saved Birchill though, so maybe it's time he returned the favour.

"Are you going to object to the application?" I ask,

sitting on the wall that encircles the fountain. "I imagine you don't want a housing estate on your doorstep."

He draws on the cigarette. "It's not that simple."

"Then give the land to me. I'll never sell it to anyone."

"I know, but your sanctuary doesn't have planning permission."

"It doesn't need it. I checked. The District Planning Officer ratified the decision."

"You mean the previous District Planning Officer, who never gave you anything in writing, did he?" Birchill shivers in the cold and encourages me to walk with him. "Priddy will take enforcement action to close your sanctuary if he can. He'll claim 'your father' pulled strings. He or Rathbone will leak the story to the *Daily Mail*."

"He can't prove anything," I say.

"He doesn't need to. During the furore, as Downland District Council fights to defend its good name, Priddy and Rathbone slip through planning permission for their pals in Downsview Developments."

Whatever happened to democracy and accountability?

Then again, William Fisher and Miles Birchill never took much notice of it either.

"You cannot fight this application," he says. "Your council hates me and Tombstone Adventure Park. They know it's struggling. They want it to fail, but it won't. That's why I'm considering an offer for the hotel. The buyer thinks the sanctuary would be ideal for paintballing and corporate team building games."

He flicks the remains of his cigarette into the snowdrops before climbing the steps to the patio. "You don't seem surprised, Kent."

I should be angry and disappointed, but I can relocate to

Jevington. I won't need his handouts. I won't need his help, his influence or his favours.

I won't have to endure a blood test to see if he's my natural father.

I'm free to object to any planning application to build houses or corporate playgrounds.

Twenty-Three

On Monday morning, I'm greeted by the smiling faces of officers in my team and colleagues from Licensing, all gathered round Kelly's desk. When I head over, they make way for me to look at a photograph on Facebook of Louise and me, chatting intimately at the sanctuary.

Like me, Kelly can access Facebook to check out new businesses and find people selling food from the back of a van. Some are foolish enough to post photos of their vans, complete with registration numbers. Others talk about goods they've stolen and where they intend to sell them. In my case, George has posted photos on my animal sanctuary's page.

"Gorgeous pic," Kelly remarks. "I saw you chatting at Gemma's party."

Sylvie laughs. "I knew you'd taken a shine to the receptionist at Nightingales."

"She has a lovely smile," Nigel says.

"Looks like love to me," Lucy remarks as if it's the end

of the world. "Have you seen these photos, Gemma?"

Gemma, who's just strolled in, saunters over and stands beside me. "That's Louise," she says. "It must have been taken after I left because my car's gone. Did her son take it?"

"I told you it was her son," Kelly says with a triumphant nod.

"What were you doing at the sanctuary?" Lucy asks Gemma.

"What are you doing standing around?" Danni asks, coming out of her office. "Haven't you got work to do?"

As the officers disperse to their desks, Danni takes a long look at the photo. "About time you moved on, Kent."

When Kelly returns from the photocopier, she stops by my desk. "Louise looks lovely, Kent. Hold onto her."

"Is Danni going to *Chiefs Briefs*?" I ask.

Kelly's term for the weekly Heads of Service meetings fills my thoughts with images of managers in their underwear, talking about how to be more transparent. It's killed my one-to-ones with Danni.

"Do you want to use her office?" she asks.

"After a visit to Planning. Won't be long."

Unlike the environmental health office, bristling with banter, the planning office has a more sedate, refined atmosphere, worthy of a team, charged with balancing development and the protection of the environment and communities. I don't know how they can do this work from the office, when the land being developed is outside, but almost every desk is occupied. Regimented rows of hot desks, dominated by PCs with enormous flat screen monitors for scrutinising detailed plans, fill a room lined with large maps of Downland, showing the development areas for the next ten years.

The land between Tollingdon and Downland Manor is designated for agricultural use.

"We are honoured," Neville Priddy says, emerging from his glass cubicle. "We don't often get a visit from Downland's wealthiest employee."

Short, but self-important in a pinstripe three-piece suit, silk shirt and bow tie, Priddy's in his mid-fifties, greying at the temples, but as fit as a flea, thanks to regular five aside football with his team. He wears a perpetual smile as he enquires about your family, friends, favourite football team or the cost of living. He buys the first round of drinks in the pub on Friday and ensures he's first back in the office so he can check on everyone and record who's late. He has the cultured voice and bearing of a surgeon or a judge, so why does he work for a small, rural council?

"Are you checking the progress of your latest venture?" His smile barely creases the skin around his wolf-like grey eyes. With his prominent nose and pronounced canine teeth, he could be one to avoid during a full moon.

"Developing the last of the Fisher estate," he says, leading me into his office. He sits upright in his executive leather chair, interlocks his fingers and places his hands on the desk, filled with piles of folders, government guidance and planning applications.

"I'm relocating my animal sanctuary to Meadow Farm in Jevington."

"Are you seeking assistance with an application for a change of use?"

"You're the expert, Neville. I know almost nothing about the planning process."

"That's true. You forgot to apply for permission for your

current sanctuary." His polite laugh almost manages to hide the threat. "But we never dwell on the past in Planning, unless it's a retrospective application. We look to the future," he says after another laugh, "keen to help entrepreneurs and people like you, Kent."

"It's reassuring to know you'll support me."

"One must never overlook the vagaries of public opinion," he replies. "You never know who's going to object and stand in the way of progress. Your application for a new animal sanctuary will be dealt with as swiftly and transparently as protocol allows."

"Protocol?"

"A necessary formality for those who work for Downland. We have to demonstrate rigorous scrutiny so no one can accuse us of favouring our own. That's why I'll personally guide you through the labyrinth."

He personally guides me to the Information Officer in the corner, his hand in the small of my back. Is he searching for a suitable spot to plunge a knife into?

My application looks set for a rough ride.

Armed with application forms and explanatory notes, I retreat to Danni's office to get a measure of the task ahead. My application will take at least three months to reach the Planning Committee. Objections from locals, or unfavourable reports or questions from statutory authorities like the Environment Agency, Highways or Environmental Health, could extend the time to six months or even prompt a refusal.

I hope Birchill's not planning on a quick sale of the land.

After dealing with a long list of emails, I ring East Sussex County Council to enquire about St Cloud's Orphanage, hoping their archives are better than ours. I'm referred to *The Keep* in Brighton, a huge, state of the art facility that stores historical records and information for the county. A glance at their website shows the range of records kept, but my search for 'orphanages' nets me three generic results that don't help. A search for St Cloud's reveals more results, but none relate to a home in Litlington.

The telephonist at *The Keep* refers me back to the county council, whose officers originally inspected care homes. A more persistent call to the county gets me through to an officer, who passes me to another, who passes me to his superior, who suggests I make a request using the contact form on the website.

I could have driven to Litlington, had lunch, interviewed half a dozen locals, nipped into Alfriston for a cream tea and returned to the office in the time I've spent ringing around.

I need to visit Litlington, but not during work time. With Neville scrutinising me, I can't afford to give him any reasons to smear my name or application.

Kelly consults her multi-coloured spreadsheet. "You have ten days leave outstanding and seven weeks to take them. Danni will only allow you to carry leave into the next financial year in exceptional circumstances, like a marriage, say."

"Does being best man count?"

"Leave it with me, lover. It won't be easy because Danni usually returns from *Chiefs Briefs* with her knickers in a twist."

As predicted, Danni's not feeling generous when she summons me at one thirty.

"I'm in Warwick tomorrow and Wednesday, so you're

deputising, Kent. If you finish the statutory service plans before my return, you can take this Thursday and Friday as leave."

"What about next week?" I ask.

"It's half term, Kent. Not the best time."

Fifteen minutes later, Kelly perches on the edge of my desk. "Danni's granted you Thursday and Friday this week and Monday to Wednesday next week."

"But she said next week was no go."

Kelly grins. "She remembered Louise's son, George, from the photos earlier."

"You mean you reminded her." I rise and kiss her on the cheek. "Thank you."

"You have to deliver the service plans on Wednesday or no time off next week."

"Best order me a lamp so I can burn the midnight oil then."

I'm still wading through statistics and past service plans when Kelly stops by at five thirty. "Gemma's phoned, so everyone's safe and accounted for," she says. "How's it going?"

"Danni wants an aspirational service plan."

"She means upbeat and positive, focusing on what can be achieved, with examples of good businesses that others will want to emulate." She laughs. "Did I sound like a management manual? I meant she wants photographs of good kitchens, like Nightingales."

"We only take photos of contraventions for evidence."

"Some of the old service plans have photos. Maybe you should widen your search."

When I searched the premises database for St Cloud's,

there were no matches. If I broaden the search criteria, make them less specific, I might find something. After several searches that return hundreds of records, I type in 'Saint', hoping it will pick up something I missed earlier. When it doesn't I abbreviate to 'St.' Still no joy. When I lose the full stop, the computer returns a long list, but no St Cloud's.

I'm about to give up when I notice St Hildas has no apostrophe.

I type 'St Clouds' without an apostrophe.

My whoop of delight distracts the cleaners. There's only a scanned copy of a telephone message.

St Clouds closed on 23rd January 1982. Please update your records. Kim Jaggers, Inspector of Homes, East Sussex County Council.

With any luck, she's still working, hopefully for the Care Quality Commission. I don't recognise her name, but the date looks familiar.

Trimble also died on 23rd January.

Is it a macabre coincidence or is the killer trying to make a point?

Twenty-Four

Tuesday morning flies by in a haze of meetings and briefings, leaving me little time to phone the Care Quality Commission about Kim Jaggers. I leave a couple of messages, but by the time Kelly and I finish work at six that afternoon, no one has returned my call. At least we completed the Food Safety Service Plan, adding photographs culled from Google and business websites. Tomorrow we'll tackle the Health and Safety Service Plan and I can extend my annual leave into next week.

That should give me plenty of time to submit a planning application for Meadow Farm.

"You should take a photograph of Nightingales for the back cover," Kelly says.

We're sitting at the meeting table in Danni's office on Wednesday morning, ready to start work on the Health and Safety Service Plan.

"It's such a beautiful location," she says, "and it's going to be sunny tomorrow."

I can imagine Louise's reaction if I turn up in reception. Miss Rudolf's too.

"Taking photographs is hardly protecting public health," I say. "Imagine what Councillor Rathbone would say."

"Go in your lunch break, lover. Take Louise to the Tiger afterwards."

Back at my desk at lunchtime, I phone the Care Quality Commission once more, determined to talk to someone. After a couple of dead ends, where I'm forced to explain the reason for my call to each person I talk to, I reach Human Remains. A polite young woman tells me Kim Jaggers is not an employee. That's all she's prepared to tell me due to confidentiality. When I ask to talk to Malcolm Knott, care homes inspector, I'm greeted by his voicemail message.

I fire off an email to him and then set about the long list of messages that have accumulated in my Inbox during the morning. I clear most of them after little more than a cursory glance at the subject line, including the one from Gemma, who's taking an extra hour for lunch to evaluate wedding venues.

For some reason, her email leaves me deflated. I lean back in my chair, unable to hold back the memories, including the time when she was shot. For an awful moment, which seemed to stretch into hours, I thought she might die.

Never before had I felt so scared, so empty, so helpless.

Even now, a few months later, the memory chills me, reminding me what a fool I was to lose her in the first place.

The most attractive woman I ever met was crazy about me. She loved me more than life, she said, as we showered together that Sunday morning.

An hour or so later, I ran like a scalded cat.

And when I missed her like crazy, I lied to myself.

When I knew I'd made the biggest mistake of my life, I found excuses. It was too soon, too impetuous, too awkward with the difference in age. How would her friends react? What would her parents think? How long before she grew bored?

Would people think I'd taken advantage of someone much younger?

That excuse, I'm ashamed to say, stopped me going back to her.

I pick up my phone and select my favourite photograph. Gemma's sitting at the table, a bathrobe shrugged over her shoulders, wet hair tumbling around her young face. Her chin rests on her hand, her head tilts to one side, and her dreamy smile matches the mood in her dark, sexy eyes as they look deep into mine.

"I never realised how much she loved you," Kelly says, leaning closer.

"Me neither."

She places a hand on my shoulder. "You have to move on, Kent."

"Or put things right."

She shakes her head. "You have someone else now. Don't let what's happened mess up what's possible."

My phone rings, flashing up Louise's name. Kelly squeezes my shoulder and retreats, encouraging me to go for it.

I take a deep breath. "Louise, how are you?"

"I wanted to apologise for Saturday," she replies, sounding formal. "George showed me your Facebook page. I didn't know ... I never realised you built the sanctuary from nothing. I should never have accused you of showing off."

"No problem," I say, barely listening.

"And I'm sorry for messing up lunch."

An uneasy silence starts to spread between us. I should tell her it was nothing, if only to be polite, but I don't care, if I'm honest.

"Will you let me make it up to you?" she asks, her voice quickening. "I'm not Nigella Lawson by any stretch of the imagination, but I can make a passable chilli con carne, though you're probably busy at the sanctuary this evening, or making plans for the new one, so I won't be offended if you can't make it."

She runs out of breath and gasps.

I should decline, but Kelly's words chip at my conscience. Don't let what's happened mess up what's possible. Have my regrets held me back these past seven years? Gemma's planning a wedding. She couldn't make her intentions any plainer, could she?

"We could have lunch tomorrow at the Tiger," I say, trying to sound enthusiastic.

"I don't want Miss Rudolf to …"

"Why are you worried about Miss Rudolf?" I ask, a little sharper than intended.

She hesitates. "I've already made the chilli for this evening. It's in the slow cooker. George is at football practice so we can … talk."

I realise she's gone to some trouble to plan this evening. If only she'd rung me earlier or yesterday. Maybe she intended to, but lost her nerve. Maybe she has more than talking in mind.

As I reach for my pen, I spot Gemma in the doorway. "Where are you?" I ask Louise.

"My flat's in Hampden Park at the back of Sainsbury's," she says before rattling off the address. "Six o'clock?"

Gemma strolls over, dressed in a tight white sweater and skinny designer jeans. With fingernails and lips painted, thick glossy hair tumbling over her shoulders, and a smile to tell me what I'm missing, she slides into the chair beside my desk.

"Who is it?" she mouths.

"Kent, is six o'clock okay? Is it too early?"

"No, it's fine."

I end the call and pocket the note before Gemma can read it. "How did the evaluation go?" I ask, settling back in my chair.

"Did I interrupt a conversation with Louise?"

I shake my head. "Danni, checking to make sure I haven't destroyed the place. Wedding all planned?"

She sighs, a dreamy smile spreading across her face. "Herstmonceux Castle's perfect for the wedding and reception. Richard's father knows a few people there."

I know the chef and contract caterer that provides the meals for the students. Owned by Queen's University, Canada, the red brick 15th century castle, originally built as a family home, is picture postcard perfect with its moat and woodland setting.

Perfect for a white knight on a steed …

"Shall I inspect the kitchen before the wedding?" I ask, dismissing the thought.

"And get your morning suit dirty? I'd visit a couple of days before."

"Does that mean you're accepting me as best man?"

She purses her lips. "Will you be bringing Louise?"

"You've fixed a date then?"

"We're synchronising diaries," she replies, sounding like Danni. "Richard's family are scattered around the globe."

"Maybe you need a spreadsheet."

"Already done for the gift list. I'm not leaving anything to chance, Kent. I want everything to be perfect," she says, gazing into my eyes.

"I'm sure it will be," I say, turning back to my computer.

She helps herself to one of the crisp white grapes I bought earlier. She grimaces as the acidity hits her tongue and then nods with pleasure. "Do you remember the morning we –"

"I'm busy," I say, remembering exactly which morning.

She takes another grape. "Too busy for an update on Anderida Villas?"

"If it's quick," I say, leaning back in my chair.

"I've found someone who worked for Anthony Trimble. We're meeting her at five thirty tonight."

"Why can't we visit tomorrow during the day?"

"You're on leave," Gemma replies. "And Miss Jaggers goes to bingo at seven and stays over with a friend in Eastbourne."

"Jaggers? Kim Jaggers?"

"You know her?"

Yesterday, I learned that Kim Jaggers inspected St Cloud's, the orphanage. Today, she turns up living opposite Anderida Villas, where she worked for Trimble.

She's known the man for 35 years, probably more.

For someone who doesn't believe in coincidence, I must be looking at karma.

Should I cancel Louise or reschedule for later?

"We'll go at five," I tell Gemma.

Twenty-Five

At four fifty-five, I park behind Anderida Villas, facing Kim Jaggers' dark and empty-looking bungalow. She could be at the back, I guess. My mother insisted on watching TV in the dark, though I never understood why. As long as Kim Jaggers hasn't forgotten our visit.

I note down a few questions, curious to learn more about St Cloud's before and after it closed. What did Trimble do between running St Cloud's and owning a hotel and hostel in Pevensey decades later? Why didn't he sell St Cloud's? How did he make his money? I can't imagine an orphanage generating much profit.

Maybe Kim Jaggers will know why Trimble lost everything to the Sherlocks.

Or did he?

Richard drops Gemma off at ten past five. She leans across to kiss him before hauling herself out of his Audi TT. Looking chic in a bomber jacket and jeans, she saunters across the road and slides into the passenger seat, clutching a small handbag.

"I had a flat tyre," she says, waving to her fiancé as he drives away. "You'll have to drop me back at the flat because Richard's with the bonsai brigade tonight."

"It's one way to keep trim," I say. "I don't know if Kim's home."

"She lives in the back," Gemma says as we head through the rotting front gate. A light above the door bursts into life, blinding me for long enough to clatter into her. The aroma of leather mixes with her perfume as she leans into me, her hair soft against my face.

"I remember the first time you groped me," she says. "You were more excited in the trouser department, but just as clumsy."

I step back and straighten my jacket, wishing she wouldn't keep arousing memories.

"I'll do the honours," she says, walking up to the door. She ignores the bell and reaches for the knocker, mounted on a mullion between two glass panes. The door and glass shake and rattle as Gemma makes enough noise to wake the dead in the nearby cemetery.

A few moments later, a light goes on in the hall and a shadow shuffles closer. The door opens a few inches, releasing a waft of stale tobacco smoke that makes me wince. The rounded and wrinkled face of a small but plump elderly woman appears in the gap. Heavy eyelids almost obscure her pale, weary eyes as she studies us. The rollup cigarette between her flaccid lips went out some time ago.

"If you're selling stuff you can ... oh, it's you. You're early."

"This is Kent Fisher."

"I know who you are," she says, opening the door.

"Handsome devil, aren't you?"

Her wheezing laughter becomes a smoker's cough, shaking thin grey hair out from under a loose scarf. Yellow fingers pull the cigarette from her mouth and flick it over our heads into the garden. She wipes her hands on her tired cardigan, stiff with stains, and hoists her tracksuit bottoms to reveal fluorescent pink trainers.

"In case I want to give you the run around," she says with a sly smile. "Come on, let's get on with it. Bingo awaits."

The reek of cigarettes, combined with the damp, almost stagnant odour of the bungalow, intensify as we follow her down the hall. The feeble light from a lonely low watt bulb can't hide the bald greasy carpet, which sticks to the soles of my shoes, or the mould creeping along the peeling wallpaper.

"Seen better days," she mutters, "but ain't we all?"

I've smelt better days too, detecting the acrid undercurrent of cat, emanating from the litter tray in the corner of the small and cosy kitchen. She's managed to squeeze a drop leaf table and armchair into one corner. Filled with chipped Formica worktops, plywood cabinets and a freestanding larder unit with a drop down door from the 1960s, the kitchen reminds me of my mother's basement flat. This one has a vinyl tiled floor rather than a damp one.

Kim drops into the armchair. She stretches up to the table for her tobacco pouch, cigarette papers and Zippo lighter, narrowly avoiding the saucer filled with cigarette butts.

"You knew Anthony Trimble," I say, standing between the cat litter tray and the larder unit. Gemma remains by the hall door for a quick escape.

"Lots of people knew Tony. He was a popular man in his

prime."

She finds a rolled cigarette in the pouch and studies it with surprise. Then, with a shrug, she lights it with the Zippo, almost setting fire to her scarf with the lively flame. As soon as she breathes in the smoke, she coughs. The rasping noise makes me shudder.

"They'll be the death of me," she says, wiping stray tobacco from her lips. "So, what do you want to know about Tony?"

"When did you meet?"

"Fifth of May 1970. Tony wanted me to look at a house he wanted to convert into a home for orphaned children. He wanted to look at me," she says, her eyes lighting up. "I was slim and elegant in those days with long blonde hair, shapely legs and juicy tits, as Tony called them. He liked my legs too, the randy old sod."

She pauses to draw on her cigarette, a smile on her lips. "He was like a car salesman – all flannel and wild promises, but so good looking. He smelt divine too. He followed me round during my inspection, standing so close I could smell his hormones."

Her laughter degenerates into a coughing fit. While Gemma fetches a glass of water, I sneak a look at a framed photograph on top of the larder unit. Taken in an office, Kim's at the front with a party hat and a glass of wine. Though not slim, she's shapely enough to gain the attention of the older man behind. He has one arm draped over the shoulder of a redheaded woman, his hand resting on her breast. His eyes stare down at Kim's cleavage. She has an arm over the shoulder of the younger man beside her. He's staring at his feet as if he wishes he were somewhere else. A third man, short and officious-looking, stands on the other side of the redhead, keeping his distance.

No one looks that cheerful, considering it's a party of some sort.

"You inspected St Cloud's," I say, once Kim's calmed her cough.

"It was a wonderful place, filled with happy smiling faces and laughter. You'd never have guessed it was a refuge, a safe haven for children the world didn't want. Most were runaways, kids with no parents, boys and girls as young as seven and eight, begging in the streets. Tony would have taken them all in, but he could only accommodate ten. I was strict about that."

"What did the locals think of the place?"

She looks up. "Why are you interested in a home that closed over 30 years ago?"

"I'm interested in Tony Trimble," I reply. "He owned Anderida Villas, didn't he?"

She struggles to her feet. "Still does. Why are you interested in my photo?"

She grabs hold of the larder unit for support and catches her breath. She removes the photo, polishing away the dust with her sleeve.

"My last day as an inspector with East Sussex," she says, moving the photograph back and forward until it's in focus. "They joined the new regime, but I was 62, hopeless with computers and too old to change. Tony found me a job across the road."

"That was handy, you living here."

"Tony owns this place. The hotel manager lived here. When I took over, it became mine. But the bookings fell away so we turned it into a hostel for refugees and asylum seekers."

"When was that?" I ask.

"2008 or 2009, I don't remember. I know we upset everyone in the village. They said we'd all get burgled, but it never happened. These were poor families who'd lost everything, not thieves. Tony wanted me to keep an eye on things."

"Can I take a look?" I ask as she returns the photograph to the larder unit. "One of the men looks familiar."

"That's Margaret," she says, pointing at the redhead. "Martin and Malcolm are on either side, and that's Walter with me. He did our admin work. Margaret left soon after me to breed Dalmatians. Martin retired when the Care Quality Commission took over. Malcolm still works for them, running the local office. You can see he's ambitious."

"What about Walter?" I ask.

"He was only with us a couple of months. Never saw him again. Not sure I'll see Tony either now he's moved to that posh home."

Gemma and I exchange a glance, realising Kim doesn't know.

"I'm sorry, Kim, but Tony died on the 23rd January."

"Died?" Confusion fills her eyes. She looks at each of us in turn, clutching the photo to her chest. "He can't have died. He's still paying me."

"He's gone," Gemma says, going over to her. "We buried him."

"Does that mean I have to move out?"

When she wobbles, Gemma takes her arm. "You need to sit down, Miss Jaggers. Or would you prefer to lie down?"

Kim continues to look confused and lost, glancing around as if she's in a strange place.

"Is there anyone we can call?" I ask, taking the photo

before it slips out of her hand. "A friend or relative?"

"There's no one, now Tony's gone. I think I'd better lie down."

While Gemma escorts her into the hall, I fill the kettle and scout around for a cup and some tea bags. While the water comes to the boil I check the names on the reverse of the photograph. At the back are Margaret Jones, Martin Bell and Malcolm Knott, the inspector I left a message for at CQC. Walter has no surname.

Admin officers never get the recognition they deserve.

When Kim calls for her tobacco, I slide the photograph into my pocket and take her pouch and lighter to her. She's sprawled out on the bed, slumped against a couple of yellowing pillows. I almost stand on the cat, who hisses before sprinting out of the room.

"Are you sure there's no one we can call?"

"Give me my baccy." She snatches it from my hand and slumps back, wheezing from clapped out lungs.

"How about Violet?" I ask, remembering the woman who undercooks Victoria sponge. "Shall I see if she can come round?"

Kim falls silent, staring at the pouch in her hand. Her eyelids droop and close. Her shoulders relax. Her wheezing ceases. As the pouch of tobacco slides from her fingers, her head slumps forward.

Gemma reacts first, her fingers seeking a pulse in Kim's neck.

"Walter!" Kim cries, jerking awake, her eyes wide and wild. She grabs my arm and pulls me close. "Is that you, Walter?"

Trimble asked me the same question at Nightingales, a week before he died.

Twenty-Six

When Kim Jaggers dozes off again, Gemma insists we remain.

"Maybe Violet will keep an eye on her," I say, heading for the door.

I don't catch Gemma's remark, but it didn't sound complimentary.

Outside I ring Louise to explain. "I'll ask one of the neighbours to keep an eye on her. Then I'll be with you."

"Wouldn't it be better to call a doctor?"

"Gemma said that, but I –"

"You're with Gemma?" Louise cuts in. "Can't she stay with Kim Jaggers?"

The tension in her voice irritates me. She means, what's Gemma doing there?

"Gemma had a puncture and doesn't have a car. Once we've taken care of Kim Jaggers, I'll drop her home and be with you as soon as …"

I sigh, realising Louise has hung up.

No dinner for me. I'll have to make do with some of Violet's fruit cake.

"One for you and one for your lovely fiancée," she says, popping two large slabs into sandwich bags. "You look so handsome together."

I pop the cake on the rear seat of my car while Violet heads for Kim's bungalow, armed with her knitting and some puzzle books. When I join them, Violet's found a tin of cat food in the larder unit. Gemma's trying to shoo the cat away as it strokes itself against her leg.

It takes another twenty minutes before Violet's settled beside the bed, puzzle book in hand, cup of tea on the bedside cabinet. No one's eaten any cake at this point, though I suspect the cat will be on the table the moment we're gone. Kim's sleeping, her breathing shallow but rhythmic, still sounding like an effort.

"We should have rung the emergency doctor," Gemma says again as we race along the Pevensey bypass towards Tollingdon. "She'll need one if she eats any of Violet's cake. It's half-cooked inside."

"Half-baked," I say.

"Like your ideas," she says with a grin. "Have you rung Louise?"

"She's cool," I reply. "I was going to offer her the second slab of Violet's cake, but it was meant for you. We make such a handsome couple. I don't know what gave her such an idea. I mean, you can hardly see your engagement ring, it's so small and insignificant."

She covers it with her hand. "Richard likes big displays of affection."

It looks more like ownership to me. "He wants the world to know how lucky he is," I say. "I imagine the bonsai people are itching to meet you."

"Don't," she says with a shudder. "I'm sure they're lovely people, but I'd rather talk about murder."

"Who's?"

"Yours, if you keep looking at me like that."

"Like what?"

"You know what I mean."

Within minutes we're in Tollingdon town centre. I take a left opposite Station Road into a street with terraces of grand Victorian houses, converted into flats many years ago. Students tend to occupy the basement and attic flats, swamping the streets with their old cars and recycling boxes filled with beer bottles. The flats are comfortable, reasonably priced, and a short walk from the shops, train station and work, which might explain why she's the last to arrive in the morning.

Due to the lack of parking spaces, I stop in the middle of the road. Gemma unbuckles her belt and turns to face me.

"Why did Kim Jaggers think you were Walter?"

"Soft hands," I say, holding them up.

"Cold," she says, placing a hand over mine. The warmth of her hand and the electricity from her touch catch me by surprise. "Like the trail we're following. Kim Jaggers and Trimble were up to no good. She inspects his orphanage, giving him more than a pass mark."

"When she retires, he lets her run his hotel and chucks in a bungalow for good measure," I say.

"Hardly a professional relationship, is it, Holmes?"

But an enduring one, I muse, wondering if I'm missing something.

Gemma squeezes my hand. "You're supposed to say, No, Watson, and amaze me with a brilliant insight."

"I'm too hungry to think straight."

"Then you'd best get over to Louise."

"I'm not going," I say as she's about to exit the car. "She wasn't impressed with my time keeping."

"You explained about Kim Jaggers, right?"

I nod. "We could order in a pizza."

"I'm not sure that would be a good idea," she says, her eyes gleaming. "Richard goes home after bonsai. They meet in Alfriston, near his parent's house."

I look into her eyes. The messages they're sending make me nervous. Excited too. In my mind, we're already in the shower. I vowed never to come between people in a relationship, but if she was my fiancée, I wouldn't be trimming plants in the evening.

"We should discuss the case," I say, turning to face her, to look into the dark eyes that make my stomach turn somersaults. "Work out where we go from here."

She smiles and nods. "I enjoy investigating murders with you. Do you remember when we broke into Collins' house? It was scary, but exciting."

"But not when someone pushes a shotgun in your face."

She gazes into my eyes, making my heart pound. "No, but you saved me, Kent."

I recognise the desire in her eyes, the longing so deep it hurts, drawing me closer till I can feel the purr of her breath on my face.

"I can save you again, Gemma."

Our lips meet and the passion and longing surge through me. The touch of her lips electrifies me. Seven years of regret and recrimination tumble away. My fingers slide over her stomach, pushing inside her bomber jacket, seeking out her breasts.

"No!"

She grabs my hand. She stares at me, tears running down her cheeks.

"What's wrong?" I ask, afraid suddenly.

"I thought you'd changed. I thought you were in love with me."

She pushes my hand away and scrambles out of the car, stumbling along the pavement. I should go after her, but I'm not sure what went wrong. We were kissing like we used to, unable to control the desire and passion, and she freezes.

I lower the window to call out, but a car pulls up behind me, wanting to pass. I drive off and turn around at the end of the street. When I come back, she's gone inside, the house dark.

Did she have an attack of conscience? Did I push her too far? Too fast?

No, I messed up a long time ago.

It's time I came to terms with that.

As I'm about to drive off, a text arrives.

Sorry.

Twenty-Seven

Louise's second floor flat overlooks the railway line in Hampden Park. Though a regular shopper at Sainsbury's, I'm unfamiliar with the estate at the back of the supermarket. By the time I've driven back out, around the industrial estates and found the correct road into the estate, I'm 35 minutes late.

I'm not even sure why I'm here.

When I press the buzzer and announce myself, I'm surprised when Louise lets me in. She waits in the doorway, looking stunning in a coffee coloured blouse and skinny jeans that stop short of slender ankles. Though she seems unsteady in high heels, there's nothing uncertain about her appearance. Her deft use of makeup enhances her slender cheeks and delicate jaw, highlights the gentle curves of her glossy lips. I'm no expert, but she's spent several hours, maybe all afternoon, and most of this week's wages, to look good.

I look and feel shabby in my crumpled work clothes,

which smell of cigarettes and cat.

"You look amazing," I say, looking her over from head to toe. "I'm a mess."

"Emotionally or physically?" she asks. "Don't look so worried," she adds quickly. "It's a joke. You said you were a mess. You didn't say you looked a mess. How's Kim Jaggers?"

"A neighbour's keeping an eye on her."

"And Gemma's safely home?"

I nod. "Something smells good."

I follow her inside, leaving my jacket on a coat hook in the hall. The aroma of chilli, tomatoes and onion intensifies as I enter the lounge diner. It's dominated by a worn sofa and a large old-style TV that takes up as much space as the small table. Like mine, the uncoordinated furniture comes from second hand shops and auctions. Despite the weary carpet and faded magnolia walls, she's brightened the place with poppy-patterned throws on the sofa, big, bright cushions, and a matching table cloth.

She pulls on a Sport Relief apron and skirts around the breakfast bar into the kitchen, heading for the microwave. "The rice won't take long. Can I get you something to drink?"

"Mineral water," I say, eyeing the slow cooker. The environmental health officer in me wants to know if she browned the mince before placing it in the cooker. The cynic in me wonders if she used a slow cooker because she knew I'd be late.

It also makes her a sound judge of character.

Am I totting up points to compare her to Gemma?

I take the mineral water and smile, knowing I should say something to diffuse the tension between us. "When's

George back from football?"

"Soon."

"In that case, how can I help with the food?"

"You can help by not inspecting my kitchen. I know it's old and clapped out, but I don't need you telling me what nasties lurk in the corners."

While she dishes up, I wander around, admiring the French Impressionist prints on the walls. Their erratic positioning suggests they're hiding cracks or holes in the plaster. Photos of George gather on the shelves of a 1980s wall unit with drinks cabinet and slots for LPs. The photos reveal a confident lad with wild hair, long lashes and serious eyes.

"Is this Ben?" I ask, holding up a photo of the boys on their bikes.

She nods. "And Tracey's in the next one."

The bleached blonde looks rather fond of herself and her cleavage. Short, buxom and cheeky, she seems an unlikely friend and not someone I've met before. I'm not a fan of tattoos, no matter how detailed or artistic they look. I like large tattoos on shoulders and biceps even less.

"She's not the shy, retiring type then?"

"No, she's an outrageous flirt, always trying to fix me up. She keeps telling me to get out and have fun, as if I'm shrivelling up from neglect in here, but I don't need a man. Sorry, I didn't mean …"

Her cheeks don't quite match the colour of the chilli con carne, but they're generating as much heat. She turns away and takes a few mouthfuls of mineral water before bringing the bowls to the table. She lets me scatter some Doritos on a plate, while she fluffs the rice.

"I hope it's cooked enough," she says when we're seated.

"I'm not used to wholegrain."

"How did you know I preferred wholegrain?"

She lowers her head. "I rang Niamh and asked her what your favourite dish was."

"And when you couldn't make chicken jalfrezi, you went for chilli."

I spoon a healthy amount over the rice, enjoying the fiery scent of chilli. "And you used baked beans," I say, nodding in approval. "Niamh briefed you well."

"Not quite. She originally suggested pizza and wedges with chilli sauce, but I wanted to cook something."

"Thank you," I say, appreciating the effort she's made. If only I hadn't arrived late in my work clothes. "You didn't need to go to all this trouble."

"You went to so much trouble on Saturday, trying to include me in your investigation and I messed it up for you."

"You found St Cloud's for me."

She swallows. "Miss Rudolf called me in. I'm sure she's found out what I did. I'm not cut out to be your assistant, Kent. I'm sure Gemma's much better."

An uneasy silence allows me to tuck into the food. The fiery chilli makes my taste buds sing before leaving a hearty afterglow on my tongue. Before I know it, I'm on my second helping, aware of the apprehension behind her smiles. Whether she's not sure what to expect, or what she wants, I can't tell, but Gemma's in there somewhere, coming between us.

"Have you had the locks changed?" I ask when I can eat no more.

"Mr Sherlock's put it in hand," she replies, placing her bowl on top of mine. "He's offered me a flat near the seafront, but I'm close to Sainsbury's and the train station here. Then there's George's school."

"I can do it for you."

She shakes her head. "I don't think anyone's coming back. Whoever it was, wanted to look at the book. Why bother to return it if there was anything else?"

Why bother to return it? Why not throw it in a bin?

"As long as they don't take too long," I say. "Can I see the book?"

"It's in the bedroom," she says, rising.

Moments later, she returns and hands me the hardback. *The Cider House Rules* has a faded and torn cover and damage along one side of the spine. As someone who spends most of his time reading on a Kindle, I'm a stranger to hardbacks with rough pages and musty odours. At least no one's folded down page corners.

To Little Lisa, my favourite.

The bold, flowing strokes, written in fountain pen, suggest confidence and authority. The words tell me Louise's mother was one of several children. The capitalisation implies a pet name for Elisabeth. What made her special – special enough to be given a book? Why a novel about an orphanage? Was it a leaving gift? Did someone adopt Little Lisa?

"Have you read the story?" I ask, flicking through the pages.

"Not since school."

"Any sign of the missing photograph?"

"I stripped out the wardrobe and dressers, but I can't find it anywhere. I thought I'd rip up the carpets tomorrow and take out the bathroom on Friday."

"Don't forget the loft," I say with a smile.

"I'm hoping to leave Miss Rudolf up there, tied and gagged." Louise laughs and then blushes, realising what she's said. "I'd best clear away."

I fetch the framed photograph I took from Kim Jaggers and show it to Louise after she's cleared the table. "Was the man in your photo any one of these?"

She takes a close look, studying each face in turn, and shakes her head. "Where did you get this?"

"The woman at the front is Kim Jaggers."

"What did she tell you about Mr Trimble?"

"Not much. We can go back and talk to her when she's feeling better."

"You and Gemma, you mean."

Having upset Gemma, I doubt if she'll be interested. "You and me, Louise. I've taken a few days off work, so we could go anytime."

She shakes her head. "Gemma's your assistant."

"We're not joined at the hip, you know."

"No, she just pops into your bedroom to enjoy the views."

Louise groans and turns away, shaking her head. I should tell her Gemma's history, but I can't find the words.

"Gemma's a good friend," I say.

"She hates me," Louise snaps. "And don't tell me I'm overreacting. I saw the way she looked at you when we were chatting at the party. She gave me the same look on Saturday. Why would she do that if you were only friends?"

"You think there's something going on between us?"

Her hands plead with me. "I saw the way you looked at her at the party, Kent."

"Yeah, me and every other man in the room. She looked amazing," I say, lowering my voice. "She always does. I could have spent the evening with her, but I came here, didn't I?"

Her eyes widen. "You think I should be grateful?"

"No, I didn't mean it like that."

She snatches the book from the table and marches back to her bedroom. Moments later, the door slams.

Why do I always struggle with words when it comes to feelings?

I spent my teenage years keeping my feelings and opinions to myself, pretending to be someone I wasn't to ward off the bullies at school and those who were quick to judge me. I learned to remain objective, to keep things simple, to keep my distance. Commitment meant having to explain who I was, how I felt. I'd rather have fun and move on because sooner or later another woman will stroll past to remind me there's always something better over the horizon.

That's what my English teacher told me after she read one of my despairing stories of failure and humiliation. She told me to believe in myself, to stop comparing myself to others, to stop wanting what they had. 'Never stop hoping,' she said, 'because there was always something better over the horizon.'

When things went wrong at school or at home, when my mother put me down or beat me when she was drunk, I told myself this.

It's what keeps me moving forward, hoping for a better future.

Yet I haven't found anyone better than Gemma, have I?

Maybe I haven't tried. Maybe I've never given anyone a chance.

I get to my feet and pick up the photograph from the

table. As I draw level with the bedroom door, I'm tempted to knock, to tell her Gemma's history, but I walk past. I lift my jacket from the hook and sling it over my shoulder. I pause in the doorway, wondering whether to say goodbye, but what's the point?

I can't be someone I'm not.

I pull on my jacket as I descend the stairs. Outside, the biting wind cuts through the weary fabric, spurring me back to my car. I'm about to climb in when I spot a folded note, flapping beneath the wiper.

Why would you want to hurt the ones you love, Mr Fisher?

Twenty-Eight

When I reach home, Columbo hurtles down the stairs from the kitchen and leaps up at my legs, barking and wagging his tail. When I scoop him up, he licks the side of my face and ear.

"At least you're pleased to see me," I say, ruffling his fur.

I carry him back to the kitchen and set him down. He scurries over to Frances, who's standing by the kettle, ready to make tea. He paws her leg and barks. She's opened the door to his food and treats cupboard and he's not prepared to wait. She pulls out a small dog biscuit, which he devours whole. He barks for a second biscuit, even though she's closed the door.

"You can't always have what you want," she tells him.

That makes two of us.

"He's been restless all evening," she says, dropping teabags into the mugs. "Did you find out anything useful from Kim Jaggers?"

"Not really. She passed out and gave us a fright."

Frances hands me my mug. "Us?"

"Gemma found Kim Jaggers and arranged the visit."

"Then you went out to eat," she says, pointing at a sauce stain on the front of my shirt.

"Sleuthing makes me hungry," I say, not wanting to complicate things by mentioning Louise. "And now I'm ready for Miss Marple."

"I thought we were watching Morse," Frances says.

We're midway through the box set of Inspector Morse, which we're watching on 'Crime Nights' every Wednesday and Thursday. When we reach the end, we'll start with another crime series. Though we've seen every episode and series many times, we play spot the clues, pointing them out as they occur, sometimes spotting details we haven't noticed before. Halfway through the episode, we break for tea and digestives. Columbo rouses for his snack before going back to sleep on the sofa between us. As soon as the closing titles come up on the screen, he leaps to the floor, ready for a tour of the grounds before bedtime.

"I'd rather watch Miss Marple," I say, in need of some of her clinical logic and deduction.

The next episode of Morse, *Dead on Time*, features Susan Fallon, the woman he desperately loves even though she broke off their engagement many years before.

"Let's watch *A Murder is Announced*," I say, plucking it from the DVD rack.

It seems appropriate as Trimble announced his murder to me, but something else is prompting me to watch the episode. I have to wait until the closing titles before I realise what's nagging me.

"I still say she took a risk," Frances says in the kitchen.

"By announcing a murder to prevent people discovering her secret, she's drawing attention to herself."

Trimble said, 'They know who I am, but they'll never learn my secret.'

Of course they knew who he was. They took all his property from him.

So, what's his secret? The numbers he left me? Or where they will lead me, if I ever work out their meaning?

Or maybe he's not who they think he is – like Miss Blacklock in *A Murder is Announced*.

I smile. What if Trimble isn't Trimble?

Though keen to explore the possibility, I need to deal with the windscreen notes first. Before tonight, they were innocuous notes that could mean anything. Tonight the notes became personal.

Once scanned onto the computer, I look at the three notes with their identical paper, font and central positioning of the words. The same person sends them. I call him Wiper, confident it's a man, though it could be a woman. Wiper places them under the same windscreen wiper, as if he wants the passenger to see them first. He also leaves the notes when I'm with Louise – twice at Nightingales, the third at her flat.

Either he knows where I'm going or he follows me.

I'm not sure which is worse.

If he knows where Louise lives, he could have taken the book. But his latest note refers to more than one woman.

Why would you want to hurt the ones you love, Mr Fisher?

It sounds like a warning, a threat even.

A scampering of paws signals Columbo's return from outside. He bounds into the room and leaps onto the bed, his damp paws and undercarriage leaving muddy smears on the duvet. After an obligatory bedtime treat, he's soon asleep, leaving me to my deductions and a cold mug of tea.

Wiper's notes started when I visited Nightingales. They're linked to Trimble and Louise, who's helping me investigate his death. Someone wants me to stop.

Miss Rudolf?

"Yes!" I cry, punching my fist into the air.

Columbo barks. Frances leans around the door a moment later. "Are you okay?"

"I may have to take up knitting and call myself Jane," I reply, enjoying her puzzled frown. "Jane Marple."

She nods and leaves me to my knitting.

Armed with a fresh mug of tea, I turn my attention to Trimble.

If he's not Trimble, who is he?

And who's Walter?

I scan Kim Jaggers' photo and enlarge the image. Walter's my height with short dark hair and an indifferent, almost cynical smile, but he looks more like Martin Bell, who stands behind him. They both have long faces and share the same taste in bright ties, but that's insufficient for a conviction.

I zoom in on the grainy image of Bell. Have we met? Did we once make a joint visit to a care home?

Maybe Kim Jaggers can tell me more tomorrow.

Or Malcolm Knott, if he ever returns my calls.

Though ready for bed, I look at Trimble's numbers.

17	9	7
2	26	4
26	15	6
26	15	6
9	13	6
11	14	7

Should I read them down or across? Are the seven rows significant? Why are the third and fourth rows identical? Are they items on a takeaway menu?

"Why didn't Trimble leave us a clue?" I ask Columbo.

He left six clues, I realise while brushing my teeth.

"Crosswords," I tell Columbo when I climb into bed. "Trimble liked crosswords."

Maybe I should take up knitting.

Twenty-Nine

In the office the following morning, Sylvie becomes defensive. My unexpected appearance prompts her, and everyone else, to remind me I'm on leave, even though my chinos and polo shirt give me away.

"You had no right to bin them," I repeat, my voice rising. "They're part of his estate."

"Who's going to want a pile of smelly old crossword books?"

She's right, of course. I'm annoyed because I didn't make the connection sooner.

Gemma strolls over and gives me a smile as if nothing happened the previous evening. "Old crossword books?"

"His new girlfriend prefers the intellectual type," Sylvie replies.

Gemma laughs. "Then she's bound to be disappointed. Kent's so clever he came into work on his day off."

While Danni's in a meeting, I use her office to ring the Care Quality Commission. Once again, Malcolm Knott requests me to leave a message. "Can we talk about Kim Jaggers?" I ask, hoping that will prompt him to ring back.

On my way out, Gemma emerges from the office and walks beside me. "Do you want to tell me about Trimble's crossword books?" she asks.

"It's nothing," I reply.

"You were getting pretty steamed up over nothing."

"It's becoming a habit," I say, stopping by the stairs. "Look, about last night ..."

"I overreacted," she says. "You took me by surprise."

"It won't happen again, I promise. You're engaged to Richard, not me. I –"

She presses a finger to my lips and looks into my eyes. Then, hearing someone cough nearby, she glances down the corridor. "Damn!" she says, pulling away.

Sylvie watches with interest, but remains by the office. "I kept an itinerary," she says, holding up her notebook. "Trimble had six crossword books."

"Did you make a note of the publisher?" I ask.

Her frown suggests I should get a life. "If you'd asked me on Tuesday, I could have given you the books," she says. "I put them in the recycling bin when I left for home."

Gemma walks over to the green wheelie bin and peers inside. "It's almost empty."

When the bin's full, the caretaker moves it to the basement for collection, replacing it with an empty one. He must have taken the full bin yesterday afternoon.

"Or first thing this morning," I say, heading down the stairs.

On the first floor landing, I hear a reversing alarm in the yard. I peer through the landing window at a collection wagon, heading into the recycling area. Taking two steps at a time, I'm soon in the basement, hurtling past the caretaker's office. I burst through the basement doors and come to a halt in the yard. A beefy man, cigarette wedged into the corner of his mouth, attaches two green bins to the back of the wagon.

I call out to him.

Brian, the caretaker, officious in his orange hi-vis jacket, steps out from the covered refuse storage area. "Restricted area, Fisher. Hard hat and hi-vis required."

I brush past him and approach Beefy. "I need to check the bins."

"Lost your bullshit manual?" Brian laughs as he steps up alongside. "Once it enters the bin, it becomes the property of Downland District Council. Doesn't it, Angus?"

Beefy rolls his eyes and unhooks the bins from the hoist mechanism.

"If you rummage in there, you'll be in breach of ... of health and safety," Brian says.

"Why isn't Angus wearing a hard hat and hi-vis jacket?" I ask.

"They're knackered," he says in pure Glaswegian. "I asked you for replacements last month, Brian."

"Don't you keep spares?" I ask.

Brian retreats to the cluster of wheelie bins in the corner and pulls one out. "You can decant into this empty one," he says. "What are we looking for?"

"Crossword puzzles."

"Don't you have enough to do in environmental health?"

I could explain, but I'd rather help Angus transfer cardboard, envelopes and paper to the empty bin. "Is this one?" he asks, holding up a paperback.

I nod, taking it from him. A few minutes later, we have

all six.

"What's with the books?" Brian asks when Angus returns to emptying the bins.

"Haven't a clue," I reply, heading for the car park.

In my car, I flick through the pages. Trimble filled the margins with scribbles and notes to solve anagrams and list possible answers. While most of the clues make as much sense as Danni's emails, the answer to his three columns of numbers lies in these books.

Do the numbers represent clues, or a particular puzzle?

I open the final volume. Trimble never started any of the crosswords, though the crack in the spine and smears on many of the pages tell me he leafed through the book. He also removed, with great care and precision, the answer pages for the first 30 puzzles.

He doesn't intend to make my quest any easier.

I pull out his numbers. The highest in the first column is 26. I flick to Puzzle 26 and find 15 across. The answer comprises two words of six letters.

Does that explain the two identical sets of numbers? 26-15-6, 26-15-6?

It takes seconds to confirm that the first column identifies the puzzle, the second the clue, and the third the number of letters in the answer, in case there's a 5 across and a 5 down. Delighted with my progress, I study the clue for 15 across.

Perhaps I probed price to uncover heroine's seduction. (6,6)

It might as well be written in Russian.

Thirty

I spend the rest of Thursday morning on a tour of bookshops, hoping to find a copy of the crossword book with all its answer pages. When it becomes clear that no one stocks seven year old puzzle books, I try the second hand bookshops without success. The owner of the last one I enter suggests I try the charity shops, which stock an amazing range of books, but few with crosswords in them.

While I rest my feet and enjoy a skinny decaffeinated latte, I surf Amazon.

It looks like I'll have to solve the cryptic clues.

Good job no one's life depends on it.

Though hungry, I drive over to Pevensey and park at the rear of Anderida Villas. With her photograph safely in my pocket, I rap on Kim Jaggers' door. The thud of the knocker echoes in the cold air. When she doesn't answer, I try again, hoping the dead in the nearby graveyard will forgive me. Aware of curtains twitching, I decide not to sneak down the side passage.

I walk along the road to Violet's bungalow. She comes straight to the door and invites me inside. She looks even thinner than last time with a dress that hangs like curtains from her stooped shoulders.

"I've got a sponge in the oven," she says, flapping a bony hand at the bowls, whisk and spoons on the table. "Cup of tea, love?"

"I only popped by to see if Miss Jaggers was okay," I say, spotting a stack of puzzle magazines on the worktop. "Thanks for helping out last night."

"She ordered me out as soon as you left and went to bingo."

"Was she all right?" I ask.

Violet nods. "She said you were fussing over nothing."

I flip open a copy of *Take A Puzzle* magazine, wondering if Kim Jaggers pretended to pass out to get rid of us. "She's not answering her door," I say.

"She stays with friends after bingo. Won't be back until the weekend, I imagine. I'm saving the puzzles for her. She likes the cryptic crosswords. I can't make any sense of them."

"Interesting."

"What's interesting, love?"

"Nothing," I reply, wondering if Kim Jaggers and Trimble spent evenings solving puzzles. "I'll pop back over the weekend."

"Do you want me to tell her you called, love?"

"It might make her anxious. We don't want her passing out again."

Back in the car, I search the glove box for business cards, but they're in my work jacket, of course. Then again, if Kim Jaggers is withholding information, do I want to give her advance warning of my return?

Maybe I should ask Gemma to drive past on Friday.

I sigh, relieved she's not angry with me. She has every right after my impulsive behaviour yesterday evening, but she didn't protest when I kissed her. I'm sure she wanted me to kiss her. And in the corridor at work, there was a hint that she ...

I sigh again, wondering if I'll ever understand her, or any other woman for that matter.

I can understand Louise feeling uptight because I was late. Okay, slotting in a visit to Kim Jaggers wasn't a good move, in hindsight, especially with Gemma helping me. Louise clearly enjoyed helping me when she hacked into her boss's computer, but she doesn't want to share the role with Gemma.

As Louise works at Nightingales, she could still help me, but can I tempt her back?

I pick up my phone and text her. Hopefully, she'll be intrigued and ring me back.

Perhaps I probed price to uncover heroine's seduction. (6,6)

Louise doesn't ring me or text.

On Friday morning, the planning application beckons. While the questions on the application form make more sense than the crossword clues, the answers require more thought. I study the forms and notes while Frances seeks help from Google. After a couple of hours, we've produced a half-completed form and a location map.

"Get an architect," she says as we eat lunch.

After lunch, I ring Richard. "Can you recommend a good architect? One who's sympathetic to environmental concerns and highly respected by the council?"

"I might know someone," he replies. "Simeon Humboldt's retired, but he's often tempted by the more unusual projects. Your sanctuary might pique his interest. I'll take soundings."

"Thanks, Richard. I thought you'd know someone."

"Before you go," he says, "can I ask you about last night?"

A knot forms in my stomach. "Last night?"

"Yes, Gemms sent me a strange text, so I went back to her flat when bonsai wound up. She was a tad tetchy – and rather tipsy when I found her. Nothing serious," he says, after a nervous laugh, "but she'd polished off a bottle of Prosecco. Not like her at all. Then, after I put her to bed, I discovered rather a lot of tissues in the waste bin. At first, I thought she was coming down with something."

"She seemed fine when I dropped her off," I say, maybe a little too quickly.

"Oh," he says. He sounds disappointed, but it could be a trap. Solicitors aren't averse to leading witnesses. "I was rather hoping you could point me in the right direction. You know her so much better than me."

Sweat begins to run down my back. "Kim Jaggers collapsed while we were talking to her. We thought she'd had a heart attack."

"Gosh, that would shake you up, wouldn't it? I mean, I wouldn't know one end of a defibrillator from the other."

"People don't normally keep them at home."

"No, quite," he says. "Gosh, how scary. Gemms likes to pretend she's tough, but she's rather sensitive, as I'm sure you know. Neither of you likes to admit your feelings."

Richard's more astute than I thought.

"At first, I thought the two of you had fallen out," he says, catching me off guard.

I shift in my seat, still sweating. "You did?"

"I know you two drive each other bonkers, so don't deny it. She's always complaining about how you disagree at work. I'm not taking sides, Kent, but I wonder if it's because you're like the father she never had."

I try to keep my tone frivolous. "Maybe I should walk her down the aisle instead of being your best man."

A little after four, a storm howls over the South Downs, driving torrential rain that stings our eyes as Frances helps me secure the horses, donkeys and goats in the barn. After making sure they're safe, she retreats to the rusting caravan she calls home. Four years ago, after a similar storm had abated, she arrived in a Range Rover, driven by a man with longer dreadlocks than her. She climbed out, straightened her camouflage jacket and trousers and said she'd come for the job.

"I don't want money," she said, twisting a braid in her fingers, "just a place to pitch my van, fresh air and three meals a day. I got no references, but I understand animals."

She strode across the yard to the kennels, where the dogs had barked since the Range Rover arrived. Moments later, the barking stopped. When she came out of the barn, three excited dogs followed at her heels.

"They need more exercise," she said, glancing towards the Downs. "I can take them now, if you want. All you got to do is help Titch unhitch the Bitch."

She gestured to her caravan and strolled off with the dogs.

"Frances won't let you down," Titch said as he climbed

out of the Range Rover. "You look after her because she's all I got."

We agreed a site for the small caravan, bruised with numerous dents, and moved it into place. When she returned an hour later with three weary dogs, he'd long gone. She walked around the caravan, nodded her approval and introduced herself.

"Why do you call your father Titch?"

"He's small."

I never asked her any more about her family or her past and she never told me anything. Now I can't run the place without her, though I'm sure Titch will return one day, hitch up the caravan and take her with him.

Back in the flat, I check my phone to see if Louise has replied to my text. I soften my disappointment with a plain chocolate digestive or three and ring Malcolm Knott at CQC. Four fifty on a Friday afternoon isn't the best time to call, but to my surprise, he picks up on the first ring and announces himself in a dry, slightly pompous tone.

"How can I assist you?" he asks after the introductions.

"I met Kim Jaggers on Wednesday. She sends her regards."

"I'm not familiar with the name."

"You worked with her and Martin Bell, I believe."

"Oh, that was a good many years ago, Mr Fisher. I barely knew the woman. She retired shortly after I started."

"I went to see her about Anthony Trimble." I pause to see if Knott reacts. When he doesn't, I mention St Cloud's in Litlington. "You may remember it."

"When was this?" Knott asks.

"In the 1980s, though Mr Trimble continued in the business for many years."

"Well before my time, I'm afraid."

"Unlike Nightingales in East Dean. You carried out the last inspection."

"If you know that you must have read my findings," he says, unfazed by my change of direction. "It's an exemplary home, Mr Fisher. Do you have a concern about hygiene?"

"I'd prefer to discuss my concerns in person."

Impatience creeps into his voice. "Perhaps you could give me an indication, Mr Fisher. Or is there something you want to show me at the premises?"

"I'd rather meet at my office. It isn't far from Nightingales."

"It is if you live in Maidstone. I'd like to oblige, Mr Fisher, but with a huge district and a backlog of inspections, I need a good reason to make a 50 or 60 mile round trip."

"I'm concerned about the wellbeing of the residents, Mr Knott."

"Can you give me some examples?"

"Mr Trimble died."

"Are you saying his death was suspicious? If you are, isn't that a matter for the police?"

"I don't believe he was properly assessed."

"In that case, let me check," he says, clicking away at a keyboard. "I have inspections in the Downland area, but they're planned for next month. If I bring one forward, we could meet afterwards. How about I ring you back with a date and time?"

"Thank you, Mr Knott. Does Walter still work for you?"

"We don't have anyone called Walter working here."

"Kim Jaggers told me he was an admin officer. She gave me a photograph of you all."

"Why did she do that?"

"I said I would be contacting you about Nightingales. She asked me to mention her to you and gave me the photograph. Walter's in the front row with her."

"It's not ringing any bells, Mr Fisher. Do you have a surname for Walter?"

"No, that's what I was going to ask you."

"I'll be in touch," he says and ends the call.

"Interesting," I tell Columbo, who's watching me from under the table.

But not as interesting as the text Louise sends me at midnight.

Bodice ripper.

Thirty-One

Malcolm Knott telephones the sanctuary around 9.15 on Saturday morning. I'm with Frances on the roof of her caravan, armed with a mastic gun, trying to fix the several leaks.

"We can meet you at your office next Wednesday at four," he says. "I appreciate you may not have access to your diary at the weekend."

"No, the internet hasn't made it to Downland yet, but we live in hope."

"Let me know if you can't make it."

"Are you okay?" Frances asks, releasing the pressure on her mastic gun.

"I have an itch I can't scratch," I reply.

Once finished with the caravan, Frances and I clear the debris from yesterday's storm. Columbo attacks the broom as I sweep, despite repeated instructions to stop. He bobs from side to side before lunging forward to bite the broom and tug it out of my hands. If I shake the broom at him, he simply barks and wags his tail more. In the end I find an old broom head among the cobwebs at the back of the barn and let him play with it.

Thirty seconds later, he's back, attacking my broom.

The sound of a bicycle bell distracts him and he hurtles across the yard. George swings into the yard, a rucksack on his back, his grin as wide as the handlebars. He skids to a halt and dismounts in one fluid movement, almost landing on Columbo. George props his bike against the barn and pulls out a treat.

"Mum thought you might need some help," he says, removing the cycle helmet.

I pull out my phone, wondering if I missed a call from Louise. I can't believe she would let her son ride from Eastbourne to the sanctuary.

"I'll ring your mother to let her know you arrived safely."

"She's out," he says. "That's why she said I could come here. I caught the train to Tollingdon." He shows me the ticket, as if he expected me to doubt him.

Now I do.

"How did the football go on Wednesday?" I ask, deciding to ring his mother once I know what brought George here.

"I missed a penalty, so I was substituted at half time. Mum said shit happens."

I can't help feeling she wasn't referring to his penalty miss.

"It happens to dogs too," he says, following Columbo upstairs. "That's why you're here to make it better, isn't it?"

"We do what we can," I say.

"I wish you could make it better for my mum."

Tears well up and he hurries into the kitchen. His distress turns to embarrassment when he finds Frances in there. He mutters something about the bathroom and scurries down the hall. She gives me a shrug and offers to make lunch.

"Let's use the leftover sausages," I say, opening the fridge.

While I reheat the sausages and fry them with some onion, Columbo sits by my feet, hoping food will drop into his dribbling mouth. Frances prepares the granary rolls and salad, stopping only to get George a diet cola from the fridge. They chat about orphaned lambs, the injured foxes and badgers we sometimes take, and how he can become a volunteer. The conversation continues while we eat.

George eats as fast as Columbo, devouring his hotdog before I've taken more than a couple of mouthfuls.

"Why do you think I can help your mother?" I ask as he reaches for a second roll.

"She was crying when I came home from football." He tears off a chunk of roll and sausage with his teeth and chews as if he's in a race.

"Do you know why?" I ask.

"It's my dad." His scowl tells me all I need to know. "He's always ringing, asking for money."

Louise claimed his father left before George was born. Why didn't she mention he was still sniffing around?

"He came over for tea on Wednesday," George continues. "That's why Tracey took us to MacDonald's after football. When we got back, I knew mum had been crying. Ben and I were sent to my bedroom. We couldn't hear that much, but Tracey kept saying, I told you he's not worth it."

Why didn't Louise tell him I came to tea? "Are you sure

it was your father?"

He takes another bite, considering his answer. "I spoke to him on the phone when mum was with Tracey. Don't tell her."

"What did he say?" Frances asks, no longer eating.

"He wanted us to be a family. He said he would take me to watch Brighton play. Then we could go for a burger. He told me not to say anything to Mum because she wouldn't let me go."

"Did you tell her?"

"Nah," he says, reaching for the remaining roll. "I said I didn't need a dad because I'd managed fine without one."

He looks from Frances to me, puzzled by our laughter, no doubt.

"Are you going to tell my mum?" he asks, looking worried.

"She needs to know," I say.

"Mum won't mind. She likes you. That's why I know you'll make her feel better."

I wish.

Thankfully, George is more interested in what Frances is doing. Once we finish lunch, he follows her downstairs. I load the dishwasher, make myself a mug of tea, and then settle on the sofa and ring Louise.

"I'm at work," she says, her voice little more than a whisper. "Miss Rudolf will be back any moment."

"Did you tell George he could come over to the sanctuary?"

"What? He plays football on Saturday morning and spends the afternoon with Peter, one of his friends from school. What's he doing with you?"

"I don't know. Do you want me to take him to Tracey?"

"She's away. Did he ride over?"

"He caught the train and rode from Tollingdon Station. Why don't I pick you up from Nightingales?"

"I don't know what time I'll finish. We're short staffed. Miss Rudolf's already in a foul mood because the Sherlocks are back."

"So what do you want me to do?"

She hesitates. "I'll text you when I'm home, if you don't mind bringing George back. You wait till I see him."

"Go easy on him. He's upset at the moment."

"He's not the only one."

She ends the call before I can ask about George's father.

Thirty-Two

I reach the Plough and Harrow shortly after 2.30 and ask for Fred Bailey, who could be the font of all knowledge concerning Litlington. He accepts the pint of best I place before him.

"Thought you wanted to talk to me last weekend," he says. "You and that girl. You want to buy Barten Mill, don't you?"

Like his faded jeans and threadbare corduroy jacket, his face has seen better days. Dried and cracked, his skin's the colour of rawhide, punctured by grey bristles that almost reach as high as his dismissive eyes. He raises the glass to his thin, cracked lips and gulps back half the beer before wiping his mouth on his sleeve. His lips make a slapping sound as he settles back in his chair, closing one eye while he regards me with the other.

"But you're really interested in St Cloud's." There's a chuckle in his voice as he speaks in a broad Sussex accent.

I sit opposite and pull out a notebook. "What can you tell

me about the place?"

"About Anthony Trimble you mean?" He laughs. "He died recently and you have a side-line in murder, Mr Fisher."

I settle back with my mineral water, pleased he's saved me a lot of explanation. "Tell me about Trimble."

"Have you ever wondered why someone would set up an orphanage in the back of beyond?"

I shrug, wanting him to continue.

"Me neither. The whole village was talking. Everyone believed he'd bring homeless kids from London or Brighton. The ones that play loud music and stick needles in their arms, I mean. We were already drawing up a petition when the youngsters arrived. Wouldn't say boo to a goose, none of them. Quiet as a mouse. St Cloud's, I mean."

He drains the remainder of the beer and smacks his lips together. "They were well mannered, the children. Respectful, you'd say, though some of them seemed timid – frightened like. But if you were taken away and put in a home in the back of beyond, how would you feel?" he asks, rubbing his leathery hands together.

While I consider buying him another pint, he says, "People lost interest after a few months. Children came, children went. They were fostered or moved to new homes. An inspector visited regularly to keep a check on things. Handsome woman, with the filthiest laugh I ever heard."

I show him the photo of Kim Jaggers on my phone. "Is this her?"

He studies it for a moment and nods. "She was here so much, I thought she was moving in," he says, nodding to emphasise the point.

I lean forward. "What do you mean?"

"Just seemed odd, I suppose. Then again, she was religious. They both were. They always made sure the children went to church on Sundays, all dressed smart and proper." He sighs, his expression solemn. "Then that poor boy drowned and she seemed to go to pieces. Mind you, the whole village turned out for the funeral. Sad it was. Only twelve years old, bless him. Place was never the same after that."

"I can imagine."

"No one was surprised when the place closed. The inspector had tears in her eyes when she locked the gates behind her."

"She closed it?"

He nods. "Doubt if she had much choice. Number of children dropped, money was tight. Trimble claimed he had money of his own, but they all say that, don't they? People who don't have money, I mean."

"Do you remember when it closed?"

He rubs his chin while he thinks. "1982. Saturday morning. That's right. The inspector came and took two children with her. Place stayed empty for years. Trimble's twin brother opened it as a home for the elderly. Oak Tree Lodge he called it. Strange name for a place with no oak trees."

"Trimble had a twin brother?" I make a note to trace him in case he's alive and unaware of his brother's death.

"Marcus Trimble. He pronounced it Trimbell, as if he was important," Fred says in a posh accent, exaggerating the last syllable. "Filled the place with rich widders."

"Widders?"

He reaches to one side and picks up a dirty, hand-knitted woollen scarf. "Widows," he says in his posh accent.

"When Marcus disappeared, Tony came back. Kept it going for years, filling the place with asylum seekers. Thankfully, we hardly saw them and they didn't mix with us."

It sounds like a forerunner to Anderida Villas.

"Placed closed a couple of years after the Millennium, I reckon. Trimble stayed there, on and off. More off than on, I'd say. Then about three years ago he sold it. The new people spent money doing it up, but never moved in."

"Do you know who they were?"

"Not a clue. City people, I expect. They think they can move to the country and then discover it's noisy, smelly and doesn't have gas. More money than sense, I'd say."

He rises, one hand firmly on the table for support. He wraps the scarf around his neck and pulls a cap from his pocket.

"When did the name change to Barten Mill?" I ask.

"Didn't know it had."

He gives me a nod as he passes, walking with short steps. He waves to people in the main bar and they all wish him well. Moments later, the barman collects the empty glasses from the table. "If anyone knows, Fred knows," he says.

I can't help thinking Fred's left me with more questions.

He suggested Kim Jaggers and Trimble were partners, which supports what she told me. Then there's the mysterious twin brother, Marcus. Does he exist, or was Trimble pulling a tax dodge? Then there's the boy that drowned.

Maybe the rector will remember.

Outside, the wind howls across the car park. I drive to St Michael's church and pull into the narrow layby by the front gate. The wind pushes me back as I enter the graveyard, whistling around my ears and through my clothes while I check the headstones, scattered across the grass. By the time I reach the last headstone, I'm frozen to the core and no wiser.

The hedge along the boundary wall offers some protection as I walk around the church. At the back I find a few more headstones in a smaller grassed area. Again, I move from headstone to headstone, thinking about Louise to distract me from the chill. It won't be easy, asking her about George's dad.

Head bowed, I hurry back to the front, eyes almost closed against the wind. When I swing around the corner of the church, a malicious gust propels me towards a yew tree. I grab a branch and halt my fall, avoiding a nasty collision with a small headstone by the trunk. I missed the headstone earlier. When my eyes adjust to the poor light, I take a closer look at the weathered inscription. I have to turn on the torch on my phone to decipher it fully.

Martin Bell, born 2nd April 1946, died 14th December, 1957. Missed, but not forgotten.

I pull up the photograph of Kim Jaggers and her colleagues.

In the middle of the back row, large as life, stands Martin Bell.

Thirty-Three

If I had a telephone directory, I'd find plenty of Martin Bells in Sussex. Yet the name links to Kim Jaggers, who links to Anthony Trimble, who ran an orphanage in Litlington, where there's a grave bearing the name, Martin Bell.

It's hardly a perfect circle, but the possibilities intrigue me.

Sussex Police has teams of officers, forensic scientists, specialists and support workers to uncover and analyse evidence, to make connections. I follow a trail from person to person, place to place, relying on imagination, deduction or guesswork. Occasionally, someone offers me a baffling set of cryptic clues that are starting to look like a cruel hoax.

Why am I letting Trimble lead me from beyond the grave?

Then a text from Louise arrives and I know why. Despite my mixed feelings, I'm pleased we're talking again.

Dusk swamps the land as I reach Wilmington, reminding

me I'm still fumbling in the dark. But the unspoilt darkness that surrounds my sanctuary will soon be lit by rows of small, but expensive houses. Water supplies, already struggling to cope with demand will be stretched to breaking point. Sewers that struggle with peak flows will choke and overflow, leading to floods of complaints. With no additional schools, GPs, dentists or libraries, a small supermarket with an off licence and a National Lottery point will have to cater for everyone's needs.

It's no way to build a community.

Not that George has any such concerns. The future's bright if he can spend time with Frances. Tired, but excited by his afternoon clearing out the stables and walking the dogs, he doesn't stop talking until we reach his home in Eastbourne.

"Remember to apologise," I say as he secures his bike in an enclosed communal area on the ground floor. "And ask before coming to the sanctuary next time."

"What if she won't let me come?"

I could tell him you can't always have what you want, but he'll learn soon enough, if his mother's expression is anything to go by. I nudge him forward.

"I'm sorry," he says, head bowed.

When he looks up, her scolding expression melts away. She pulls him into a tight hug, which he's keen to escape. The moment she steps back, he swerves past her and into the flat, his rucksack thudding against the door.

"Thank you," she says, straightening her jacket. "I hope he behaved himself."

"He's welcome anytime, provided he asks you first."

"I'm not sure that's a good idea." She pulls the door behind her and looks straight into my eyes. "He already has the wrong idea about us."

"Why didn't you tell him we argued on Wednesday? Why did you let him believe it was his father?"

She looks away and groans, fidgeting with her jacket sleeves.

"Why didn't you tell me his father was sniffing around?" I ask.

"Have you any idea what it's like being a single mother?" She looks up, her eyes defiant. "Men run a mile when they find out. Or they think you're lonely and desperate for sex. I can't trust anyone."

"Can't or won't?"

"George thinks you're cool, the dad he's always wanted. He wants us to be a happy family. I don't want him to get hurt, Kent. Surely you can understand that."

"And what do you want, Louise?"

"I want what's best for my son."

"Then let him come to the sanctuary and see what I'm like. He loves animals, being with them in the fresh air, doesn't he? Most teenagers would rather play computer games in their rooms and waste days on social media, but he wants to make a difference."

Her voice rises. "How do you what he wants?"

"Louise, that's how I was at his age. I didn't fit in with the crowd. I wanted something different. I didn't want to be inside when the world was out there, full of things to learn and see. I wanted to explore it, understand it and be part of it. But I had no one to help me, no one to guide me and tell me it was okay to be different."

I sigh, surprised by how sharp the memories remain. "I did three paper rounds to earn enough to buy a bike, so I could ride into the countryside and …"

Her arms slide around my neck. Her smile stops me in my tracks. She kisses me so softly, so exquisitely, I tingle with pleasure. Too soon, she pulls away and looks into my eyes.

"You bastard," she says. "I was about to tell you I never wanted to see you again."

"You could try again," I say, pulling her closer.

She shakes her head. "I'm not sure I'm ready for this."

She tries to pull away, but I hold her close. "Ready for what? We kissed, that's all."

"It's not that simple."

"Does it have anything to do with George's father?"

"No, this is about how I feel."

"How do you feel?"

"Scared. Anxious." She pushes my hands away and steps back. "I don't know if I trust you."

"Why not?"

She draws a breath and looks me in the eye. "Gemma. No," she says, as I start to talk. "You asked me how I feel. She intimidates me because she's everything I'm not. She's gorgeous, witty, confident, sexy and so amazing it makes me gag."

She draws a breath and flaps her hands to cool her reddening cheeks. "It's like she's here between us, if only in your thoughts."

"You're the only woman in my thoughts," I say. "You're bright, kind, caring, considerate and if you don't mind me saying, rather sexy for a mum."

For a moment, she looks ready to strike me. Then she realises I'm teasing and laughs. The tension eases from her shoulders. Another kiss later, it's gone altogether.

"Besides," I say, nuzzling her hot ear, "I can't wait to

find out what you mean by bodice ripper."

"It's the only answer I could come up with. It's a type of steamy romance story, isn't it?"

"Or something we could try," I say. "If you have a bodice, that is."

"Don't push me too fast, Kent."

"I'm only teasing. Why don't we go for a stroll along the cliffs to Birling Gap with George and Columbo tomorrow?"

"What if I'm working tomorrow?"

"I can't believe you'd be heartless enough to disappoint a cute little Westie."

My smile lasts until I reach Pevensey and find Kim Jaggers' bungalow as dark as the sky. My gut tells me something's wrong, but rather than sneak around the back of the bungalow, I go to see Violet.

"Do you know if she's back?" I ask.

"I don't, love, no. Why don't you step inside?"

"Do you have a key to her place?"

She nods, but doesn't look certain. "I'm not sure where I put it. Do you want to come in while I look for it?"

I glance at my watch, keen to return home. In truth, I don't want to hang around while she takes ages to make a cup of tea. She'll chatter away, forgetting all about the key to Kim Jaggers' bungalow while she cuts a huge slice of whichever cake she's underbaked.

When I look up, she's already on her way to the kitchen. I follow and close the door behind me. The smell of burnt food intensifies when I join her in the kitchen.

"It's in here somewhere," she says, pulling open a drawer.

I spot the electric ring glowing bright on the cooker. As I

switch the ring off, I spot a pan in the sink. The blackened, burnt on residue at the bottom of the pan could be soup. From the heat it emanates, I realise she took the pan off the cooker a moment ago. I turn on the cold tap to let a trickle of water cool the pan.

The hissing distracts Violet. "What are you doing, love?"

"You forgot the pan on the cooker."

She nods as if it's a regular occurrence. "I'd forget my head if it wasn't screwed on, love. Now, what was I looking for?"

"Do you have any relatives who can help you? A son or a daughter?"

"No, love, I couldn't have children. Someone's always popping in for a chat, so I'm okay. If you've got good friends you want for nothing, love."

She opens another drawer, filled with old bills and letters, which she decants onto the worktop.

"Would you be offended if I asked someone from the Council to pop round for a chat?"

"Of course not, love. Now, where did I put those keys?"

"Do you like fish and chips?" I ask. "I could pop down the road and get some for supper. You're hungry, aren't you?"

She glances at the cooker and nods. "I don't want you going to any trouble, love. Not on my account."

"It's no trouble, Violet. And while we're eating, you can tell me why people wanted to harm Anthony Trimble."

"Did they?"

"That's what you said."

She looks worried now. "Did I?"

"You said he loved children and couldn't understand why people wanted to harm him."

Her forehead furrows with concentration. She sweeps the letters back into the drawer, unaware that most of them fall to the floor around her feet. Then her hand goes to her mouth. She stares into space, her eyes wide and frightened.

"He only gave the children sweets. Two men beat him up." She walks over to the window and points to Anderida Villas. "Over there, in the garden. I didn't see them. I only realised when Tony staggered out, covered in blood." She shudders, tears in her eyes. "His poor face."

"When was this, Violet?"

She looks down, distracted as water overflows from the pan into the sink. She turns off the tap. "When was what, love?"

"I'm going to call someone to come and visit you," I say, guiding her towards the lounge. "Now, what would you like – cod or haddock?"

Her brows dip for a moment and then she smiles. "Hake. My Bert always got me hake. She'll be back tomorrow. Kim Jaggers, love. She'll be back tomorrow, you'll see."

I hope she's right.

Thirty-Four

On Sunday, we park in the layby at Horseshoe Plantation, on the road beneath the old Belle Tout lighthouse on top of the cliffs. Columbo leaps down from the parcel shelf and begins pawing the door when I switch off the engine. We often walk around here, enjoying the views across the cliffs to the modern red and white lighthouse at the foot of Beachy Head.

"Here, Columbo," George says, dangling the harness. He slips it on and fastens the side clips before attaching the lead like a pro.

"Fasten your coat," Louise says when we step outside into the brisk wind. "It might be sunny, but it's still February."

He zips his matching parka and then races off with Columbo, who takes a sharp left and plunges into the long grass to investigate a scent. Louise straightens her snug coffee-coloured sweater over her skinny jeans and then slips on her parka, zipping it up to her chin. With the fur trim of the hood nestling around her slim face, she looks enchanting. Aware that I'm watching, she bends to check the laces of her weary trainers.

A gentle breeze sweeps salty air down the grassy slopes, rough with bare hawthorn and ragged gorse bushes. The naked trunks and branches of ash and sycamore trees huddle together in a small copse that creeps up the hill. The trees look young, rather than remnants of the ancient woodland that once coated the hills. In summer, they provide welcome shade. In winter, their upper branches flicker in the sun as it hauls itself above the cliffs for a few hours.

Once on the path, I look across the undulating fields towards East Dean and Friston, visible between the hills. Louise walks on, eager to visit the Belle Tout lighthouse.

"Why was he called Mad Jack Fuller?" he asks when we stop to take photographs.

Built from grey granite blocks, the lighthouse is topped with a circular glass room that once housed the lantern. It remains as spectacular as it did when local squire, John Fuller, built it in 1832. Later, someone added a two storey extension to provide accommodation.

"He built lots of unusual buildings," I reply, "like a watchtower in a garden and a pyramid over his grave. He provided employment for the locals, so I don't think he was mad. Eccentric, I guess."

"He means weird," Louise adds when George looks puzzled.

"Is the pyramid like the ones in Egypt?" he asks.

"It's much smaller, but it still dominates the cemetery."

He looks at his mother. "Can we go and see it? I'm doing local history at school."

"Maybe. Please don't fill his head with too many ideas,"

she tells me once George is out of earshot.

"Aren't you pleased he's interested in local history?"

"Sure, but we can't do everything at once."

She's telling me to slow down, which we must to climb to Belle Tout.

"I'm not sure who's got the most energy," I say, pausing to take more photographs. "How about one with you in the foreground?"

She raises her hand to cover her face. "I look ghastly."

"How about a selfie then? We could post it on Facebook."

"No," she says, pushing me away. "I don't want Miss Rudolf to find out."

"Why not?"

"I said I'd go in today. I called in sick."

She scoots up the slope with ease, joining George and Columbo at the corner of the flint garden wall. With another short climb ahead, I give Columbo a drink. He laps a small amount of water from the bowl, more interested in the surroundings and the other dogs on the hills.

"Frances said they lifted the lighthouse out of the ground and wheeled it away from the edge on tram lines," George tells his mother. "If they move it again, can we watch?"

"It could be years from now," she replies. "We might have moved."

"Are we moving to the sanctuary?"

She sighs and casts me another look that says this is my fault. "The only place we're going is the top of this hill," she says, setting off. "Let's see who can get there first."

While they race, I pack the water bowl into my rucksack and set off with Columbo at a more sedate pace. The vistas open up in both directions, stretching gently and peacefully into the distance. To the west, the grassland dips into Birling Gap, before undulating across the Seven Sisters, shimmering white against the glistening sea that laps at their feet. To the east, the land falls and rises towards Beachy Head as it overlooks the vast sea, drifting to a hazy horizon, punctuated by the occasional ship on its way along the English Channel.

With only the rush of wind in my ears, and the shrieks of the gulls to spoil the solitude, this is about as close to heaven as I can imagine. Even Columbo stops to admire the views, his ears pricked, alert to any sounds that could mean something to chase.

"It's so beautiful," Louise says, gazing towards the Seven Sisters.

"It gets better as we approach Birling Gap," I say, taking her hand.

"I can't believe six months have passed since I moved to Eastbourne," she remarks as we dodge between the rabbit holes and sheep poo.

"What brought you to Eastbourne?"

"Miss Rudolf," she replies. "She took me on as a receptionist at Skylarks in Tunbridge Wells a few years ago. When she transferred to Nightingales she asked me to come with her. The flat above Tracey was vacant, so she arranged for me to live there and job share."

"Miss Rudolf must have thought a lot of you," I say.

Louise stops and shudders, her cheeks paling. She turns around and gasps, letting go of my hand.

"What's wrong?" I ask, following her gaze.

"It's Miss Rudolf. I knew this would happen!"

I use the zoom on my camera to scan the people milling around the base of Belle Tout. "Are you sure it was her?"

"She was standing at the foot of the tower. She followed us."

"Why would she do that? Anyway, you couldn't see her face from this distance."

"What's she doing here, Kent? She should be working."

Or on her lunch break, I want to say.

I turn my back to the wind and phone Nightingales. "Could I speak to Miss Rudolf?" I ask when the receptionist finishes her greeting.

"She's busy. If you give me your name and number, I can ask her to ring you back."

"No, don't trouble her," I say, aware that Louise is listening. "It's not urgent."

"Thank you for your call."

When the receptionist hangs up, I say, "If she's come off the phone, put me through. Miss Rudolf? It's Kent Fisher. Sorry to bother you on a Sunday, but I wondered if you'd reached a decision on the Pets as Therapy visits. No, you haven't," I say after a suitable pause. "No, no, I understand. You have procedures. Well, thanks for your time, Miss Rudolf."

I return my phone to my pocket and turn to Louise. "Looks like you were mistaken."

Louise doesn't look convinced, but starts walking.

"Tell me how you solved the cryptic clue," I say. "How did you get *bodice ripper* from *Perhaps I probed price to uncover heroine's seduction?*"

"It's an anagram of *I probed price*."

I should have spotted that straight away. "How does that tally with an orphanage named after a book?"

She links her arm through mine and snuggles up. "Maybe the staff had a steamy time. Imagine all that passion, smouldering beneath their starched white uniforms."

"I could starch my white coat. In case, we want to enact what we think happened," I add with a grin.

"I'll let you know once I solve the puzzle that's you, Mr Fisher."

"There's nothing cryptic about me."

She gazes into my eyes for a moment and then shakes her head. "Perhaps the bodice ripping will make sense when we solve the remaining clues."

I like the way she says we'll solve the clues. "I'll bring the puzzle book with me – next time I visit."

"Or you could email me the clues. We wouldn't want to spend all our time together solving them."

We stroll down the slope towards Birling Gap, taking in the views along the coast of the Seven Sisters, rising and falling in gentle scallops of white, topped with green. The cliffs stand white and erect above the mellow sea, retreating from the beach. We weave our way through the students and ramblers, the sightseers and day trippers, descending to the National Trust car park. I'd like to stop for a cup of tea and a flapjack, but George is already descending the steps to the shingle beach below.

On the stony beach, we wander some distance behind him and Columbo. They dodge in and out of the surf that seeps over and between the rocks and polished chalk, visible only at low tide. Ahead, a couple of Labradors dive into the icy sea to retrieve sticks. When George tries the same trick, Columbo ignores him like a typical Westie.

"Miss Rudolf's in the office," I say when I catch Louise looking over her shoulder.

"I know," she says, sounding anything but convinced. "But what about the people who work at Nightingales?

What if one of them sees us?"

"No one's going to report you." I take her hands and pull her close. "No one's going to hurt you, Louise."

"Does that include you?"

With my record, it's highly likely.

I slide my arms around her waist. "Screw Miss Rudolf."

"Screw Miss Rudolf," she says, resting her head against mine.

In the distance, at the top of the steps, I spot a familiar figure. Miss Rudolf raises her sunglasses and smiles at me.

Then she's gone, lost in the crowd of visitors.

Thirty-Five

"Someone's had a good time," Frances remarks when I return home a little after nine thirty.

Dare I blow my reputation and tell her Louise and I spent the evening watching *Notting Hill* with George?

We also talked about Nightingales. With Malcolm Knott coming to see me, I wanted to glean as much information as possible about the place. I discovered more about Miss Rudolf and the tight control she exerts over every element of the business.

"You'd think it was her own money, the way she checks every little detail," Louise said, relishing the chance to sound off.

Not for the first time, I wanted to mention seeing Miss Rudolf at Birling Gap. I wanted to warn Louise, in case Miss Rudolf confronted her at work. Then I remembered Louise wasn't back till Wednesday. When George flopped on the sofa a few moments later, my chance had gone.

"Tell Kent what Tracey told you about the last

inspection," he says, grabbing the remote. "Tell him about lunch."

Miss Rudolf took Malcolm Knott out to lunch at one. They didn't return until after four. A few minutes later he left.

Hardly the detailed two-day inspection recorded on the Care Quality Commission website.

On Monday morning, while I'm enjoying oat granola for breakfast, I realise I have to prepare for my meeting with Malcolm Knott on Wednesday. I need a better idea of the fiddles and games the owners of Nightingales might play. I've seen occasional reports on TV about abuse and cruelty to elderly residents in care homes, but the Sherlocks seem to be ripping off their residents. I want to find out how they might do this. With Louise and the boys at the zoo, I ring my favourite American in Herstmonceux and arrange to pop over for lunch.

Yvonne Parris, the new partner in Summer Breeze retirement home, is so delighted with the microwave ovens and washing machine Mike and I sold her, she wants us to supply a couple of commercial fridges.

Dressed in a baggy sweater, tired jeans and faded trainers, she towels her damp hair as she talks. She looks different without glasses, her eyes bigger, accentuating the mischievous glint that matches her sharp tongue. She leads me past the kitchen to a small, windowless store room, which also acts as her office.

"It's small, but it's mine." She tosses the towel onto some boxes and retrieves her glasses from the cluttered desk. "That's better," she says, sliding them over her petite nose. "Not working today?"

I shake my head, glancing at the wall planners, duty rosters, health and safety information and supplier details that smother the wall areas between the upright freezers and shelving units. The space left allows just enough room for a desk and chair.

"I can only offer you a sandwich while we wait for Andi. She should be finished with the accountants any time now."

"As long as it's not peanut butter."

"With the amount of false teeth in this place?"

Yvonne checks her phone for messages and then leads me to the kitchen. "Now tell me why you're interested in how to rip off residents? Has the market in second hand catering equipment bottomed out?"

"Shall I make tea while you astound me with your culinary expertise?"

"You want your pickle artistically arranged over the cheese?" She pulls on her apron and heads for the fridge. "I suppose you would since you moved up in the world. I hear the property came with its own housekeeper."

"Alice," I say, searching the cupboards for fresh mugs.

"Now all it needs is a lady of the manor."

"That's Niamh."

"You can't marry your stepmom!" Yvonne stares at me in disbelief. "No, you need someone like the intriguing but desirable Miss Parris, who stole your heart during a food hygiene inspection. Why, I never saw a probe thermometer like it," she says, clasping her hands to her chest like Scarlett O'Hara. "But frankly, you don't give a damn, do you?"

"I'm not the marrying type."

She opens the fridge. "Me neither after two divorces. So, what have you uncovered this time? Some kind of scam?"

While Yvonne makes sandwiches, I explain about Nightingales' equity release scheme, careful not to mention the name of the home.

"Talk about vested interest," she says, smearing two slices of granary bread with thick layers of salad cream at my request. "You sure it's legal?"

"It's a contract, I guess. No one's forced to sign it."

"Tell that to a relative who's lost their inheritance." She reaches for the block of cheddar. "We rely on savings and council funding here. We struggle, but we're legal. But when I spoke to Andi after you called ..." She whistles and shakes her head. "Man, can you make some serious money."

She cuts a thick slice of cheese. "It's a question of scale. If you run a chain of homes, you can scale up the overcharging and scale down on things like staffing."

"I thought you had to have a certain number of people on duty."

"Sure, and you have to train them, which costs money, right? If you have a core of trained staff that you can move between homes, you can meet legal requirements and cut the training bill."

Louise moved to Nightingales from another of the Sherlock's homes. Many of the workers multitask – across multiple sites maybe. "That's more an economy than a rip off."

"Not if you promise a high standard of care."

She finishes slicing the cheese, slapping my hand when I pinch a piece. "Then you got to look at services provided. Not that type," she says, raising a warning finger. "We're talking beauty treatments and hairdressing."

"Hairdressing's hardly lucrative."

"Says the man who gets his mom to cut his hair. How much do you think it costs for a simple shampoo and set?"

I shrug, enjoying my cheese.

"Let's say it costs £15 if it's done in your room. Maybe more if the home has a salon. But you charge £30."

"Wouldn't the hairdresser need to be part of the scam?"

"If they're paid a set rate, I doubt it. If you bill the relatives for the whole package, things like hairdressing charges are tucked out of sight. Better still, get power of attorney and look after a resident's finances."

"£15 a time isn't going to make you rich."

"How good is your math, Kent? Twenty residents have a weekly shampoo and set at £30 a go. That's £600 a week over 50 weeks equals £30K a year. And the home pockets half," she says, sprinkling onion slices over the cheese. "Then there are outings, bingo, clothes, medication not on prescription. You buy the cheapest incontinence pads in bulk and sell them at the price of the most expensive."

While Nightingales clientele may not need incontinence pads, they have a hairdressing salon on the premises and pay for expensive menu choices, produced by an overworked young chef with a couple of low paid East European helpers, imported from another home.

"You employ the cheapest and charge for the most expensive."

"I do believe he's got it," Yvonne says, wafting the pungent odour away.

"Temporary residents provide the easiest pickings, Mr Fisher."

The soft voice with a hint of Lancashire belongs to Andrea Deacon, Yvonne's business partner. Somewhere in her fifties or early sixties, Andi's formal grey suit and brogues make her look like a headmistress from one of those old black and white films. There's nothing strict or frightening about her rounded, smiling face though, or the soft blue eyes that betray the compassion essential for running a care home. Her warm, firm handshake tells me she's friendly and fair, but not someone to be messed with.

"How were the accountants?" Yvonne asks.

"Expensive," she replies, helping herself to a tomato. "Do we have any crisps?"

"In the stores," Yvonne replies.

"No, I'm on a diet," Andi says, pulling a face. "Mind you, after meeting the accountants, we have to slim down our expenses too. Do you know any cheap hairdressers?" Her wink tells me she overheard the conversation. "I'd love to know which home you're talking about, Mr Fisher."

"I'd love to tell you, but I have a care homes inspector to talk to first."

"Don't mention inspectors," she says with a shudder. "Ten years ago, I almost lost everything thanks to them. At one point I thought I was going to prison."

Her fingers ball into fists as she explains how she was accused of stealing jewellery from residents. "One kept her jewellery in her room, despite my advice to put it in our safe. She was always misplacing it and then claiming it was stolen, only for us to find it a few hours later, tucked away down the back of an armchair, say. I didn't spot the pattern until the damage was done."

Yvonne slides my sandwiches across the counter while Andrea composes herself, still clearly upset by the incident.

"The jewellery always went missing after her son visited," she says. "I'm sure he hid it. His mother would notice it was missing and complain. We'd search the room and find it."

"Until the time you couldn't find it," Yvonne says.

"Because he'd taken it," I say. "Clever."

"He doesn't want to report it to the police as the jewellery's only worth a few thousand pounds, so he suggests I reimburse his mother. That's when I knew it was a scam," Andrea says, nostrils flaring. "I refused and told him to go to the police. They arrived the next day."

She declines the sandwich Yvonne offers and continues with the story.

"The police interviewed every member of staff, searched the home from top to bottom, but found nothing. They checked staff for criminal records, uncovered an illegal immigrant and … I'm sure you can imagine how upsetting it was, having your life and business turned inside out. At my lowest ebb, I wondered whether one of my staff had stolen the jewellery. Thankfully, the police never found anything to charge us with, but the reputational damage was immense. Then the care homes inspectors descended for the audit from hell."

"No smoke without fire," I say, offering her my tea.

She takes a sip and sighs. "The police were thorough, but they were pussycats compared to Martin Bell."

"Martin Bell?"

She looks up. "You know him?"

I pull out my phone. "He worked with Malcolm Knott."

"Another useless, nit picking …" Andi closes her eyes and takes deep breaths. "I'm sorry, Mr Fisher, but I work 100 hours a week to keep my head above water and those people … Now, where was I?"

I show her Kim Jaggers' photograph and she nods. "That's Martin Bell, and Knott. Bell looked much older in the flesh. He dyed his hair so black, it looked ridiculous, but he knew all the tricks. Poacher turned gamekeeper. Knott was his understudy, watching, writing the reports, pretending to be sympathetic. He implied we were guilty of mismanagement without actually saying it. Chinese whispers did the rest."

"What do you mean?"

"We lost nearly half our residents once word got round. It took a change of name and nearly five years to get back to full occupancy. And no sooner had we let the final room than who should turn up?"

"Martin Bell?"

"Malcolm Knott from the new Care Quality Commission. New job title, new suit, same old pettiness. He scored us good in most areas, but when you read the report it sounded so begrudging. So forgive me if I seem a little resentful, Mr Fisher. I know most inspectors are good people."

Andi walks out of the room, her back stiff.

"I'd better make sure she's okay," Yvonne says. "Stay and finish your lunch."

I would, but I've lost my appetite.

I drive across the marshes to Pevensey, keen to talk to Kim Jaggers about Martin Bell and Malcolm Knott. Instead of seeking Knott's help as an inspector, I need to expose him as a fraud. If Louise will give evidence to support Andi's claims, we could set a ball in motion. Other home owners might come forward then.

There's no answer when I knock on Kim Jaggers' door. The front room curtains are drawn. I'm sure they were open on my previous visits, but not certain enough.

"I haven't seen her since the doctor called," Violet says,

beckoning me inside. "Would you like a rock bun, love?"

"When was that?"

"Let me think," she says, her forehead wrinkling. "Where are we now?"

"Monday," I reply, wishing she would hurry up.

"The doctor called Saturday evening, not long after you left. He wasn't her usual doctor, but he was a real gentleman – ever so polite and well mannered. When I went over, he told me not to worry because he'd given her antibiotics for her bronchitis."

"So she was home all the time?" I shake my head, wishing I'd been more persistent. "Did you see her?"

"No, love. The doctor said it was best to let her rest."

"Have you been around since?"

"No, love. Do you think I should? I could take her some rock buns. Are you sure you won't take some too, love?"

I decline and open the front door. "Must dash, Violet."

"That's what the doctor said. Must dash, Violet." She looks confused for a moment. "How did he know my name?"

Thirty-Six

DI Briggs draws on his cigarette. His cold, disbelieving eyes observe me from under drooping eyelids. Everything about him seems weary, from the downturned mouth and sagging jowls to the unkempt grey hair that lies flat over his high forehead, etched with deep lines. After 30 plus years in the police, he's winding down to his pension, indifferent to the frayed cuffs of his jacket or the crumpled trousers that bulge at the knee.

"I wore this suit on my first day with Sussex Police," he tells colleagues.

At least his shoes have worn better, making a healthy noise on the pavement as he taps his toes in frustration. He points a yellowed finger at me.

"Why are you interested in an old bird who popped her clogs in her sleep?"

"Shouldn't you wait for the post mortem to determine the cause of death?"

"You think her death's suspicious? I should have guessed

when I saw your name on the incident report."

That's what brought Briggs here.

When Violet finally retrieved her key for Kim Jaggers' front door, we went inside to find her slumped in an armchair in the front room, clutching a book to her stomach. Her skin was cold and grey. I didn't touch the empty bottle of Jack Daniels on the floor in case we'd walked into a crime scene.

"Her GP, Dr Jones, treated the old bird for the last ten years," Briggs continues. "He visited last week, trying to persuade her to go into St Wilfrid's Hospice."

"Was it lung cancer?" I ask as he draws on his cigarette.

"What made you go into her bungalow, Mr Fisher?"

I wonder whether I should mention the on-call doctor knowing Violet's name.

"The front room curtains were drawn," I reply. "They were open when I called on previous days. As she didn't answer the door, I thought she might be injured."

I pause while the undertakers carry the remains of Kim Jaggers from the bungalow to their hearse. Violet and a few neighbours in her front garden bow their heads. She's offering everyone rock buns, but so far only the police officers have accepted.

"Why did you think she was injured?" Briggs asks. "She could have been out."

"Violet said a doctor called on Saturday."

"Dr Puncheon, the on-call doctor. He left a prescription for painkillers on the sideboard."

"Dr Puncheon?"

He flicks his cigarette into the bushes. "You know him?"

Dr Puncheon certified the death of Anthony Trimble.

"It's an unusual name," I reply. "Did you find anything

of interest?"

"Anything suspicious, you mean?" Briggs laughs as if I'm nothing but trouble. "There's no sign of forced entry or a struggle. You saw the old bird in her armchair with a puzzle book, the Jack Daniels beside her." He reaches inside his jacket and pulls out an evidence bag containing a photograph. "We found this inside the book. Recognise him?"

"His name's Walter. He worked with Kim many years ago."

"Take a look at the back," he says.

The untidy, faded writing says, 'Forgive me, my darling son'.

"Did the old bird mention a son?"

I shake my head. I'd like to know why Kim Jaggers wanted forgiveness.

"Dr Jones says she had a child, but gave him up for adoption, hence the forgive me. Do you know where he is?"

I shake my head.

"That's a shame because you seem to know a lot about the old bird. Why the interest?"

"We're investigating noise and antisocial behaviour complaints at Anderida Villas."

"Thieving scumbags and scroungers," he says, glaring at the rundown property. "I know you think they're victims, but the women go shoplifting between having babies. Their husbands fence the goods, deal drugs, and piss away the cash down the pub and the bookies."

He raises a warning finger. "I've been in there. They're little more than glorified squatters. It doesn't take much to keep a place clean, does it?"

"I'll pass your observations onto our housing people."

"Don't bother."

"If you locate Walter, would you let me know?" I ask, sensing we're through.

"You worried you'll have to bury the old bird if we don't?"

I'm worried who Walter might kill next.

Thirty-Seven

I collect Louise, George and Ben on Tuesday morning and drop the kids at the sanctuary around eleven thirty. They don't stop talking throughout the journey, barely pausing to breathe, let alone give my ears a break. Louise too seems excited, her grin suggesting happy thoughts. Or if I'm lucky, thoughts she can't share in front of the children.

I'm surprised at how good I feel after her nervous demeanour on Sunday. I know I should tell her about Miss Rudolf's appearance at Birling Gap, but why spoil the day before it's started?

The kids race into the barn like heat-seeking missiles, homing in on Frances. Columbo makes a growling sound and chases after them. When they emerge, she looks exhausted already, trying to fend off questions, delivered like machine gun fire. Louise silences them, but they're pestering the moment we climb the stairs to the kitchen.

A splash of sun bursts through a crack in the clouds, flooding the stairs. Louise slips inside, looking cosy in a sweater and trim jacket that complements her skinny jeans. While we haven't decided what we're doing today, she's chosen sensible shoes.

Once inside the kitchen, she wraps her arms around my neck and kisses me.

"I missed you," she says, stroking my face with tender fingers. "Would you take me to your bedroom?"

"The Downs look better at sunset. Or did you have something else in mind?"

She gazes into my eyes, playing havoc with my hormones. "Google," she says.

"Google?"

"Google Maps. There's somewhere we need to find. Your computer's in the bedroom, isn't it?"

I nod, not sure I put yesterday's underwear and socks in the linen basket. Since Niamh moved out, I've slipped back into a more relaxed routine.

"What are we looking for?" I ask, taking her hand as I lead her down the hall.

"Patience, Kent. All will be revealed."

I'd like to think so, but not when her son and his best friend are so close.

Thankfully, I tidied the room and straightened the duvet earlier. She goes straight to the window to check the view and steps back almost immediately. "Shit," she says, patting her chest as she retreats from the window. "Frances looked up. I hope George didn't see me."

She sits on the bed to catch her breath. I stay in front of the computer, waiting for it to boot. I keep a laptop in the kitchen, but the view out of the window isn't as good. The view inside the bedroom couldn't be better, even if she seems a little nervous.

"Time to reveal all," I say, once the computer has booted.

She pulls a piece of paper from her small black bag. Slowly, and somewhat seductively, she opens the paper out to reveal Trimble's puzzle.

17	9	7	Collins
2	26	4	Farm
26	15	6	Bodice
26	15	6	Ripper
9	13	6	Breast
11	14	7	Reveals

Collins Farm Bodice Ripper Breast Reveals.

"You solved the clues. What does it mean?"

She shrugs. "I'm sure I've got the correct answers. If we can find Collins Farm on Google, we could check it out."

The search throws up Collins Farm north of Lewes, about fifteen miles away, but nothing closer.

"That's the only one," I say after refining the search and spelling it a few times. "We could drive out there, if you want, or we could make some local enquiries first."

"Litlington, you mean?"

"If it's anything to do with Trimble, it makes sense to enquire locally. If Collins Farm has changed its name, the locals might remember. Fred Bailey in the Plough and Harrow should know. Do you mind going back there?"

She gets to her feet and walks over. She smiles and rests her hands on my shoulders. "You want to finish the chilli cheese ploughman's you left behind."

I get to my feet and slide my arms around her waist. "You should compensate me for the loss - plus interest."

Her kiss arouses more than my interest.

"No, not now," she says. "Not here."

I kiss her, enjoying her eager fingers as they push through my hair.

She pulls back and raises her hands. "No, we have things to do. Is that George?"

She laughs as I pull away, almost falling over my chair.

After a flick of the comb and a splash of cold water on my face, we're ready to go. I brief Frances, who gives Louise a wink, making her blush.

The sun continues to push back the clouds and warm her cheeks as we drive down the A27. Louise rests her hand on my thigh and smiles.

"What do you think the puzzle means?" she asks.

Collins Farm Bodice Ripper Breast Reveals.

Trimble could have a filthy mind or a stash of pornography at Collins Farm. If that's his secret … I stop the thought, knowing I need to remain positive.

"No idea," I reply, reflecting on what I've discovered so far. If Kim Jaggers had a son, Walter, then I'm confident his father is Trimble. If Walter was given up for adoption, his bitterness and resentment would make a good motive for murder.

If he left the notes on my windscreen, it means he knows what Trimble told me. Either Walter works at Nightingales or has an accomplice there.

Miss Rudolf probably. She saw us at Birling Gap. But how did she know we'd be there?

I glance at Louise, wondering if she's feeding information to Miss Rudolf or Walter. No, Louise wouldn't be with me now if she was. All she needed was the crossword clues, which I emailed to her on Sunday evening.

Once solved, she and Walter could track down Collins Farm without me.

"What are you thinking?" Louise asks, gazing into my eyes.

"I'm thinking how lucky I am to be with you."

She gives my thigh a squeeze to tell me I could be luckier later.

I'm distracted long enough to miss the left turn to Wilmington. I ease off the accelerator, knowing there's no rush. We have the rest of the day together to find Collins Farm and reveal Trimble's secret. Maybe then, I can put an end to Walter's notes and games. Miss Rudolf too.

My thoughts return to her appearance at Birling Gap. How did she know we would be there? If Louise didn't tell her …

Everything falls into place when I realise her friend, Tracey, is the leak. She took the book from Louise's flat and gave it to Walter. Then Tracey returned it, but not the photograph. Is he the man in the photograph? Or is there something else about the book that could point to him?

Either way, Walter's keeping tabs on me, which means I'm getting close.

I glance in my mirror, wondering if he's following me. He must be to leave the notes on my windscreen. Is he in the red Nissan behind me or the black car that's pushing out, eager to overtake?

"Is something wrong?" Louise asks, twisting to look over her shoulder.

"No, someone's determined to overtake," I reply, slowing as we approach the road to Milton Street. Let's see if anyone follows me.

No one does.

"What are you thinking about?" she asks, her fingers playing games on my thigh.

"I was wondering whether Trimble had a passionate affair with Miss Rudolf and took some revealing photographs of her breasts."

"Be serious, Kent."

"I guess he's a little too old."

"No. Can you imagine Miss Rudolf in a bodice?"

We laugh so much I scuff the verge. Once back in control, I cruise along at a steady 30 mph, in case anyone wants to catch me up.

"Tracey said Miss Rudolf sprang an internal audit yesterday," Louise says. "She's checking phone and internet records, finding out how many free coffees and meals we have, that kind of thing. Tracey's furious because she spends hours on the shopping channel."

"Let's hope she covered her tracks."

Louise nods and sighs, studying the expensive brick and Sussex tile houses, set back from the road. "It must be heavenly living in the countryside."

"You wouldn't say that if you saw the complaints we get. Muckspreading, overflowing septic tanks, noisy cockerels, clay pigeon shooting, people using chainsaws, farmers leaving manure heaps next to gardens."

"It wouldn't bother me if I lived there," she says as we pass a low thatched cottage with a window in the roof. "It's so romantic. Imagine the history and people who've lived there."

"And the spiders."

"You must have had plenty at Downland Manor."

"Most of the creepy crawlies were politicians."

"What was it like, mixing with people like that?"

"No idea. I spent my time with the girls at the stables."

She smirks. "Why doesn't that surprise me?"

"Can I help it if I like horses?"

"But what was it like, living at Downland Manor?"

"Not much different from living anywhere else," I say, wondering why people always think I led some kind of magical existence. When I tell them how ordinary and mundane it was, they're always disappointed. It must be like meeting your hero and realising they're human like you.

We drift into silence, enjoying the countryside as we pass the Sussex Ox public house and then weave our way south. Though the sky's a dirty grey, the silvery light adds a sinister sheen to the views across the Cuckmere River and valley as we wind our way towards the clusters of houses that make up Lullington. Conscious of the silence, I ask Louise about her family.

"I'm an only child like you," she replies. "There's not much to tell before George came along."

"I'm all ears," I say, stopping at the junction with the Wilmington to Litlington road.

She explains how she didn't mix with others at school, feeling left out, not like them. She never invited anyone for sleepovers, scared of what they would think of the small flat she shared with her mother. Louise became so lonely, so desperate to belong, she fell in with the wrong crowd.

"I was fifteen when I got pregnant. I don't know who was more disappointed, my mother or me. All those hopes and dreams. Then she passed away and it was just me and the baby."

"Did your mother ever say anything about St Cloud's?" I ask, not sure Louise wants to talk about the place.

"No."

"What about the book and the photograph? Do you think Trimble gave them to your mother?"

"He must have."

"Then she meant something to him."

Louise shrugs, lost in thought as she watches the trees and hedgerows blur past. As the road narrows on the approach to Litlington, I slow down. The muddy banks at the foot of the woodland have crept onto the tarmac, adding a slippery border.

"Do you think we'll find the answer in Collins Farm?" she asks.

"I hope so."

When St Michael's church comes into view, she calls out. "Stop!"

I slam on the brakes. We slide to a stop, testing the seatbelts. After a glance in the mirror, I reverse into the small layby outside the entrance gate.

"What is it? Did you see something?"

"Divine intervention," she replies, pointing. "The noticeboard."

"What about it?"

"Maybe the local rector's heard of Collins Farm."

The noticeboard gives me a phone number for the rector, who's based upriver in Alfriston. An elderly sounding woman answers on the first ring.

"Could I speak to the rector?" I ask. "I'm Kent Fisher, an environmental health officer from Downland District Council."

"Could I ask the reason for your call, Mr Fisher?"

"I'm trying to find a farm that was once located around here. I'm hoping the rector might remember it."

"Don't you have maps and records at the council?"

"I'm not in the office. Has the rector worked here long?"

"He's ministered for over 40 years."

"Can I speak to him?"

"He's busy at the moment. If you give me your number, I'll ask him to ring you."

"It's urgent," I say, walking back to the car. "Tell him I'm interested in Collins Farm."

With a sigh to emphasise her displeasure, she puts me on hold. I stand by the car, back to the wind. Moments later, a deep, cheerful voice booms in my ear.

"Mr Fisher? Geoffrey Hinchcliffe, Rector of St Andrews, the Cuckmere and all who overlook her. Martha said you were enquiring about Collins Farm."

"That's right."

"How interesting," he says. "You're the second person to ask about the place in as many days."

Thirty-Eight

The rector suggests lunch in the Smugglers. "It's perfect for what I have to tell you," he says.

I turn around and drive north, taking the left turn onto the road that goes over the Cuckmere River. We join the road south to Alfriston and soon enter the village. The road narrows as we reach the bottom of North Street. I stop to let oncoming traffic pass.

An older lady in her best coat and hat waits while a group of Asian tourists take photos with their tablet computers and selfie sticks. On the left they can photograph the red brick terraces of Victorian houses with their small front gardens. On the opposite side of the road, the flint and brick cottages are much older. Mostly residential, their doors open onto the raised pavement, teeming with a torrent of tourists.

One group congregates outside Badgers Tea Rooms, which has transformed the traditional façade into contemporary white walls and moulded grey frames that show off the Georgian windows and imposing front door.

"They serve heavenly scones," I tell Louise as we drive past.

"Which play hell with my waistline," she says.

"You don't mind having lunch with the rector, do you?"

She smiles. "Do you think he'll tell us who the other person is?"

"We'll see," I say, enjoying a challenge.

We drive into Waterloo Square, where an elongated island occupied by a memorial stone cross, benches and a tree, splits the traffic. On the left, tall flint buildings with red brick trims have a more affluent appearance than their contemporaries on the right. But that's Alfriston – a pleasing pastiche of styles and architecture from timber framed buildings dating back centuries to more recent Victorian additions. They live in harmony, surviving the back up of traffic, especially in summer when the coaches squeeze along the High Street, rumbling over the narrow brick pavements.

Alfriston attracts all ages, even on a cold winter's afternoon. The locals scurry into the village stores and post office or congregate outside Ye Olde Smugglers Inne for a cigarette between pints. The pub snuggles into the corner of the square, its original building predating most of the buildings around it, I imagine. The different-sized sash windows, crosshatched by Georgian glazing bars, don't line up with one other. White weather boarding covers part of the first floor, blending into the painted tile finish on the older, original building.

We're lucky to find a space in the free car park, but I take it as a good omen. It takes a couple of minutes to walk back along West Street to the pub. I open the door for Louise and follow her inside, taking in the aroma of food and the sound of laughter as we weave between the tables and chairs. The bar stretches its polished oak splendour along the back wall, filled with bottles of spirits and colourful liquors.

A portly man in a sports jacket sets aside his walking stick and raises his trilby. Though his rounded shoulders and slight stoop betray his advancing years, his red, smiling face and bright eyes reveal an energetic spirit, transmitted through a firm handshake.

"Kent Fisher," he says, as if I'm an old friend. "I follow your exploits with interest and can't help wondering whether our meeting is part of another adventure."

"That depends on what you have to tell me," I say, distracted by his crooked teeth.

"Martha, my housekeeper, tells me I'm too old for adventure. I may be 76, but my enquiring mind and spirit keep me young."

His voice fills the room, bouncing off the brick floor to the dark oak beams that tramline across the ceiling from pillar to pillar. A wide smile crinkles the corners of his mouth as he turns his attention to Louise. He preens the soft grey down on his bald head as I make the introductions.

"You make a handsome couple, if you don't mind me saying," he says. "Let's celebrate that in the time honoured tradition of a pie and a pint."

He's disappointed when we refuse the local ales in favour of mineral water. I'm not sure my choice of chicken salad fits in with his image of an adventurer, but he makes no objections when I pay for everything.

We follow him up the step and across the polished stone flags to a table by the window, overlooking the square. Geoffrey waits for Louise to sit before he lowers himself into a chair, using his stick for support.

He gestures at the square. "Like the smugglers who made this their home centuries ago, I like to keep watch in case my enemies come for me."

"I can't believe you have enemies," she says.

"As I'm sure Mr Fisher knows, people with conviction always have enemies. These days my greatest foes are arthritis and cholesterol."

While we wait for the food, I ask Geoffrey about his work and life in Alfriston. He tells us about his forty plus years as a rector and what he loves about the village, breaking off every few seconds to wave to someone crossing the square.

"The smugglers fascinated me when I first arrived," he says, accepting a half pint of bitter from one of the locals. "They give this hostelry its name, of course. Are you aware that the local gang landed contraband at Cuckmere Haven on the coast?"

Louise nods. "Didn't they bring their goods up the river by barge?"

He smiles, clearly enchanted by her. "The river was much wider then. They stored their goods here and in other places along the High Street before moving them inland." He leans closer and lowers his voice. "Some of the rooms upstairs had hidey holes in case the customs officers turned up."

"Like priest holes?" I ask.

"No, much smaller. Secret compartments in chimneys mainly. There was one upstairs, but I can't remember which room. It may not be there anymore, removed in the interests of health and safety, I expect."

He laughs before taking a sip of beer. "The gangs used the hidey holes for their paperwork. They had to keep accurate records and accounts, even though they didn't pay duty."

When the food arrives, he's forced to focus on the sachets of brown sauce that refuse to yield to his fingers. After several failed attempts, he uses his teeth to break into the sachets, emptying three of them into the heart of his pie. He fans the steam as he tells us about the many tunnels that spread contraband far and wide across the valley.

"One led to Downland Manor," he adds.

Louise smears ketchup over her burger. "Do any of the tunnels remain?"

"No idea," he replies before sampling a small portion of pie. "Scalded my tongue once and couldn't eat for two days. Now, let me get to the point so we can enjoy our food. The Alfriston gang, which met here, were led by Stanton Collins."

He watches my reaction and smiles. "That's right, Mr Fisher, Collins Farm was named after this village's most notorious smuggler. It was never a farm, as far as I can tell, and it was built long after Mr Collins died. I'm told it's an empty shell at the mercy of the elements since the roof collapsed."

"Where is it?" I ask, enjoying my chicken salad.

"On the road to Milton Street, there are two semidetached cottages, set back from the road. On the right you'll see a farm gate and an overgrown track that looks like it leads to a garage at the rear of the houses."

He reaches inside his jacket and pulls out a folded sheet of paper. He spreads it on the table, revealing a printout from Google maps. An arrow points to an area behind two houses we passed on the way to Litlington.

"I checked it out yesterday and the gate's padlocked and

covered in brambles," he says. "Not that you'd dream of climbing over the gate in those lovely jeans of yours, Louise. And you wouldn't bother knocking on the doors of the adjoining houses because they're unoccupied during the week. Londoners," he adds with a hint of contempt.

"Is that what you told the other man who asked about Collins Farm?"

"I never said it was a man." He slides a large portion of pie and mash into his mouth, smiling as he chews. "But you're right, Mr Fisher. He claimed Collins Farm was owned by his father, Anthony Trimble."

Louise stops eating. "Mr Trimble had a son?"

"I didn't ask him to show me a birth certificate," Geoffrey replies, "but I had no reason to doubt him. Do you know him, Mr Fisher?"

"No," I reply, retrieving my phone from my jacket, "but I think I know who he is."

Louise gives me a look that says I could have shared my suspicions. But as I discovered on previous investigations, it doesn't help when too many people know too many details.

"Trimble seems to have owned a few properties around here," I say.

Geoffrey nods. "He was also a generous benefactor to the church. He made sure the children in his care attended every week."

I slide my phone across the table. "Is Trimble's son in this photograph?"

Geoffrey pulls his reading glasses from inside his jacket and perches them on the end of his nose. He studies the photograph while he chews and gives me the briefest of nods.

"Is he in the back row or the front?" I ask.

"I couldn't possibly say, Mr Fisher."

"Back row?"

"Really, I cannot betray a confidence."

"Front row?"

Geoffrey hands back the phone without answering. He shovels the last of the mash into his mouth and settles back in his chair.

"What can you tell me about St Cloud's in Litlington?" I ask.

"I'd advise you not to listen to any rumours you might hear." He slides his fingernail between his teeth to remove some stray beef, using the time to consider the rest of his response. "You'll hear tales of children who ran away, never to be seen again. If you check with the relevant authorities, you'll find most of the children were placed into foster care or transferred to other homes."

"Most?"

"There was a tragic death."

"Martin Bell."

He looks surprised. "You're aware of it."

"I've seen his grave."

He finishes the last of his beer and rises, his chair scraping across the stone flags. "Mr Trimble was a polite, well-educated man, generous to a fault, but intensely private. This didn't endear him to the locals, but it's how I will remember him."

He dons his trilby and holds out his hand. "Thank you both for your company and I wish you well in your endeavours."

He nods and smiles his way across the room, declining several offers of beer.

I pinch a chip from Louise's plate. "What did you make

of that?"

"I don't know." She dabs her mouth with her napkin and settles back. "It seemed too easy, too convenient. He gave you a map and encouraged us to trespass onto private property. He'd already gone there himself. Why would he do that?"

I nod, wondering how my conspiracy detector had missed that. "Maybe he was curious after Mr Trimble's son contacted him."

"Or there's nothing at Collins Farm." She drains the last of her mineral water and gets to her feet. "Mr Trimble's son may already have found whatever it is we're looking for."

"But how would he know? You haven't shown the code to anyone, have you?"

Her eyes narrow, telling me to watch my step. "I didn't know Mr Trimble had a son until ten minutes ago," she says, her tone sharp. "When were you going to tell me?"

"I wasn't sure myself."

"You had a photograph of him, Kent. When were you going to tell me about it?"

Some people nearby tune into her raised voice. "Let's talk outside," I say.

She holds out her hand. "Can I have a look?"

I pull the phone from my pocket. "It's a shot of a leaving party, that's all."

"Who's leaving party?"

"Kim Jaggers."

"The woman you went to see with Gemma?" Louise nods as if it all makes sense. "Has she seen the photograph?"

I pass her the phone.

Her deep sigh holds as much disappointment as the look

she casts me.

"He's the one in the front row," I say.

She studies the photo, zooming in to take a closer look. She stares at the photo for a few moments. Her brows dip into a frown. When she hands the phone back, her expression is grim.

"I think I've seen him at Nightingales."

Thirty-Nine

Outside, a storm's brewing. The air feels tense. We walk side by side, Louise holding onto my arm, almost skipping, telling me she can't wait to explore Collins Farm. She took another look at the photo and said she was mistaken. Walter didn't work at Nightingales. How could he? His photo wasn't in any of the galleries. Maybe she caught sight of a delivery driver who looked like the man in the photo.

Do I believe her?

I can't think why she would lie.

Yet it feels like a lie. She's too excited, too eager, too …

I can't shrug the feeling that she's competing with Gemma.

Then again, I'm hopeless at knowing what women think or want.

Like all other issues where I'm undecided, I set it to one side and concentrate on certainties. I'm now sure Walter left the notes on my windscreen. While it suggests he works at Nightingales, where he left the first two notes, he could be using Tracey to get his information.

"Was the lock to your flat changed?" I ask, pausing to cross West Street.

Louise nods. "Only Miss Rudolf and I have keys. Hers is locked in the safe and mine is in my purse," she says, patting her bag.

"What about Tracey and George? Won't they need keys?"

She kisses my cheek and then looks into my eyes. "I love it when you worry about me, but I'm a big girl now. I brought up George without any help, didn't I?"

I nod, making a mental note to check her lock later.

"We're stronger than you think," she says, sliding her arms about my neck. "We run police forces. We balance careers and motherhood. We even ask men out and take them to bed these days."

Her lips almost brush aside my doubts.

When we reach the car, I glance around the car park, wondering if Walter's watching.

On Sunday, he approached the rector about Collins Farm. I didn't email the crossword clues to Louise until Sunday evening. If Walter didn't have the clues, or the solution she worked out later, how did he know about Collins Farm?

Is that why he stole *The Cider House Rules*? Is there a reference to Collins Farm in the book?

Or were the numbers on Trimble's laptop, which conveniently went missing?

I'm back to Nightingales and Miss Rudolf once more.

Then again, Louise had a copy of the numbers from the moment Trimble passed them to her, long before she gave them to me.

I dismiss the thought, but not fast enough. It lodges in my

head, hanging on with grim determination, posing questions I don't want to consider.

Louise smiles when I settle in the driver's seat and places her hand on my thigh. The nervous, self-conscious woman I first met seems determined to get me under the duvet. While she could be trying to outdo Gemma, Louise might also believe my brains live in my trousers.

"Are you okay?" she asks.

"Maybe we should go back," I say. "Frances must be run off her feet with those two."

"What about Collins Farm?"

"It'll still be there tomorrow."

"But I'll be at work." She pulls her hand from my thigh. "Are you planning to visit with Gemma?"

"Of course not," I reply. "If you're happy to clamber over gates and wade through brambles, let's do it."

The flicker of doubt in her eyes before we kiss tells me she doesn't trust me either.

A large spotted laurel, planted in front of the house, obscures almost half the gate that leads to Collins Farm. It offers some protection from the wind, which penetrates my fleece with stronger and stronger gusts as the storm gathers in the valley. The wind whips up the bramble stems that smother the gate. They haven't moved in a long time, so no one's clambered over the gate. There's no sign of any flattened grass or weeds on the driveway beyond. I switch on my Maglite and point its powerful beam into the dark chaos of branches and stems until I spot the padlock. It's locked fast, preventing anyone from opening the gate.

"Unless there's an alternative way in, Walter hasn't beaten us to Collins Farm," I say, retrieving a large screwdriver from the boot.

I'd like to know why he hasn't used his two-day advantage.

I use the screwdriver to pull the thick, spiky stems back and clear a small section of the gate. I pull back a few more stems, ignoring the cuts and scratches to my hands and forearms.

"After you," I say.

Louise pulls down her hood, rubs her hands together, and attacks the gate with an agility that's fearless. When she straddles the top rail, she leaps into the bramble below, flattening the stems as she lands. She swivels and plants her elbow on the rail. She rests her chin on her hand and gives me a smouldering look. "Let's see how fit you are, Mr Fisher."

I lob the screwdriver into the boot, hand her the Maglite, and then clamber over, feeling the hinges creak and groan. I land beside her, glad the brambles peter out within a couple of paces to reveal a concrete drive, impregnated with clumps of spiky grass and dead weeds. Further along, the ivy that covers the boundary wall of the house has crept over the drive.

I hold out my hand for the Maglite. "I'll take that."

"Does it double as a light sabre?" She turns on the beam and swings the torch through the air. "I love Princess Leia. Feisty but compassionate."

I loved Carrie Fisher, though for different reasons. As we shared the same surname, I used to pretend we were married – when we weren't saving the universe, of course.

I manage to trample enough stems down for us to reach the concrete with only minimal cuts and snags. Unimpeded, we walk along the drive, sheltered from the worst of the wind by the garden wall. Once around the corner, the drive's bounded by trees and shrubs. To our right, hawthorn and elder sway and creak in the wind. Sycamore and ash stretch up to the clouds behind them. To our left, the trees are ornamental. Cherries mingle with apple trees in what looks like an orchard, overgrown with grass, more brambles and a couple of gorse bushes.

The drive swings back to the right, revealing a small flint cottage between the trees. With no roof, the gable walls have collapsed, making the cottage look more like a bungalow. Gaping holes reveal where the windows and doors once protected the interior from the weather. The doorway leads into a small hall and what's left of the staircase. The handrail clings to the wall, now denuded of plaster. A doorway to the right leads into the front room, where the floor's a mess of slates, flint and rotting timbers, smashed when the roof collapsed.

I shine the torch around the walls, bare now except for the chimney, protected by a small area of the first floor that hasn't collapsed. Many of the ceiling joists have survived, unlike the floorboards, which rotted away decades ago.

"Is it safe?" Louise asks, looking down at the rubble, visible between the floor joists.

There's enough intact flooring around the edge of the room to take us into the kitchen. I test the boards first and then follow them along the wall, blotting out the smells of rot and decay that fill the air.

"What are we looking for?" she asks, following me to the kitchen, which has a brick floor that follows the contours of the earth beneath. The floor above, still intact, protected the room from the collapsing roof. The wind whistles through the window and back doorway, fanning the grass that's squeezed between the bricks.

"Careful," I say, putting my hand on her arm as she steps into the kitchen. "Tons of slates are lying on the floor above, so stick close to the walls.

I walk along the wall of the front room to the chimney, forced to clamber over rubble in places. I check the fireplace, but no one's had a fire here. The stone hearth has sunk, resting on rubble and rain has streaked the soot inside the chimney. The outside remains dry and intact, protected by the floor above. Even the wooden mantelpiece, coated with dust and debris, remains anchored to the wall.

At the end, I spot a fallen candlestick, about three inches high with a twisted stem. It's the only sign that anyone lived here.

Or did they? Trimble would have lived at St Cloud's, surely. Maybe he used this place to meet Kim Jaggers. As an inspector, she couldn't afford to stay at the orphanage or be spotted there. Maybe she lived here, waiting for him.

"There's nothing here," Louise calls from the kitchen.

I clamber over the rubble and join her. The old stone sink, supported by brick pillars, remains beneath the window. The lead water pipe, which once fed a tap, stops halfway up the wall. There's an opening into a pantry and what appears to be the remains of an old cupboard, rotting in the corner.

"Did anyone live here?" she asks, stepping through the door into the rear garden. "I can't see any plugs or lights," she says, peering back inside. "It was probably quite romantic with candles and a fire in the grate."

"Romantic enough for bodice ripping, you mean?"

Outside, a small courtyard is flanked by beech hedges, their brown leaves waiting for spring and new life. Ahead, a dense forest of evergreen shrubs, ivy and more bramble, block our way to what's left of the garden. To the right, a small outbuilding clings to the main wall. A braced door, held up by the upper hinge, moves in the wind.

"Toilet," I say, not needing to check. "That means there should be a cesspool somewhere beyond the bushes.

"What's so important about this place?" I ask, trying to imagine it with a roof, a fire in the hearth and food cooking in the kitchen. "It's abandoned, derelict and worthless, but Trimble specifies it in a code."

"We'd better go," Louise says, glancing at the sky.

We head back, reaching the gate as the first drops of rain begin to fall. Within minutes, the rain hits the car with venom. She wriggles out of her parka while I sit there, wondering if I missed something in Collins Farm. Maybe the answer's upstairs in the bedroom. Is that where Trimble and Kim Jaggers conceived Walter?

I turn on the engine and pull away between the rivulets of water that stream down the drive. Louise settles in her seat and checks her phone.

"Tracey's sent a text. She's going to be an hour late. Can we take care of Ben?"

"We could take them for something to eat," I say, checking my watch. "I know it's a bit early, but it would give Frances a break."

"Did you tell her when we'd be back?"

"No."

"Then how will she know if we're late?"

An hour or so later, I lay there, my arm wrapped around Louise, her breath soft against my chest. Exhausted but exhilarated, I continue to smile, recalling the clumsy way we began. The moment I closed the front door of her flat, she flung herself on me, hands everywhere, pulling at my clothes as her lips crushed against mine. Like a beast released from a cage, she flattened me against the wall, ready to devour me.

But arms caught in sleeves. Her bra refused to unhook. Our noses bumped together.

It hurt for a split second before we laughed. We laughed so much, it hurt. Then, as the laughter faded, I gazed into her eyes, so bright, so alive, so uncertain.

"It's been such a long time," she said.

It didn't seem like it.

"We need to get moving," I say, dragging myself back to the present. "Frances must be wondering where we are."

Louise groans and kisses my lips. "I just want to stay here."

"Then lie here while I shower," I say, sliding out from under her arm.

She lays back and groans. "Don't use all the hot water."

I head into the small bathroom which has a full width shower unit. I step inside, thinking about the past hour, surprised by how soft and gentle she was, even when she took control. Then again, every woman is unique, with her own ways and tricks. That's what makes life so exciting and unpredictable.

Once the water's hot enough, I step under the shower, reminded of the moment Gemma slid open the door to join me. She wrapped her arms and legs around me, kissing me like she'd never kissed me before.

"I never want this to end," she said.

I'm still not sure why I ran when she was everything I wanted and more.

The shower door slides open and Louise steps inside. "Tracey's still working," she says, wrapping her arms around my neck.

"Perfect."

"Don't say that. I don't want to disappoint you."

"You won't," I say, knowing I'm more likely to disappoint her.

Forty minutes later, I do.

Forty

When Louise spots the note beneath the windscreen wiper, I'm sunk. She unfolds the paper and reads. Without a word, she hands it to me.

You have immaculate taste in women, Mr Fisher.

The paper's dry, yet it only stopped raining five minutes ago.

Walter's close, lurking in the shadows, hiding behind the slatted door of a bin shelter. He followed us here, waited for the rain to stop. If we'd skipped out of the front door a few minutes earlier, we would have seen him.

"Must be a crank," I say. What else can I do? Admit it's the fourth note and explain why I never said anything before? "I wouldn't pay any attention to it."

"Then why are you looking around?" she asks, her voice cold.

"I thought I might spot the kids who left it."

"Kids don't say immaculate. They don't know your name."

"No," I say, pocketing the note as it starts to rain.

"It sounds threatening. You have immaculate taste in women, Mr Fisher."

I open the passenger door. "Come on, let's go."

She stamps her foot. "Don't treat me like an idiot. What's going on?"

"Let's talk in the car," I say, transferring the note to the glove box for safe keeping.

She glances around, pulling her jacket tight. "He's here, isn't he? Walter Trimble."

"Get in the car," I say, more firmly than intended.

"No!" She slams the door shut with both hands. "I'm not going anywhere until you level with me, Kent. I saw your face when you spotted the note."

The rain runs down her hair and face as it did in the shower a short time ago. Only then it made her smile and groan with pleasure. Now, her eyes are filled with fear and anger. I doubt if she'll believe anything I say. Why should she? Even though I did it to protect her, I haven't been entirely honest.

I'm not the only one.

"This isn't the first note, is it?" She steps closer, her face inches from mine. "How many are there? How long has he been leaving them?"

"I didn't say anything because I knew you'd ..."

"What? Overreact? What do you expect me to do when he leaves threatening notes outside my home? Laugh as if it's a big joke?" She stares at me, her hands raised, pleading with me. "The guy broke into my flat and stole a book. Then he came back to replace it."

"So why haven't you replaced the lock? You told me you had, but I checked on the way out."

"I said I had because I knew you'd only go on about it."

A low growl of thunder echoes through the buildings, unleashing more rain. It stings my face and bounces off the tarmac. Rivers of water surge down the gutters and into the gullies.

"George will be wondering what's happened to us," I say.

"He's not the only one," she says.

Nearby, out of the rain, Walter Trimble's watching, enjoying his moment. He couldn't have timed it better. Louise won't trust me again. She won't want anything to do with me after this.

Maybe it's for the best.

If Walter sees us argue and break up, he might leave her alone and concentrate on me. It's a long shot, but if I can lure him to Collins Farm and persuade DI Briggs to help me …

But Walter hasn't visited Collins Farm, even though he knew about it two days before me.

"What haven't you told me, Louise?"

"What are you talking about?" Despite the defiance in her voice, she won't look me in the eye. "I'm not the one keeping secrets."

"If someone broke into my home, the first thing I'd do is change the locks. I offered to do it for you, Louise, but you refused. Why?"

"Why didn't you tell me about the notes?"

"You said Tracey was at work, but the lights are on in her flat," I say, pointing. "Why did you lie?"

Louise stares at me, her chest rising and falling. Mascara runs down her cheeks. She could be crying, but it's hard to tell with the rain beating down.

"I don't know. I wanted to make love to you." She looks up and gives me a helpless shrug. "Haven't you been so excited, so desperate to be with someone, you'd do or say anything to be with them? I loved solving those clues, even if they didn't make sense. And then today, when I told you and we went to Collins Farm …"

"How did Walter Trimble know about the place two days ago?"

She stares at me in disbelief. "You think I told him?"

"Did you? Collins Farm isn't on Google. But you knew that before we looked, didn't you?"

"I don't even know who Walter is. How could I tell him?"

I don't remind her she recognised him on Kim Jaggers' photo and then denied it. "You suggested we talk to Hinchcliffe," I say. "I thought it was such a good idea."

"It was a good idea."

"Only because it worked two days ago." I shake my head, realising how stupid I've been. "Well, you fooled me, Louise, pretending you were scared of Miss Rudolf when you knew she was following us all the time. She even smiled at me."

Louise gasps. "You saw her? You said she was working."

"Drop the act, Louise. You've already given me a masterclass in the bedroom."

"You bastard!"

An angry growl rises through her, becoming a scream. She thuds both hands into my chest and pushes me back.

I stumble, crashing into the car. My legs buckle. As I drop, the back of my head thuds against the wing mirror, a split second before I hit the ground. Dazed and surprised, I stare down at the puddle that's seeping through my trousers.

Louise gasps and drops to her knees. "I'm so sorry, Kent. I didn't mean to …"

"Leave it, Louise. Just go."

She stares at me as if she's wondering whether I'm worth the trouble. Clearly not, she decides, hauling herself to her feet.

"Until a few minutes ago, this was one of the best days of my life. I thought I'd found someone who cared for me, but you're in love with Gemma, not me."

A few moments later, the entry door slams behind her.

Nearby, a car screeches away. I drag myself to my feet, trying to ignore the throb at the side of my head. I run my fingers along the base of my skull. There's no blood, as far as I can tell, but a bump's starting to form.

I open the boot and pull out the bag with my running kit. I keep it there in case I fancy a run, especially somewhere different. Today, I need a change of clothes if I'm to avoid pneumonia and sopping car seats. I hurry over to the communal bin area, relieved when the door opens. The smell of rotting vegetables and waste fills my nostrils as I strip off my wet clothes in the dark. I pull out a towel and dry myself as best I can before pulling on leggings, a long sleeve shirt and my trainers.

Outside, the rain's diminished to drizzle. Water continues to stream across the tarmac into the gutters. I lob the bag of saturated clothes into the boot and head round to the driver's door. Before I climb in, I look up.

The lights are on in Louise's flat, but not in Tracey's.

I don't realise how stupid I am until I'm home.

Cold, disappointed, but mainly annoyed with myself for letting Louise trick me, I almost collide with a taxi that's pulling out of the lane to the sanctuary. A few minutes later I turn into the sanctuary and stop behind Niamh's Mazda MX-5 convertible, wondering why she's here.

Armed with my bag of wet clothes, Walter Trimble's note, and a range of explanations, I pause at the kitchen door. Inside, Columbo barks and paws at the door. He leaps up as soon as I walk in, panting and making all manner of excited sounds. The aroma of pasta sauce, laden with onion, garlic and basil, greets my nostrils. Unable to calm my dog, I drop the bag and scoop him into my arms so he can lick my face.

Niamh stares at me, numerous questions furrowing her brows.

"I got caught in the rain and changed into my running clothes," I say, strolling over to inspect the sauce. "Was that George and Ben in the taxi?"

She nods. "Is Louise okay? Only her friend rang to say a taxi was on the way to pick up the boys. Has she caught a chill?"

"No, it's me that went cold on her." I lower Columbo to the floor. "Looks like I misjudged her, but it's a story for another day. Anyway, it's good of you to come over and cook tea, but I've had a filling lunch."

"When you and Louise didn't show, Frances called me, wondering what she should do. I told her to leave you two love birds alone and came over to feed the boys. Then the taxi arrived and off they went. You look terrible," she says, looking into my eyes. "Go and freshen up. There's enough pasta if you want any."

And that's when I spot the laptop on the table.

That's when I realise Walter Trimble stole his father's laptop. Walter didn't need a set of numbers. He didn't need to work out what they meant. All he had to do was find the right file on Trimble's laptop to learn about Collins Farm.

Forty-One

Though clean and refreshed after my shower, the side of my neck aches and my mood hasn't improved. I should ring Louise and apologise, but what's the point? She's right. I'm in love with Gemma. It's just about the dumbest, most pointless place to be because I'm probably in love with the memory of our brief time together.

I eat a small portion of pasta, grateful that Niamh and Frances don't ask me about today's events. As Niamh mops up the last of the sauce with a hunk of baguette, she tells us about a plastic surgeon called Roland and his wife, Felicity, who's five years older than him, but looks half his age.

"People think she's his daughter," Niamh says. "That's how skilled Roland is. He works with celebrities from those shows on ITV2 and helps out at the Burns Unit from time to time. To put something back into the community, he said. He thinks Belmont is going to be perfect for his retirement.

"He might even throw in a nip and a tuck," she adds, tightening the skin on her neck with her fingers. "I'm thinking I might be treating myself to a boob job."

"We get the picture," I say as she lowers her hands. "But before you get too many ideas, Birchill's selling Downland Manor."

"Isn't it just the best news?" She laughs and raises her glass of Prosecco. "You can't imagine how good it will feel to be rid of him."

"Not if we need his help."

She shakes her head. "Once we move to Meadow Farm, he's history."

"It could take six months, Niamh, more if people object."

She dismisses my concerns with a flap of her hand. "I know almost everyone in Jevington as most of them voted for William. No one's going to object. I'll talk to the parish council and sweeten them up."

"What if Birchill sells quickly and wants us out?"

"It'll take him years to evict you through the courts. He'll have to wait. Anyway," she says, topping up her glass, "I've spoken to Richard and he assures me it'll take at least three months to sell the hotel, probably longer, so don't go worrying yourself."

Frances, who's remained quiet during the discussion, sighs. "There's so much to do, Mrs Fisher, and so little time to do it."

Niamh's having none of it. "I've organised parties and celebrations for dignitaries and diplomats from all over the world. I'll even make sure Neville Priddy delivers planning permission on time. Nothing's going to go wrong, Kent. Trust me."

While she drinks her wine, my phone rings.

"Sorry to disturb you in the evening," Richard says, sounding tense, "but Gemma thought you'd want to know right away. This afternoon, I received a letter from solicitors representing Daniel Church."

"Who's Daniel Church?"

"He's a former soldier, living in a hostel in Portsmouth. He has a letter from Colonel Witherington that promises him a share of the estate."

Corporal Daniel Church claims he saved the Colonel's reputation and career when a young soldier died in suspicious circumstances at Princess Royal Barracks, Deepcut. In return, the Colonel promised to look after the corporal and make him a beneficiary in his will.

"But when he married Daphne, the Colonel changed his will," I explain at Belmont after a meeting in Richard's office on Wednesday morning. "Not that there was any mention of Daniel Church in the previous will."

"So, he's trying it on," Niamh says, looking relieved.

"He has a letter from the Colonel. Richard believes it's his writing and signature. Would you take a look, Alice?"

She studies the photocopy for a few moments, her expression telling me it's genuine. "What does he want?" she asks in a resigned tone.

"His fair share of the estate, whatever that is."

"We'll fight him," Niamh says.

Alice sighs and looks down at the letter. "He came here a long, long time ago. A scruffy looking man with long hair and beard, like those people you see on the street, begging with a mongrel. It took me days to get rid of the smell. They argued in the office and Colonel Witherington gave him some money."

"Did he tell you anything about the man?"

"No, but he told me never to put myself in anyone's

debt."

"We fight!" Niamh bangs her mug down, slopping tea over the table. "What does Richard suggest?"

"He says we can mount a robust defence," I reply.

"He means pay the man off." She sighs and pushes her untouched cake away. "That's what solicitors do. They drag everything out, charge you a fortune, and then compromise."

"I've asked Richard to find out as much as he can about Daniel Church."

"If he's a vagrant, we'll discredit him," Niamh says.

I shake my head. "If he's an ex-serviceman, who's suffering from stress or fallen on hard times, we –"

"That's not our fault," she cuts in. "How do we know he's not making it up?"

"The Colonel gave him money."

"Or Church blackmailed him." Niamh's on her feet, eyes flashing with anger. "I've already lost one house, Kent. I'm not giving up Belmont or Meadow Farm to some vagrant who thinks we owe him a living."

"They were never ours in the first place," I remind her.

"You earned them, Kent. You solved Daphne Witherington's murder. I'm damned if I'll let you give it away to some loser with a sob story."

"What about Alice?" I ask. "She stands to lose more than any of us."

Niamh raises a hand in apology. "I'm sorry, Alice. What do you think?"

"I think we should settle this quickly or we may lose everything," Alice replies. "If this drags on for months, or years, Mr Birchill's not going to wait."

"If it wasn't for *him*, we wouldn't be in this mess."

Niamh marches out of the room, slamming the door behind her.

"Oh dear," Alice says, shaking her head.

Back at the sanctuary, I split my time between the washing machine and the computer. If we have to pay compensation to Daniel Church, how will that affect my plans for Meadow Farm? How much am I prepared to pay? What will I do if he won't accept an offer?

A reminder pops up on my phone for my 4.30 meeting with Malcolm Knott and I realise I haven't even rung the office to reserve a meeting room. As soon as I log into Downland's systems, I can't help checking my emails. Within seconds I'm drawn into work problems, checking the amendments Danni wants to the service plans, while balking at the number of meetings she's scheduling into my diary for the next two months.

When Frances pops her head around the door to ask me what I'd like for lunch, I've been working for over an hour.

Back in the kitchen, I unload the washing machine and put the clothes in the tumble dryer while she makes sandwiches. Columbo only moves to catch stray crumbs of cheese that fall to the floor. Then he takes up position by my feet at the table.

"Does it mean you can't sell Belmont?" Frances asks, after I've explained the implications of Church's claim.

"Not until we resolve the claim."

"What about Meadow Farm?"

"We proceed as planned," I reply. "I'm meeting an architect there this afternoon."

"What if Church wants the farm? It's only a short walk to the pub."

I'd like to ask Richard to say nothing about Meadow Farm, but he'll have to. Church's solicitors will demand a full valuation of the Colonel's estate. If we can't agree a settlement, a judge will have to decide, adding to the cost.

"It looks like we can't do anything," I say, a sinking feeling in my gut. "But if we do nothing and Birchill sells the land, we're homeless."

I head into the bedroom and text Birchill.

Would you evict your son from the land he loves?

He rings straight back. "Does that mean you accept I'm your father?"

"It means I'll take a DNA test."

A few minutes later, Malcolm Knott from the Care Quality Commission rings.

"I'm sitting on a bench in Hampden Park, Mr Fisher, between the café and the lake, watching the herons while I eat my lunch. In half an hour, I leave for Gatwick Airport."

Forty-Two

Fifteen minutes later, I park on the slip road that weaves between the woods and the lake. Hampden Park's a magnet for birds, dog walkers and mothers with their toddlers. Though mainly woodland, there's plenty of grass for picnics and family games, ornamental gardens, and a play area for infants. On the couple of occasions I've visited with Columbo, he's taken a shine to the grey squirrels, happily chasing them back into the trees.

I remain in the car, watching the elderly couples in their thick coats, sitting on the many benches that overlook the lake. The young mothers sit with their coats open, heads bowed as they stare at their phones. I scan the area, wondering if Walter Trimble's also watching, but everything and everyone seems normal. Even the pigeons beside the lake have stopped scrapping over the crumbs thrown by an elderly man. On the island in the middle of the lake, close to the water, I spot one of the herons, waiting there, its sharp beak pointed at the water like a bayonet.

With less than ten minutes to Knott's deadline, I stroll down the path furthest from the edge of the lake. A cacophony of crows sweeps down from the bare trees to overwhelm the grass below, paying me little attention, much like their cousins, the jackdaws, more interested in the scraps of food people drop or throw to them. Feral pigeons, accompanied by ducks and small gulls, mob many of the occupied benches overlooking the lake, including the one where Malcolm Knott sits.

He's a short, stocky man with hunched shoulders, wrapped in a gabardine-style raincoat. His rounded, sagging face reminds me of Alfred Hitchcock, though he has a full head of silver hair, combed back over his head. His left hand rests on a soft leather briefcase, propped against the arm of the bench. In his right hand, he holds the cup from a thermos flask. After a glance at his watch, he tips the remaining liquid onto the ground and twists the cup back onto the flask.

I step back behind a laurel as he rises and looks around.

I watch him place the flask and a sandwich box inside a supermarket carrier bag, which he pushes into the waste bin. Then, he takes gloves out of his coat and slides them over his fingers, which he interlocks to get a snugger fit. He takes another look at his watch and then glances around, pausing as he looks across the lake to the opposite bank. He picks up the briefcase and strolls to the fence at the edge of the lake.

Knott places the briefcase on the ground and retrieves a couple of slices of bread from a sandwich bag. While he feeds the noisy gulls and ducks that race across the water towards him, I stroll up alongside.

"Bread sinks to the bottom and poisons the water," I

remark.

Apart from the greying hair, he looks the same as the photo I have of him from fifteen years ago. His small dark eyes regard me like a nuisance he must tolerate. He continues to feed the birds until he has no bread left. He drops the sandwich bag inside the briefcase, snaps it shut, and straightens.

"I've read a lot about you in the past couple of days, Mr Fisher. That's why I've taken these somewhat elaborate precautions." His half-hearted smile reveals a flash of gold incisor. "In a few hours, I'll be on a plane and free at last."

"Free from what?"

"Free from looking behind, wondering when someone like you will put a hand on my shoulder." He sets off along the path. "The nightmare began when I met Martin Bell. He joined the inspectorate shortly after the millennium. Much older than the rest of us, he was a poacher turned gamekeeper, a man who'd run care homes and knew every trick in the book. He told me we were going to clean up the industry and get rid of the charlatans."

Knott follows the path that leads back to the road and café. He takes no interest in his surroundings, walking in slow, measured steps, his rotund stomach pushed forward and his shoulders pulled back for balance. He speaks as if addressing an audience.

"Bell considered himself a mentor, but sadists and bullies often see themselves as heroic, do they not?"

We stop at the kerb and then cross, heading in the direction of the indoor bowls club.

"He put many homes out of business," Knott says. "The owners complained and objected, of course, but one by one, he beat them down. Many closed or sold up. Others worked with him and spent fortunes improving their homes."

He pulls back his sleeve to check his watch. "Bell sailed close to the wind, but he got results. Senior management welcomed his no-nonsense approach, ridding the district of substandard care. With the media on his side, no one dared challenge him, Mr Fisher. He acted with impunity, treating homeowners like criminals, always scathing in his assessments. As his reputation spread, home owners stopped challenging him."

"Why?"

"He frightened them. He frightened me. He sensed your weakness and homed in like a heat-seeking missile. He uncovered your mistakes." Knott walks in silence past the car park to the bowls club, his head bowed. "It took one relationship with a nursing home owner whose care standards were a little patchy, shall we say."

"You gave her the benefit of the doubt?"

"And much more, I'm ashamed to say." He brings his arms around from his back. "It was the start of a long, slippery slope. I turned the proverbial blind eye and falsified records. I accepted inducements and remuneration. They've weighed heavy on my mind."

"So heavy, you're leaving them behind while you jet off to sunnier climes."

"I don't expect anything, Mr Fisher, but you must believe me when I say I didn't take the road willingly. When Bell discovered my affair, I intended to confess my sins and resign, even though I had a young family to support." He stops to watch two mothers in the play area, pushing their toddlers on the swings. "But Bell said it would be our secret. He'd taken care of my problem and I had nothing to worry about."

"Until he wanted something in return," I say.

Knott's laugh is hollow. "It's surprising how quickly you sweep aside your values. That's why I'm leaving you the evidence to do with as you think fit."

"You should testify against Bell," I say.

He shakes his head. "He's dead now and I intend to spend what time I have left as a free man. If you try to stop me, you'll never see my files. I've left you enough evidence to close down every home in the Sherlock group, and many others."

"While you enjoy the proceeds."

"No one said life was fair, Mr Fisher."

"And if I call the police to arrest you?"

His laugh mocks me. "On what charges?"

"Then I'll take your briefcase."

He offers it me so quickly, I know it's empty, but I check anyway.

"I left another briefcase in a safe place. I'll text you the location when I'm in the air. Now, if you want to see those files, I must dash."

I step in front of him. "Tell me about Walter Trimble."

"Kim's son, Walter, worked with us for two months. Why are you interested in him?"

"I think he's working at Nightingales."

Knott checks his watch. "Nightingales runs one of the smoothest, most efficient operations I've seen. They're rather good at moving their staff around to make it look like everything's up to standard."

"You're saying they don't employ enough qualified staff?"

"Their management systems are flawless, Mr Fisher. I know because I wrote them. It was ten years ago, but I'm sure Marina Rudolf's updated them since."

"What about the equity release scheme? Was that your idea too?"

"The Sherlocks paid me to provide outstanding reports on their homes. No more."

"Tell me about Anthony Trimble," I say.

He pushes past me. "Never heard of him."

"He owned St Cloud's orphanage in Litlington during the 80s," I say, following. "Then he ran a care home on the site. He also ran a hostel in Pevensey."

Knott stops at an old Mercedes, opens the door and flings his briefcase on the passenger seat. "Anthony Trimble. Walter Trimble. Who are they?"

"They're father and son."

Knott settles in the driver's seat, sliding the seatbelt across his bulging stomach. "Oh no, Mr Fisher. Walter was Martin Bell's son."

Forty-Three

Knott's revelation takes over my thoughts as I rush from Hampden Park to Meadow Farm in Jevington.

If Walter is Martin Bell's son, where does Trimble fit in?

Why did Trimble call me Walter? Why did his lover, Kim Jaggers, call me Walter?

I don't even look like the guy in the photo. Well, I don't think so.

There could be two Walters, I guess, but I doubt it. Maybe Walter worked for Trimble in his care home in Litlington before joining his father at the inspection unit. Then again, if Bell was poacher turned gamekeeper, he must have run a home. Maybe he met Trimble through a care homes association or through the chamber of commerce.

Whatever the reason, it wrecks my theory that Trimble was Walter's father and Kim Jaggers' lover. It looks like she had an affair with Bell.

Why do I keep picturing the grave at Litlington church

when I think of Martin Bell?

And why don't I ring DI Briggs and report Knott?

It feels like I'm turning a blind eye to his misdemeanours. Though I tell myself I'm waiting to collect the evidence he offered, I'm wondering whether it exists. Then again, why would Knott bother to meet me if he had no evidence to give?

"All he had to do was head straight to Gatwick. I would have been none the wiser."

Saying it out loud doesn't help.

I turn left at the lights and take the road to Jevington, trying to focus on my meeting with Richard's friend and architect, Simeon Humboldt. When I arrive, I park next to a bright yellow Scimitar with white wheels. It looks as old as the man at the gate, taking photographs of the farm. From behind, he looks like a mad professor with wild grey hair as thick as a sheep's fleece, a rustic tweed jacket and baggy purple corduroy trousers that stop short of his walking boots to reveal Tartan socks. When he turns to greet me, his yellow shirt and purple silk tie seem to burst out of his tweed waistcoat, revealing a complete disregard for colour coordination. His small dark eyes regard me with a haughty, almost arrogant gaze as we shake hands.

"Are you seeking something traditional or something … contemporary?" he asks after some initial discussion.

"I want to spend money on the wellbeing of my animals, which is my main priority."

"I'm an architect not a vet, Mr Fisher. What exactly do you have in mind?"

"I don't want to waste money on unnecessary flourishes. Less is more, especially if it keeps costs down."

"Ah," he says with a disparaging sigh.

"I'm talking value, Mr Humboldt, not bargain-basement. I want an environmentally friendly, sustainable sanctuary that makes use of the latest ideas and technologies to show others how we can live in harmony with our surroundings."

"You want to be a beacon for others," he says.

"Do you?"

"Let me make a preliminary survey and assessment. I'll need some idea of what you wish to do and incorporate. Ah, you come prepared," he says, taking the folder I hand him. "Then we can discuss the details and decide from there. That doesn't mean I'll take the project," he adds, raising a finger. "I'm only here because I was asked to help you."

I follow his gaze and watch Gemma's Volvo Estate navigate a path through the puddles and potholes. She parks next to the Scimitar and winds the window down.

"Hi, Uncle Simeon," she calls. "I was just passing."

"My great niece," he says with pride as we walk over. He stoops to kiss her on the cheek. "You look lovely, my darling."

Dressed in heels, designer jeans, and a white polo neck sweater, she looks too glamorous to be a Pollution Control Officer.

She won't be with us for much longer, I'm sure of that.

"I don't have my wellingtons, so I won't get out. I was investigating a complaint about a noisy cockerel and noticed your car in the lane. Are you going to take the job? You know you're bored in that draughty old house of yours."

"Unlike your fiancé, my darling, I'm impervious to your charm."

He collects a flight case from his car, takes the keys from me and heads into the farm.

Gemma beckons me to join her. I walk around the Volvo

and smile when I spot the takeaway coffees in a cardboard tray on the passenger seat.

"I wasn't sure if I should bring one for Louise," she says, taking one of the coffees. "Where is your new Watson, Holmes?"

"She's working."

"It's half term."

"She's still working," I say, settling into the seat. "Unlike some."

"I spent my lunch finding out more about Trimble's activities at Anderida Villas. He double booked rooms to claim twice the housing benefit from the council."

"You mean he crammed two families into a single room and no one complained?"

She shrugs. "He claimed for twice the number of people living there. That's what one of the tenants told me. She said he also claimed for people long after they moved on."

"And no one spotted this?"

"Benefit Fraud lost two officers ten years ago," she replies after a sip of coffee. "The posts are still frozen. They can't monitor every landlord."

I nod, well aware of how government spending cuts have savaged public services.

"Anyway, the current tenants are homeless families, put there until the council can find somewhere permanent. Our Housing Officers keep tabs on them."

"Why didn't they tell us when Trimble sold the place to the Sherlocks?"

"Why didn't Sylvie do her job and check ownership?"

I sip my decaffeinated latte, knowing I have a lot to do to restore pride and morale to a pollution team whose manager spent almost a year on sick leave with stress.

"How's your investigation going, Holmes?"

"You remember how Kim Jaggers called me Walter? Well, it turns out he's her son. I was certain Trimble was the father, but it turns out he's not."

I give her a bullet point summary of what Knott told me. "If he's Bell's son, I don't know where that leaves me. I don't know anything about Bell."

"So, Walter could be a Bell or a Trimble," she says, looking thoughtful.

"Maybe I should call him Trimbell."

Her head jerks round. "Hang on," she says, setting her cup down. She reaches behind for her bag and pulls out a notebook and pen. "I know he's Tony, or Anthony, I suppose. Does Trimble have any other names?"

"He's Anthony Nolan Lawrence, according to his RAF record."

She scribbles a note and grins. "ANL Trimble then."

"So?"

She shows me her notebook and grins. "It's an anagram of Martin Bell."

A familiar tingle of excitement lifts my mood. "Could they be one and the same person? Trimble the care home owner became Bell the inspector, the poacher turned gamekeeper who extorted money from homeowners."

Gemma nods. "That's why he got Kim Jaggers to run his hostel at Anderida Villas."

"Then there's Barten Mill, his place in Litlington. It's another anagram of Martin Bell. I'm not sure how it helps, but we're making progress."

She raises her cup. "I love investigating with you, Kent. It beats the pants off noisy neighbours and barking dogs."

"If only it could pay the wages."

"What if we set up a detective agency? Dean and Fisher. Environmental detectives. How cool would that be?"

"Not as cool as Fisher and Dean," I say, reaching for my phone to check the text that's just arrived.

"Why don't we discuss it later? It's Wednesday, so Richard's trimming trees with the bonsai brigade. We could go for a run and then order pizza like we used to. What do you say?"

I turn my phone so she can read the text from Louise.

Found Trimble's laptop during audit. We could check it together. Louise x

Gemma forces a smile. "I just remembered. I need to talk to the wedding organiser. I'll see you at work tomorrow."

I leave, wondering why I don't tell her about my argument with Louise.

Or my doubts about the text she sent.

Forty-Four

I read Louise's text several times, hoping for some inspired insight that will explain my doubts. We argue, she pushes me over, accuses me of being in love with Gemma, and then texts me to suggest we get together. Okay, it's only to look at Trimble's laptop, but her change of heart troubles me.

In my gut, I'm sure Walter Bell would wipe the hard drive after he found what he wanted. How else would he know about Collins Farm?

Then again, I feel bad about the way I treated Louise. Had I paused for a moment and apologised for not telling her about Walter's notes, maybe she would have understood how I was trying to protect her. Instead, guilt put me on the offensive.

Now guilt demands I make amends.

If she's offering me a second chance, that is.

It could also be a cruel trick or a trap.

There's only one way to find out.

I text Louise. *Shall I collect you from work? Kent.*

Her reply is instant.

Tracey picking me up. Come round at 8. Bring pizza. Louise xx

I ring Nightingales to confirm arrangements with Louise, but she's busy working and can't be disturbed. I decline to leave my name or a message, not wanting Louise to know I'm checking on her.

That's the trouble with doubt – it makes me suspect everything and everyone.

Well almost. The truth is I'd rather run with Gemma and share a pizza with her.

I wander over to Simeon and spend another hour, discussing details and going through possibilities for the new sanctuary. He's warming to the environmental aspects of the project, throwing in ideas on ground heat source pumps, reed bed sewage treatment systems, and different ways to generate our own electricity. When we shake hands and part at 4.20, I know I'm in safe hands.

Back at the sanctuary, I take the dogs for their afternoon stroll while Frances continues to sort through the junk that's accumulated in one of the three sheds behind the barn. I've collected equipment, building materials, old fencing panels, animal cages and anything I thought would come in useful. I leave her to it, knowing I'd never throw much of it out.

After feeding the dogs, I put a spare running kit, including a larger towel, back in the boot of the car, still tempted by a run with Gemma. As I close the boot, a text arrives from Malcolm Knott.

Under the gorse.

I grab my Maglite and walk out of the main gate to a large gorse bush, threatening to burst into flower early. A quick survey of the verge reveals some scuff marks in the mud. Columbo, who's joined me, sniffs the area, but keeps away from the thorny branches and stems. I crouch and peer under the branches, spotting a dark shadow close to the main trunk.

"I'm going to need armour to get past those thorns," I tell Columbo, "or a chainsaw to cut my way through."

Five minutes later Frances and I return with a broom. While she points the torch, I try to snag the briefcase with the broom handle. After several failed attempts, I turn the broom around and use the head to snag the briefcase and drag it out, a little at a time.

The moment I pick it up I know it's empty.

I turn the briefcase upside down and shake it. "Knott stitched me up."

"Why would he drive out here to leave an empty briefcase?" she asks.

He didn't, I realise. Someone beat me to the contents.

Now certain that Walter Bell's watching me, I take a scenic route out of Tollingdon at 7.45 that evening. Every few seconds, I check the rear view mirror, aware of a black Audi two cars behind. Had I kept my wits about me, instead of letting my hormones get the better of me, I might have spotted the car before. Then I'd have a better idea of whether it's Walter Bell on my tail. The Audi pulled out behind me on the outskirts of Tollingdon and allowed a couple of cars to come between us as I drove into the town centre.

I take the back roads to Eastbourne, losing the two cars straight away. The Audi drops back and disappears from view. When I reach the traffic lights at Stone Cross on the outskirts of Eastbourne, I'm alone.

Relieved, I take Golden Jubilee Way into Eastbourne and drive along Cross Levels Way, exiting for Sainsbury's. I plan to park there and walk around the back to Louise's flat in case Walter's guessed where I'm heading. I take my time, checking the car park for black Audis with a driver inside, but everything appears normal.

If it's normal, why do I feel hot and sweaty? Why is my heart beating a little faster? Why does the slightest noise make me start and look around?

A man with a bulging carrier bag strides past, head bent as he concentrates on his phone. One day, the council will have to put direction signs on the ground or no one will notice them.

Then it's my turn as a text arrives.

Hope you find what you're looking for. Gemma.

I push aside the double meaning to her words and slow as I approach Louise's block. There are no lights in her flat or Tracey's, even though it's ten minutes past eight. I scan the parked cars on the road, but none of them are occupied or an Audi. After another ten minutes watching and waiting, I walk towards the train station, planning what I'll say to Louise.

As I reach the main shops, the aroma of kebabs reminds me I haven't eaten.

When I return and there are still no lights in the flats, I picture Louise, Tracey and the boys enjoying Big Macs, laughing at the thought of me, kicking my heels in the cold, damp air. But I can't leave yet, in case I'm wrong and they're on the way home.

I walk into Sainsbury's, thinking they may have popped in to buy wedges or dips. I walk the length of the store along the central aisle, checking each side. Then I return down the back aisle, making a final sweep along the checkouts. When a security guard takes an interest, I buy a yoghurt drink and chocolate bar before returning to my car.

When I ring Louise's mobile, I'm told I can't be connected and to ring again later.

It's now nine and I'm annoyed with my indecision. Thoughts and memories of Gemma tempt me to ring her. Thoughts of Louise make me tense as I wonder how long I'm going to wait, hoping she'll return. Twice more I ring, only to receive the same message.

Thanks for nothing.

After I send the text, I drive around and park where I can watch her flat. Still no sign of life. I listen to Barclay James Harvest while I wait, hoping to surprise Louise when she returns, though it will only confirm what a sad fool I am.

Stitched up twice in one day.

First Knott, now Louise.

At least it can't get any worse.

Columbo's pleased to see me when I walk into the kitchen. Frances wanders through from the lounge, sliding her slipper socks across the floor. She yawns and places her mug in the sink before turning to me. "What went wrong?"

"I waited but she never came home. In a minute," I tell Columbo, who's pawing at the door to go out.

"Maybe there was an accident," Frances says, watching Columbo. "Someone's out there."

The security lights come on in the yard. Seconds later, something clatters against the barn. Someone runs up the stairs.

Columbo's barking now, hackles rising.

He just gets out of the way as the door flies open.

George stumbles in, tears streaming down his face. He stares at me with bewildered eyes.

"Mum's dead."

Forty-Five

"Tell me what happened, George."

I know Walter Bell killed Louise, but I need to keep control of the maelstrom of emotions and anger swirling in my head and guts. It takes every ounce of willpower, and then some, to hold back the recriminations. If I'd collected her from Nightingales, she would be alive. George wouldn't be clinging to Frances, sobbing his heart out.

I can't deal with that now. I need to remain focused if I'm going to help this poor kid.

I should ring the police. They're bound to be looking for him. But I need to know what happened, how he got here, why he came here.

I place my hand on his shoulder, wishing I knew what to say.

Columbo sits at his feet, licking his hand. George looks down and forces a smile.

"Can I stay here?" he asks.

"Tell me what happened?" I ask, sitting opposite him.

He wipes his nose with his hand and sniffs back the last of the tears.

"We were in Tracey's flat when the police came. We couldn't hear much because we were in Ben's bedroom. When Tracey started crying I knew mum was dead."

He swallows and looks down at Columbo, who whines.

"But they wouldn't say. But I could tell from the way they looked at each other. Tracey wouldn't look at me," he says. "Even in the police car she wouldn't look at me or talk to me. It was like she blamed me."

"I'm sure that's not true," I say, considering an alternative explanation. "Where did the police take you?"

"Eastbourne District General Hospital. The mortuary's there, isn't it?"

I nod.

"Ben and I had to wait with a police woman and a nurse. The police woman wouldn't answer my questions, telling me someone would be along to take care of me." He looks up. "Can I have a drink?"

Frances hurries over to the fridge and returns with a Diet Coke.

He takes a few mouthfuls before continuing. "Tracey never came back. No one seemed to know what was happening. When the nurse asked the police woman when Social Services would arrive, I knew I had to come here. I asked to go to the toilet and gave them the slip. It's only a mile from the hospital to home, so I ran back and got my bike."

He looks from Frances to me, as if seeking approval.

"You don't know what happened to your mother," I say, picking up my phone.

He shakes his head and starts to cry again.

While Frances comforts him, I go into the lounge, closing the door behind me. As I wait for the police call centre to respond, I spot headlamps in the lane. A patrol car pulls into the yard, setting off Columbo.

I rush to intercept them, unable to stop Columbo barrelling out of the door and down the steps. Fortunately, he picks up a scent and veers into the shadows. The male police officer's checking George's mountain bike rests as I walk up.

Philip Rockwell looks fresh from training college with his boyish face, short hair and immaculate uniform. His chest swells with pride as he announces himself and his female colleague in a voice that's as eager as the sparkle in his eyes.

Amy Smethwick brushes the flyaway blonde hair, flecked with grey, from her eyes and asks, "Does the bike belong to George Watson?"

"He's in a state, as you can imagine," I reply. "What happened to his mother?"

"Are you Kent Fisher?" Rockwell asks, pulling out a shiny black notebook.

"I'm a friend of Louise Watson. What's happened to her?"

Rockwell glances at Smethwick, who nods. "About two hours ago, a body was recovered from the foot of the cliffs near Beachy Head," he says. "Identity's been confirmed as Miss Louise Watson."

"Can you tell me anything more?" I ask, amazed at how calm I am. It's like a shutter came down over my emotions.

"DI Briggs would like to talk to you as soon as possible."

"Is he on his way?"

"At Hammonds Drive, Mr Fisher."

It sounds like an order, not a request.

"I need to tell Frances," I say. "She's comforting George. How did you know he was here?"

"He told his friend you'd look after him," Smethwick replies with a wistful smile.

George shrinks into the corner when Smethwick and Rockwell follow me into the kitchen. She talks to him in a gentle, assertive way, remaining calm as he pleads not to go, slowly draining the defiance from him until his head drops. With trainers dragging across the floor, he lets her escort him away. At the door, he spins around.

"Kent and my mum are getting married," he says. "You're going to adopt me, aren't you, Kent? Tell them!"

I try to see past the despair in his eyes. "You have to go with them, George."

He looks at me with such hurt in his eyes, I feel like a complete shit.

"Don't let them take me!" he wails as Smethwick ushers him outside.

Rockwell sighs, his enthusiasm gone. "Shall I inform DI Briggs you're on your way?"

I nod. "They want to talk to me at the custody centre," I tell Frances, wrapping my arms around her. "It's routine in cases like these."

"Routine? Did you see the way George looked at us? Like we betrayed him."

Not as much as I betrayed Louise.

Forty-Six

Questions and recriminations swirl through my head during the journey to Hammonds Drive custody centre. I take a wrong turn at the roundabout and find myself on Cross Levels Way, heading towards Eastbourne District General, where Louise lies in a chiller, another statistic for the reports.

Is she dead because of me?

She left this earth, convinced I'd used her, convinced I was in love with Gemma.

Her texts seemed to ignore the argument we had. Now, in light of her death, I wonder if she sent the texts. Walter Bell seems to be one step ahead yet again.

I should have driven to Nightingales to collect her. I could have prevented her death.

At the Sainsbury's roundabout I turn around and head back, knowing I must tell the police about my argument with Louise, no matter how much I'd prefer not to.

The custody centre sits at the northern end of the

Hammonds Drive Industrial Estate at the eastern end of Eastbourne. The suite's housed in a modern building with industrial double glazed windows. It looks more like an office complex than a place to remand and interview suspects and witnesses. Late in the evening, there's little to distract me from my thoughts while I wait, sitting on a hard plastic chair in a soulless foyer that rises through two storeys. The posters on the glass screens of the reception desk and the walls behind provide some distraction with their warnings about drugs and terrorists. Sometimes, a door upstairs opens and someone walks along the balcony.

Twenty-five minutes pass before a grey door opens. Rockwell beckons me over and takes me down a familiar short corridor to the main interview room where I was questioned only a few months ago about another case. The room's neutral and modest, furnished with modern laminate tables. On the main table, there's a computer and monitor next to the seat Rockwell occupies. Another table on the opposite side of the room contains a large monitor and what looks like a DVD player. In the corner, a video camera watches and records everything.

We sit in silence on opposite sides of the main table, waiting for DI Briggs.

If Rockwell's looking at my file on the PC, he'll find a long history of incidents. I was arrested many times during anti-hunting protests and for obstruction when I chained myself to trees and bulldozers to stop developers destroying the countryside. My last incident earned me a caution for emptying the contents of a muck spreader into Birchill's Mercedes convertible.

Happy days.

Rockwell rises when DI Briggs enters. He may look

weary and ready for bed, but the cups of tea in his hands suggest it could be a while yet. He slides one cup across the table to me and apologises for the late hour. He pushes his unruly grey hair behind his ears and takes a few moments to settle. Like most coppers, he works too many hours.

Rockwell slides a folder across to him.

"I understand Miss Watson's son, George, sought sanctuary," Briggs says, loosening his woollen tie. "Poor sod."

I'm not sure if it's a comment about the boy's emotional state or his poor choice of venue.

"Thank you for coming in," he says, struggling to undo the top button of his shirt. "I'm sure you know this, but we need to talk to those close to the deceased in cases like this."

"Like what?" I ask.

"I hear you and Miss Watson were planning to marry. Please accept my condolences."

"We were only friends," I say, already distancing myself from Louise. "George didn't want you to take him away. He was frightened and bewildered, as you can imagine."

He nods. "Social Services will do their best for him. Right, let's get this show on the road as I'm sure we'd all like some rest."

Rockwell looks ready to go all night if needed. "Should we be recording this?" he asks.

"Sound only as it's not a formal interview," Briggs says. "Do you have any objection, Mr Fisher?"

"Carry on."

"You know you can have a solicitor, if you wish."

"I didn't realise this was a formal interview."

"We don't do informal, as I'm sure you know. A young

woman's life ended tragically tonight and we need to find out as much as we can."

"Of course," I say, shifting in my chair.

Rockwell signals he's ready and recites a prepared introduction to set the date and time, location, purpose of interview, and details of those present. Briggs thanks me for coming in voluntarily to help with enquiries and settles back in his chair.

"Can you describe your relationship with Miss Watson?"

"We met a couple of months ago at Nightingales, a residential home in East Dean. She works there as a receptionist. I took Columbo for a PAT visit on New Year's Eve."

"Pets as Therapy," Briggs tells his colleague. "People take pets into care homes. The residents get to fuss them and feel better. Not that my father takes any interest. He'd rather fuss the nurses. How they haven't reported him for sexual harassment, I'll never know. It's so easy to cross the line between harmless fun and harassment these days, don't you think?"

I remain silent, not sure why he's asking me.

"So, you met Miss Watson at Nightingales," he says. "When did you last see her?"

"Yesterday."

"How was she?"

I hesitate, wondering if Tracey has told Briggs and Rockwell about my argument with Louise.

"What do you mean?" I ask, certain they know more than their questions suggest.

Rockwell's itching to question me, regarding me more like prey than a witness. Despite his nonchalant, laid back approach, Briggs is about to lead me somewhere I don't want to go.

Briggs rolls his shoulders. "Was Miss Watson happy, sad, worried about anything, any different from usual?"

"She seemed fine," I reply. "Not that I know her that well."

"What did you do yesterday?"

"We had lunch in Alfriston, explored a little."

"With George?"

"George was at my animal sanctuary. He's rather taken with Frances. She manages my sanctuary," I say, realising I'm in danger of rambling.

"You wanted to spend some time alone together," Rockwell says, making it sound like we were being selfish.

"Yes."

"Tell us a little more about your time together," Briggs says. "What did you do when you'd finished exploring Alfriston?"

"We went to her flat. Without George," I say as Rockwell opens his mouth to interrupt. "Would you like a detailed account of what we did there?"

Briggs raises a hand. "Take it easy, Kent. I know you're upset, but we need to build a clear picture of events."

"Does that mean it's not an accident?" I ask, seeing if they'll bite.

Briggs takes a swig of tea. "What did you and Miss Watson do at her flat?"

From the glint in his eyes he already knows. "We made love," I reply.

"And after you made love?"

I shift in the chair, wishing I could get comfortable. If Louise confided in Tracey and I don't mention the argument, the police will think I have something to hide. If I admit to the argument, they might think that it had a bearing on Louise's state of mind.

Should I reveal my suspicions about Walter? I can't offer any evidence to support them, which means it could look like I'm trying to shift the blame.

"I went home to my sanctuary," I say finally.

"To collect George?"

"No, Louise booked a taxi."

"She didn't go back with you to collect George," he says, sounding surprised.

"No."

"How was Louise when you left her?" Rockwell asks.

I feel sweat running down my back. "We had a disagreement. Well, more of a misunderstanding, I guess."

Rockwell's almost salivating. "Perhaps you could elaborate, Mr Fisher? What caused the disagreement?"

"She found a note on my windscreen." I reach into my pocket and pull out the four notes, spreading them out on the table. "Louise spotted the fourth note," I say, pointing to it. "She thought it was threatening and targeted at her."

Briggs studies the notes, his expression giving little away. "How did she feel about the other notes?"

"She'd never seen them."

"You didn't tell her about them," Rockwell asks, making it sound like a crime.

"Until the last note, I didn't think they had anything to do with her. She thought I'd deliberately withheld them from her."

"But you didn't show them to her, did you?"

"I wanted to protect her," I reply.

"Why did you want to protect her if you didn't think the notes referred to her?" Rockwell asks.

I push my face into my hands. I failed Louise by not trusting her. No wonder she was angry. She realised I hadn't told her because I thought she'd be less likely to help me with my investigation.

How right she was.

"Do you think Louise was killed?" I asked.

"Do you?" Rockwell asks, a little too quickly.

Briggs laughs. "Don't you read the papers, Rockwell? Mr Fisher investigates the murders we miss. Isn't that right, Mr Fisher?"

I don't answer.

"Do you have reasons to believe Miss Watson was killed?"

The moment I shrug, I'm failing her again, worried about giving Briggs more opportunities to mock me.

"Do you have any idea who's sending these notes?" he asks.

"No."

"Do you believe they have something to do with her death?"

I pull out my phone. "This afternoon, I received a text from Louise. She said she'd found Anthony Trimble's laptop. He was a resident at Nightingales. I saw the laptop in his room, but when he died, it wasn't among his possessions."

"The council bury people who die without relatives," Briggs explains. "Are you sure it was Mr Trimble's laptop?"

"Can I prove it, you mean? It was in his room."

Rockwell thrusts out his hand. "Can we look at the text?"

They spend some time looking at the text chain.

"Have you recovered the laptop from the scene?" I ask.

"I'm not aware of any laptop," Briggs replies, placing the phone on the table. "In a follow-up text, Miss Watson asks you to come to her flat. Did you?"

"She wasn't home, obviously."

"What time did you arrive?" Rockwell asks.

"Just after eight o'clock."

"What time did you return home?"

"Around ten o'clock."

Rockwell can hardly hide his delight. "You stayed all that time, waiting for her to show?"

"How did you feel when she didn't show?" Briggs asks.

"I wondered if there had been an accident."

"Anything else?"

"What do you mean?"

"You sent a text, saying 'Thanks for nothing.' What did you mean by that?"

"I thought she might have played a trick on me to get her own back for the argument yesterday."

"The misunderstanding," Rockwell reminds me.

"I thought she'd gone out with Tracey and the kids, leaving me to kick my heels."

Briggs interlocks his fingers. "If you believed that, why did you kick your heels for two hours?"

I slump back in the chair. "I don't know."

"How did you feel during that time?" Rockwell asks.

"Frustrated, I guess. How would you feel?"

Briggs almost smiles. "Believing Miss Watson had misled you, would you describe your behaviour as rational, waiting around for two hours?"

"What are you suggesting?"

I'm on my feet, facing Rockwell, who's a split second slower. He stares into my eyes, willing me to take a swing at him.

"Sit down, Mr Fisher," Briggs says, sounding bored. "We're trying to verify your movements and whereabouts. There's no need to become agitated."

I drop back into the chair. "Why do you need to verify my movements? I didn't know where Louise was."

"Can anyone confirm you were in the vicinity of Miss Watson's flat between 8 and 10?"

I shake my head. Then I remember nipping into Sainsbury's and retrieve the receipt from my wallet. "You can see the time," I say.

I wait while they check the receipt. Briggs finishes his cup of tea and rubs his face.

"At 19.03 this evening, Miss Watson sent a text to her friend, Tracey Oldman, asking her to take care of George. Miss Watson went on to say she couldn't take any more of your controlling and bullying behaviour, Mr Fisher."

"That's rubbish!" I look from Briggs to Rockwell, not liking what I see in their eyes.

"Miss Watson went on to say you'd forced yourself on her yesterday."

I can barely believe what I'm hearing. "I would never force myself on any woman."

Rockwell looks at the computer screen. "Lady Sarah Whittaker accused you of assaulting her?"

"She was on a horse, whipping me with her riding crop," I retort. "I was defending myself and she fell off her horse."

"Looks like you were involved in quite a few incidents with the Tollingdon Hunt," Rockwell says. "Many of them involving women."

"Are you suggesting I assaulted Louise?"

"Did you?" he asks. "Sometimes things get a little out of

hand when you're excited. A bite here, a playful slap there …"

"It will be interesting to see what the post mortem reveals," Briggs says.

"It will reveal I had sex with Louise," I say, struggling to keep my composure. "I'm not denying that."

"You said you made love earlier," Rockwell says.

I fold my arms, furious with myself for making such a mess of the interview. "I came here to help you and you're accusing me of something I didn't do."

"No one's accusing you of anything," Briggs says, his tone calm but neutral. "When we receive information about a possible offence we have to investigate. You know that."

"You're questioning me on the basis of a text? You don't know if she sent it." My brain finally catches up. "Has someone accused me of assaulting Louise?"

"No one mentioned assault, Kent."

"Do you want me to caution Mr Fisher?" Rockwell asks.

I slump back in the chair, wondering how Walter Bell managed to stitch me up.

Forty-Seven

Briggs suspends the interview and leaves me in the company of a young officer. Ten minutes later, someone brings me a cup of tea and asks me if I'd like a biscuit. I'd prefer some ibuprofen for my throbbing headache and a shower.

I'd also like to find Walter Bell.

He sent texts from Louise's phone to lure me to her flat. If I hadn't popped into Sainsbury's I wouldn't have a till receipt as an alibi.

I never expected my activities as a hunt saboteur to come back and haunt me.

Mind you, the archives of the local press are filled with my more exuberant antics in the name of animal welfare and protecting the environment. I miss those heady days when we weren't worried about consequences.

Briggs returns after an hour and formally suspends the interview, pending further enquiries.

Outside the custody centre, the cold air makes me shiver.

I stand there for what seems like hours, lost in thought yet unable to coax anything sensible from my weary mind. One thought runs round and round on a loop.

I could have prevented Louise's death. I could have prevented Louise's death.

And unless I can identify Walter Bell and find him, I can't put that right.

I can't even make sense of Trimble's coded message.

What kind of investigator does that make me?

When I return home, a little after one in the morning, I find Frances and Columbo in the kitchen. He bounds over to greet me, tail wagging. He seems relieved, as if he thought I wouldn't return. She eases herself out of the chair, yawns and wraps the dressing gown a little tighter over her combat top and trousers.

"You look beat," she says, her voice as tired as her eyes. "How did it go?"

I paraphrase one of my manager's magical quotes.

"If making a mess of an interview was an Olympic sport, I'd be world champion."

It's a lame attempt at humour, but it's how I cope with mistakes. Pain, guilt and regret too. Denial works better, though you'll never hear me admit to that.

"Do you know what happened to George?" she asks, filling the kettle.

"Social Services will take care of him," I reply.

I can't begin to imagine how the poor lad feels, but one day he'll see Walter Bell sentenced to life imprisonment for the murder of his mother.

First, I need to see him – or a more up to date photograph of him. If he's left notes on my windscreen, he was close by. We may even have passed and exchanged a brief greeting at Nightingales.

Though tired and aching, I sit at my computer and look through the galleries on Nightingales' website. Though I've checked them before, I'm hoping to spot something or someone I missed. One by one, I study the pages for all of the homes. Either Walter Bell avoided having his photograph taken or he doesn't work for the Sherlocks.

He's too young to be a resident, though he could be a contractor. Maybe he drives the minibus that takes residents to the theatre or Glyndebourne. Photographs on Nightingales' Facebook page show many of the recent outings, but it looks like Gregor drives the minibus.

Not sure where to look next, I stare at the screen.

Walter Bell's invisibility is starting to annoy me.

When I open my eyes, daylight streams through the window. My neck and shoulders ache. My mouth and throat feel and taste like a dried out septic tank. The dull ache above my eyes is eclipsed by an agonising bolt of pain as I move my head. The swelling on my neck has pinched a nerve, making movement uncomfortable. With a groan, I raise myself up from the desk and stare at the blank screen.

"You fell asleep at the computer."

The familiar voice and wonderful aroma of coffee brings me to life. Columbo, sitting by my feet, barks, telling me there's a jam doughnut on a plate.

I reach for the cup. "Decaffeinated skinny latte?"

Gemma nods. She stands by the dresser, takeaway cup in one hand, doughnut in the other. As always, she looks amazing, her glossy hair tumbling about her face, caressing her cheeks and slender neck. Encased in a snug sweater, she tempts Columbo with a morsel of doughnut.

In the week we spent together, I loved waking up next to her, breathing in her scent, tracing my fingers along her soft, hot skin, brushing the hair from her eyes. I loved the way her eyelids flickered open. Her eyes widened as she recognised me, followed by a slow, cheeky smile that promised me more than I deserved.

"What time is it?" I ask, searching for my watch.

"Time you phoned Danni," she replies, before popping the last hunk of doughnut into her mouth. Jam oozes over her lips and she licks it away with such relish, I have to look away. She pulls out another doughnut from a bag on the window sill. "You need to tell her you won't be working today."

"I do?"

"No, that's what you say at weddings, but you wouldn't know that, would you?"

"I was late home," I say, noticing the time.

"No wonder they call you a super sleuth," she says. "I'm sorry about Louise."

"You heard."

"It's headlining on the Tollingdon Tribune website."

Moments later, I stare at a photograph of Louise, cut from the Nightingales gallery.

Mystery surrounds the tragic death of single mother, Louise Watson, whose shattered body was found at the foot of cliffs near Beachy Head.

While details remain vague, it's not clear what she was doing at the famous beauty spot or why she plunged to her death. According to best friend, Tracey Oldman, Louise was a bright, happy person who adored and lived for her son, George, who's now in the care of the local authority.

Her lover, Downland's most eligible bachelor and

amateur sleuth, Kent Fisher, is helping police with their enquiries.

Trust Tommy Logan to make me sound like a sexual predator, useless detective and prime suspect in one sentence.

"I could have saved her," I say, cradling my coffee. "By helping me, she put herself in danger, but it never occurred to me at the time. It's obvious now she's lost her life."

"How can it be your fault?" Gemma pushes the last of the doughnut into her mouth, leaving a smear of jam at the side of her mouth.

"If she hadn't helped me investigate Trimble, she'd be alive now, wouldn't she?"

"I don't wish to sound insensitive, Kent, but she chose to help you, didn't she?"

I turn my head slowly and look into her dark eyes. "Sure, but I used her, Gemma. That's what makes it worse."

"Come here," she says, opening out her arms to me.

She pulls me close and strokes my hair, pausing when she feels the bump on my neck. "Tell me you haven't been beating yourself up over this."

"Not quite."

"Last week, when I sent you the text to say I was sorry, I thought you'd turn around and come back."

Her breath tickles my ear. Her thick, lustrous hair smells of citrus as it brushes against my face. I slide my arms around her waist and hold on tight, relieved she still cares. Her cheek feels hot against mine - hot and sticky.

It's jam from the doughnut, sticking to my cheek.

When I reach up to wipe it away, she wraps her fingers around my wrist. Then, with a slow, cheeky smile, she leans closer. She licks the jam from my cheek and kisses the spot.

She kisses around my lips. Then she pauses and leans back to gaze into my eyes the way she did the first time.

I should resist. I'm crossing a line I vowed never to cross.

But I'm tired of doing what's right instead of what I want.

When our lips meet, I'm back in her bedsit, exploring her for the first time, wanting her the way I never wanted anyone else before.

Or since.

Forty-Eight

Gemma saunters across the kitchen. With her hair back in place and her make up restored, she devours the final doughnut, saving the last morsel for Columbo. She licks the sugar from her fingers and sighs. "That's almost as good as sex."

It's difficult to believe we were entwined only twenty minutes ago.

"You've learned a few tricks," she says with a wink.

"You too," I say, wondering if that's all it was – a few tricks.

She sits on my lap and wraps her arms around my neck. "You could sound a little more enthusiastic."

"I'm not sure where we go from here."

"Since when did you worry about the future?"

"Or the past," I say, "but I can't seem to shake it off."

She kisses my forehead and pulls me close. "You've had the guts kicked out of you, Kent. You're hurting and confused. Maybe you feel guilty."

"I don't regret what happened, but we've crossed a line. We can't go back, can we?"

She considers for a moment. "We can make the occasional visit."

"A reminder of what might have been? Is that all it was?"

She looks into my eyes with an intensity that reaches into my soul. "Why can't it be a reminder of what could be?" she asks.

I wish I could believe her, but I can't push Richard from my thoughts.

"Let's leave the future for tomorrow," I say. "Today, I have a killer to catch."

"Don't you mean *we* have a killer to catch? I didn't come over to sit here and twiddle my thumbs while you chase across the countryside."

"He's already killed three people, Gemma."

"And I won't let you be the fourth," she says, getting to her feet. "Come on, bring me up to speed, Holmes."

"Don't call me that, please. I can never call you Watson again."

Her hand strokes my cheek. "I know."

Back in the bedroom, Gemma's scent lingers on the rumpled sheet, filling my mind with images. I rescue the duvet from the floor. It takes me a few minutes to centre and straighten the duvet on the bed. Columbo waits until I give him a nod and then leaps up. He settles in his usual place, tail wagging in anticipation.

"You did that with my duvet," Gemma says, watching from the doorway. "Every morning while I made tea and toast, you straightened the duvet."

"I didn't know you were watching."

She smiles. "I couldn't take my eyes off you, I was so

smitten."

"I watched you," I say, settling in front of the computer. "I loved the way you flicked your hair back when something went well. And when you were reading, you rested the tip of your finger at the corner of your mouth."

"Did I?" She sits on the bed next to Columbo. "Maybe it helped me concentrate. You were quite a distraction."

Until I ran.

"This is Walter Bell," I say, handing her Kim Jaggers' photograph. "It was taken about fifteen years ago, so he may have grey hair now. He could be bald, thinning or no different. See if you can spot him in the galleries."

I move onto the bed and fuss Columbo while she checks the galleries. She's more thorough than me, taking her time, zooming in, going back to a page, reading the information as well as the names of the employees.

"I can't see anyone who resembles Walter Bell." She leans back to stretch her arms above her head. "The Sherlocks seem camera shy too, considering their names are on almost every page. What are they like?"

"I've never met them. They only got back from holiday last week. No photos of Miss Rudolf either." I say, wondering how I didn't notice before.

Why are the Sherlocks so camera shy? What are they trying to hide?

When I realise, I can't help smiling.

"Anything else you want me to look at?" Gemma asks.

"Not on the internet." I move closer and rest my chin on her shoulder. I double click to open the image of Trimble's code and solution.

She reads it and nods. "That's why you went ape when Sylvie threw out the books. What does it mean?"

"I've located Collins Farm, which is between Alfriston and Milton Street. As for ripping bodices and revealing breasts …"

My phone rings, flashing up Danni's name. "Where the hell are you, Kent? It's gone ten thirty."

I head over to the window. "I was at the police station till one this morning, Danni."

"Is this another of your nefarious activities? No, don't answer that," she says, cutting me off. "I hope it doesn't involve Gemma because no one knows where she is."

Gemma shakes her head when I glance at her.

"Like I said, Danni, I was at the police station until one this morning, helping –"

"You should have phoned me – not that oversleeping is a valid excuse for absence, I should point out."

"How about someone dying?"

I end the call and thud my fist on the window sill, setting off Columbo. By the time he's stopped barking and bouncing around, the phone rings again.

"I'm sorry, Kent," Danni says, her tone softer. "Kelly's showed me the report on the *Tollingdon Tribune* website. Is there anything I can do to help?"

"I've got people around me, thanks."

"Of course you have. Take the rest of the week off. I'll reassign your work. Let me know if you need anything."

I thank her and end the call, relieved she didn't ask for details.

"Come and take a look at this," Gemma says, beckoning me over. She's reading an article about Stanton Collins, the smuggler.

"When I searched for Collins Farm, Alfriston, this came up on Google. It doesn't help with bodice ripping, but I think I've solved the mystery of the revealing breasts. And you can cut that out," she says, slapping my hand. "You've seen enough of mine for one day."

"I was looking for inspiration," I say.

"You won't need it. Now concentrate, Kent. Your clue says, breast reveals – singular, not plural. Is that correct?"

"Go on."

"Setting aside your favourite anatomical features, where else would you find a breast?"

"On a robin."

"Does Collins Farm have a chimney?"

I sigh, wondering how I missed something so obvious. "Yes, but what does it reveal?"

She points at the screen. "Smugglers built hidey holes in chimney breasts."

"There could be one behind the plaster at Collins Farm. Let's check it out."

Columbo barks, joining in with the excitement. It lasts until we reach the kitchen. I stop, realising Walter Bell could have beaten me to the hidey hole. "No," I say, thinking aloud. "If he knew about the hidey hole, he'd have gone to Collins Farm two days before me, but he didn't. Why?"

Gemma shrugs. "I've no idea what you're talking about."

"Walter Bell found out about the Collins Farm from Trimble's laptop, but Bell doesn't know about the hidey hole. That's why he's tailing me. If he's out there, we'll lead him to the hidey hole."

Gemma peers out of the window, scanning the countryside. "There can't be many places to hide around here. We could flush him out."

"What if he goes into hiding? We may never find him

again."

She frowns, resting her finger on the corner of her mouth as she thinks. "You're forgetting the hidey hole. We might find information to identify Bell. If you ask Briggs and police to come along, we'll have protection."

"What if there's nothing there? What if it's a cruel joke? Can you imagine what Briggs will say? No, we need to get Bell there so the police can catch him in the act. He'll follow me there and let me do the hard work. But I'll be ready for him."

"He could kill you, Kent." She marches over and cups my face in her hands. "I don't want you dying on me."

I owe it to Louise, to George, to bring Bell to justice.

"I'll be fine, Gemma. There are plenty of places to hide. I'll smash a bit of plaster on the chimney and make it look like I left in a hurry out the back. He'll be so keen to recover what's in the chimney, he'll forget about me."

"And you double back to catch him by surprise?" She smiles and then shakes her head. "What if he has an accomplice?"

"That's where you come in," I reply, making it up as I go. "If you hide nearby, you can let me know when he arrives, if he's on his own or with someone else. Then we can ring the police. How does that sound?"

She hesitates and walks over to the window. "It might work, but I'm hardly going to blend into the scenery."

I look down at Richard's red Audi TT and nod. "Where's your Volvo?"

"At my mother's. If you give me time to collect it I'll … I've had a better idea," she says, becoming animated. "If you drive to Collins Farm via the Alfriston road, I'll park up at the farm with the business units, on the left side of the road."

"Cuckmere View?"

"That's the one. After you drive past, I'll follow a few minutes later. If Bell's tailing you, he should park his car at Collins Farm or in the road, right?"

"You let me know and summon the police," I say. "Sounds like a plan."

"Promise me you won't play the hero. No, Kent, I mean it," she says. "He's killed three people already. I'm not going to lose you again."

I take her in my arms, wondering why it took me so long to find her again. "You won't now I know you're waiting for me."

"Give me half an hour to retrieve my car and get in position" she says, checking her watch. "I'll be at Cuckmere View for midday."

Outside, before she climbs into Richard's Audi TT, she kisses me with such passion, I'm left breathless. "Remember that before you do anything crazy."

I wonder if she'll forgive me when she discovers what I really have in mind.

Forty-Nine

Forty minutes later, I ease off the accelerator as I pass Cuckmere View Business Park. I don't notice Gemma's Volvo estate in the courtyard, which means she's well hidden. Half a mile down the road, I take a left for Milton Street, watching as the three cars behind me go straight on. I take it easy through the bends, checking my mirror every few seconds, but I have the road to myself.

Bell may already have worked out where I'm heading.

Dark clouds race across the sky, driven by a relentless wind that signals another storm. My fleece, already scarred by the brambles on the gate at Collins Farm, won't be much use if the skies open. I should be used to the rain after my soaking yesterday, and better prepared.

When I reach Collins Farm, I reverse down the drive and stop by the spotted laurel, a few yards short of the gate. I jump out and ring the doorbells on both houses. The last thing I need is someone phoning the police because I've parked on their drive. Satisfied no one's home, I trot down to the road and peer around the hedge to look for Bell. After five minutes, when only a couple of Range Rovers and a delivery van have passed, I return to my car.

I hope he's out there, waiting for me to remove what's in the hidey hole.

Armed with my Maglite and a lump hammer, I shin over the gate and follow the flattened bramble stems from my previous visit, hoping Bell hasn't beaten me to the hidey hole. Had I read about Stanton Collins and heeded the clues the rector gave me, I'd be safe at home now with Trimble's secrets.

And so would Louise.

My pace quickens as I approach the old house, which looks even more foreboding under the leaden skies. The atmosphere crackles with tension and electricity, waiting for the storm to break. The wind whistles along the valley, buffeting my face, driving me inside the house. I turn straight into the front room and stop. My mouth falls open as I stare at the hole in the chimney breast. The door of a rusty metal box hangs from one hinge.

It hurts to know I've failed.

Have I lost my chance to catch Bell?

I cut across the room, scrambling over the rubble and debris to the hearth. I peer inside the box, half expecting to find a smug note from him. There's only dust and the remains of several candles.

I can't let it end like this.

I don't even know what *bodice ripper* means.

When the rain starts, splattering huge drops against the rubble and the few floorboards above, I shuffle to the side of the fireplace to take shelter. I rest the lump hammer on the mantelpiece and switch off my Maglite. With any luck, I can come up with a plan while I wait for the rest of the storm to pass. But I can't shift the words, *bodice ripper*, from my head. I repeat them, over and over like a mantra, hoping they will make sense.

They don't. All I can think of is how *bodice* sounds like bodies.

Bodies!

I sigh, wondering what's wrong with me. Did Trimble dispose of bodies here? Did he bury the bodies of children in the garden? Or did he leave them in the cesspool?

I close my eyes, unable to shift the unwelcome image in my mind.

Then I realise *ripper* could mean serial killer. Jack the Ripper. Trimble the Ripper.

Is that the secret he refused to share?

Why would he want people to know he was a serial killer?

With heavy heart and legs, I make my way to the kitchen and out into the rear garden, bending my head against the rain. My lump hammer proves ineffective at beating back the branches and foliage that block my way, but I keep trying.

A flash of lightning jolts me out of my trance. Soaked to the skin, teeth chattering, and in danger of getting hypothermia, I need to get out of the rain and into some dry clothes. Accompanied by a crack of thunder, I hurry through the house and run back to the car, almost vaulting the gate. Under the protection of the raised hatch, I put the lump hammer in the corner of the boot and grab my holdall. I'm about to clamber into the back of the car to change when I realise my Maglite's in the house.

There's more room to change in the house, so I rush back

and place the holdall beside the fireplace. I peel off my wet clothes and dry myself as much as possible with the towel. As I forgot to put fresh underwear in the holdall, my leggings offer a more suggestive profile than usual, but they're dry and warm. Best of all, my high visibility running jacket is fully waterproof.

As I reach to pull up the hood, a blinding flash of pain explodes in my head. My legs buckle as another blow connects with yesterday's injury, firing off more bolts of pain. Everything around me blurs as I collapse into the rubble.

The rain beats down on my head, which feels like it's in a vice. Nausea turns my stomach, leaving me dizzy and disorientated as I roll onto my back. Breathing hard, I focus to blot out the pain, like I did as a child when my mother beat me with a broom. Slowly, with each breath, I push the pain back.

My vision starts to clear as I shuffle into a sitting position. I can make out two legs in front of the fireplace. Expensive shoes beneath damp trousers that retain creases as sharp as the blade of a meat slicer. Water runs off a blue cagoule like a cascade. I see the hand, curled around a length of rough timber, about two inches square and three feet long.

My hand reaches for the swelling on my neck. The skin feels raw, sensitive to the touch, but I can't feel any blood.

The man in the cagoule watches, his face hidden by the hood. He's an expert at hiding his identity.

"Forgive me if I don't shake your hand, Mr Sherlock. You are Mr Kieran Sherlock?"

Fifty

His laugh contains less emotion than the timber he uses to prod my damp, discarded clothes. He flips the sodden fleece to one side, followed by my chinos, as if they might be hiding something.

At least he hasn't pulled a gun on me. I'm fed up with people who do this. In my last two cases I found myself staring down the barrel of a gun. Where do people get them? It's against the law to supply guns. You can't buy them in the shops.

That said, I could use a gun right now. Without one, or any other weapon, I'll have to rely on my sparkling wit and humour.

Sherlock stares down at me. "Good guess, Fisher. What gave me away?"

"It was elementary, Mr Sherlock."

"If I hadn't heard it many times before, I might credit you with some imagination."

His cultured voice contrasts with the icy indifference in

his blue eyes, as piercing as his father's. With his grey hair, greased back from a high forehead, Sherlock has a confident, sneering air, assisted by a prominent nose and cynical mouth that smiles to one side. The self-conscious Walter in Kim Jaggers' photograph may have long gone, but the long face and drooping earlobes haven't.

"You must have enjoyed playing Walter," I say.

"What are you talking about?"

"The time you worked for the homes inspectorate as an admin officer."

"I was there a month, checking on my father. He changed his identity as often as he closed and opened businesses, but you probably know that. Who's Walter?"

If Sherlock wants to play games, I'm not going to argue. "What were you after?"

He taps the timber into the palm of his other hand as he replies. "I wanted to tempt him into investing in a luxury care home that needed a substantial injection of capital."

"Nightingales?"

"That came later. No, Kingfishers. I tweaked the database so it came up on his inspection list for the following year. When he inspected the home about eighteen months later, he didn't even recognise me."

"That must have hurt, being his son."

"Or perhaps it was a testament to my beard and glasses. Anyway, he offered me a glowing report for a small consideration. If not, he would condemn the place and put me out of business. I told him I was almost bankrupt and had nothing to offer him but the business. He made me wait, I'll give him that, but he couldn't resist. He ran the place under the name of Anthony Trimble and inspected it as Martin Bell."

"Giving it glowing reports," I say, glancing around for a suitable weapon. If only I could reach my Maglite on the mantelpiece.

"Within five years my father acquired another four luxury homes, including Nightingales." Sherlock laughs, clearly enjoying the memory. "How I enjoyed taking them from him as his mind failed. My sister helped me. She's a nurse. Nurses know about medications and drugs. They know how to inflict pain too."

Having seen the state of Trimble on my first visit to Nightingales, I don't need a degree to work out how Sherlock took control of the businesses and Trimble's other properties.

"If you drugged him, why did you kill him?" I ask.

"We didn't realise he wasn't taking some of his medication. We thought he was a tough old sod, vowing he would die before he revealed his secret. Then you showed up with your dog. It didn't take me long to work out he'd passed information to you about his notebooks."

"What notebooks?"

Sherlock raises the timber above his head, turns and smashes it down, severing the metal door from the remaining hinge. The door clatters to the floor, ringing like a tin tray.

"Don't play cute, Fisher. I'll find the notebooks, whether you tell me or not."

He takes a step towards me, turning the timber to reveal a protruding nail that will easily puncture my skull. "I want the notebooks you recovered from the chimney breast," he said, oblivious to the rain streaming down his face.

"You didn't have to kill Louise," I say, feeling along the ground for a flint or half brick.

"Pretty young thing," he says, feigning regret. "All she had to do was give me the answer to the puzzle, but she refused."

"And you pushed her over the cliffs."

"Don't make the same mistake, Fisher."

My fingers close over a smooth flint, about the size of a potato. "You're going to kill me whatever I do or don't do."

He runs his thumb over the nail. "The first blow won't kill you. It'll puncture your skull, I imagine. And hurt. By the third or fourth blow, you'll be begging me to stop. Now drop whatever you've got in your hand."

The timber swings towards me. My arm shoots up to block the blow, but he stops a few inches short. "Drop it!"

I let the flint go, wishing my heart rate would fall too. It's pounding harder than the throb in my head. If I'm going to escape or overpower him, I need to get out of the house.

"Okay, you've convinced me. The notebooks are in my car. The keys are in my fleece. Help yourself."

"And leave you here on your own?" He shakes his head at me like I'm a naughty schoolboy. "Do I look stupid?"

"Can I get back to you on that?"

He raises the timber, keen to inflict more pain. "You're coming with me, Fisher. You have a date with destiny on Beachy Head."

"I throw myself off at the same spot as Louise because I can't live without her? No one's going to believe that."

"You won't be around to find out."

I retrieve my car keys from the fleece and struggle to my feet. While the nausea's gone, I feel lightheaded and unsteady. Tiredness too has crept up on me, making my muscles feel heavy.

"We'll have plenty of witnesses," I say.

He pulls on his hood. "In this weather? We'll have the cliffs to ourselves."

I take a deep breath and start walking, taking my time, hand resting against the wall to steady me. The pain eases as I move. Maybe it's adrenaline, numbing the pain like morphine. Not that I've ever taken morphine or any other drugs. Slowly, I edge my way to the front door, making my breathing as laboured as possible.

"Leave your hood down," Sherlock says when I step outside.

The rain stings my face like tiny needles. He prods me in the back every few strides as I stay close to the garden wall, which offers some protection from the wind. I look about as much as my limited head movement will allow, but my only hope rests with Gemma and the police. With the wind roaring past my ears, I can hardly hear myself think, let alone listen for sirens.

As we round the corner and the gate comes in sight, I stop for a breather.

"Come on," Sherlock says, prodding me again.

I shake my head and turn, pleased when he retreats a couple of steps.

"What's in the notebooks?" I ask. "Come on, you might as well tell me."

"You know how my mother, Kim Jaggers, procured helpless and abandoned children for the orphanage."

"Procured?" A sick feeling fills my stomach. "No, I didn't know that."

His grip tightens on the timber. "As a social worker, she selected the ones no one would miss or want to foster. She brought them to St Cloud's where they were abused and subdued. No one knew because she produced glowing reports for the place."

His head drops and I catch a glimpse of the pain in his eyes. "You've no idea what it was like, waiting in the dark, hearing the footsteps."

"He abused you? *Your own father?*"

"That's why I had to escape. I faked my death. You might have noticed my grave at the church."

"You're Martin Bell?"

"I was, but I left him behind when I escaped. Now get moving."

"So, who's in the grave?"

"No one."

"No one?"

"My body was washed out to sea after I leapt from the cliffs."

That explains why he likes to throw people off Beachy Head. "You were eleven," I say, recalling the inscription on the grave. "Someone must have helped you."

"Move," he says, raising the timber. "And shut up."

I bend my head into the wind, which gusts harder as we approach the gate. Almost blinded by the ferocity of the rain, I get my arm tangled in brambles, ripping my jacket. Raising my hand to shield my eyes, I can just make out another car beyond mine.

Gemma must have spotted it, so where are the police?

Despite the pain and nausea, and a wobble when I land, I make it over the gate. Had I felt less tired, I might have made a run for it, but I still hold hopes of overcoming Sherlock.

"Who helped you escape?" I ask as he reaches the top of the gate.

"Anastasia. She patched us up – the other children too.

She couldn't speak out or they would have killed her like the others that tried."

"Others?"

"Illegal immigrants. No one knew they were there or who they were. No one missed them." He drops to the ground and pushes me back to the car. "I begged Anastasia to come with me, but she had to stay behind to make sure I was certified dead and buried."

"What happened to her?"

"My father and mother raped her," Sherlock replies as if it was a common occurrence. "When she became pregnant, she escaped, fearing they would kill her and her baby. She had a daughter."

"Marina Rudolf?"

"Are the notebooks in there?" he asks, gesturing to the hatch.

I hold out the keys. "Help yourself."

He shakes his head. "You open it, Fisher. Nice and slow."

"What are you going to do with them?" I ask, raising the hatch.

"Read them," he replies. "I want to find out who else was involved."

"In the abuse?"

"You don't think they procured children purely for their own pleasure, do you? They supplied them to customers. Wealthy people. Prominent people. People who will pay me handsomely to protect their secrets."

People like my father, Trimble said. Dread floods through me as I think of the scandal and how it will hurt Niamh. Whatever his faults, she loved William Fisher.

"No! You have to give the notebooks to the police."

He shakes his head. "My mother and father have paid for their sins."

"That's revenge, not justice."

He snorts. "Justice? They showed no remorse, why should I?"

"What about justice for the children, for Anastasia?"

"She died, knowing her daughter would avenge her."

"Your sister, Marina. Is this what she wants?"

He raises the timber, ready to strike me. "Notebooks, Fisher!"

I lean inside, relieved to have some shelter from the storm, relieved he didn't call my bluff and look in the boot himself. I slide the sleeve of my running jacket over the handle of the lump hammer and close my fingers around the head, cradling it in the palm of my hand.

I pull out the small plastic container where I keep my car manual, spare bulbs, a spare water bowl for Columbo and an electric pump for inflating my tyres. I'm not sure why I remember what's inside the container, but it seems to help me focus. I'm about to pick it up and pass it to him when I spot Gemma, emerging from behind the spotted laurel, a wheel brace in her raised hand.

I don't know if Sherlock reads my surprise, or if he senses her presence, but he spins to face her, deflecting the brace with the timber. The brace flies out of her hand and falls to the ground, skidding into the brambles.

She flings her arms in front of her face as he raises the timber to strike her.

I slam the lump hammer into the side of his head. He staggers and stumbles, arms flailing as he crashes into the gate. He stares at me for a moment and then crumples, his head smashing into one of the metal rails as he drops. His arm flicks out as he comes to rest, dropping the timber.

I drop the hammer in the boot and grab hold of the hatch to steady myself. I can barely stand, let alone hug Gemma as she folds me in her arms. She pushes her hood back and kisses me, unaware that she's squeezing the life out of me.

When she finally lets me breathe again, I smile. "Tell me you took the notebooks."

"I came straight here from the sanctuary."

"If Sherlock hadn't waited for me, you …"

My voice falters as Marina Rudolf steps out from behind the bush, aiming a gun at Gemma's head. I pull her back and to my side, so I can step in front of her.

Miss Rudolf stares at me with cold, emotionless eyes. Her hair, tight against her head, seems to resist the rain like Teflon. She affords Sherlock a brief, almost contemptuous glance, as she gestures us to back away.

I stand my ground. "Stay behind me, Gemma."

"Get back," Miss Rudolf says, raising the gun. "I will take the notebooks."

Gemma pulls me back a couple of paces. My breathing's heavy, my eyes struggling to keep Miss Rudolf in focus. She stretches out a hand to grasp the plastic container in the boot.

"They're not in there," Gemma says, stepping out to my side.

I sway as she brushes against me and grab the raised hatch for support.

I can't pass out now. Not yet.

"I gave them to the police," Gemma says. "You're finished."

Miss Rudolf puts a hand to her ear. "I can't hear the police. I can't see them either. Now get back before I shoot you!"

I tug Gemma back, wishing I could reach my lump hammer.

Miss Rudolf lifts the container from the boot, watching me all the time. She continues to watch as she shakes the container. "What else is in here?"

"Car manuals, a pump," I reply. "I'll show you if you don't believe me."

She tosses the container to the ground. It bounces and hits Sherlock's leg. She aims the gun at Gemma. "Where are the notebooks?"

Sherlock stirs and groans. "Marina? Is that you?"

Miss Rudolf swings around and fires twice.

Gemma's scream pierces my ears.

Sherlock convulses as the bullets rip into his chest.

I heave the hatch down with all the strength I can muster. It strikes Miss Rudolf on the back, just below the head. She cries out and staggers, somehow managing to keep her balance. As she raises the gun, I crash into her, wrapping my arms around her in a bear hug. I feel the gun, wedged against my sternum.

She bites my neck.

My momentum pushes her back. Then she's falling. I'm falling.

I let go of her moments before she crashes to the ground. Air bursts from her lungs as I land on top of her. My outstretched hands hit the concrete. Pain shoots up my arms.

But it's nothing compared to the pain in my chest.

Fifty-One

In the Garden of Remembrance at Eastbourne crematorium, my wreath lies at the end of the floral tributes. I spent a few days in hospital with several cracked ribs, bruised hands, sprained thumbs and wrists, and an inflamed and swollen neck, complete with a love bite from Miss Rudolf.

The gun didn't go off, but it made an impression on my chest that's visible ten days on.

I take a final look at the flowers for Louise, hoping the arrest of Marina Rudolf will make amends for my failures. Though not as often, I still wake at night, chilled by the thought of Louise, standing on the edge of the cliff, knowing she's about to die.

I struggled for days to compose a message that summed up my feelings for her.

I only knew you briefly, but you left a lasting impression.
So lasting, I slept with Gemma the day after you died.

I wasn't going to attend, but George insisted. He said I made his mother happy.

He didn't cry during the service, attended by only a handful of people. No one from Nightingales showed, though the home sent a wreath. Tracey stayed away. Miss Rudolf confirmed she was giving Kieran Sherlock information about my investigation, gleaned from Louise.

Gemma and Richard are also here. He seems reluctant to leave her side after she nearly lost her life again.

Keen to let George mourn in private, I walk up the steps at the side of the crematorium and find a bench, overlooking the peaceful gardens. The morning dew has evaporated from the crisp lawns that surround dormant rose beds. A few sparrows squabble in the trees, looking for food, unimpressed by the show of berries from the holly bushes. Beneath bare trees, the crocus and snowbells stretch up to grab as much light as they can, knowing the buds bursting from the branches will soon become leaves.

Gemma, looking elegant in a black trouser suit, sits beside me on the bench. Short hair suits her, making her look more like the young Carrie Fisher I once lusted after. Richard doesn't approve, but it's another change, another shift in dynamics. Gemma and I haven't spoken about our morning together and I'm not sure if we will.

Some things are best left unsaid.

Richard walks up, fiddling with his black tie, looking restless and lost.

"How are you feeling?" Gemma asks, lifting my arm to examine my strapped wrist.

"I'll live. You?"

"I came out unscathed for a change – apart from a fingernail."

"I'd hardly say that," Richard says. He falls silent as she looks at him and turns away.

"Richard seems unsettled," I whisper in her ear.

"He wants to move away."

"From me, you mean."

"His uncle has a practice in the Cotswolds. He's looking for a junior partner, someone to take over in time. Chipping Campden's beautiful with its honey-coloured cottages and old buildings. You'd love it there, Kent."

"You won't prize me from the South Downs," I say.

She looks into my eyes. "How would you feel if I left?"

George walks up with Frances, saving me from another lie. He's grown up overnight, looking sombre in a black suit. Though his hair's slicked back, his face and spots mark him out as a boy. Only his eyes say different.

"Do you miss my mother?" he asks.

"We all miss her, George. She loved you so much."

Tears fill his eyes and he returns to his foster parents, his shoulders bent by the troubles and uncertainty that await him.

He deserved so much more from life.

"I'm accepting David Church's offer," I tell Richard as we walk back to the car park.

He shakes his head. "The man's an opportunist. We can defeat him in court."

"The Colonel reneged on his promise to Church. People should honour their promises."

Richard looks ready to argue, but sighs, realising how determined I am. "At least let me negotiate a lower settlement."

After a moment's thought, I nod. "As quick as you can."

"That reminds me," he says. "Why did Kieran Sherlock

wait so long to kill his parents? Why didn't he do it years ago?"

"I don't think he intended to kill them." DI Briggs steps out from behind a gleaming BMW, parked against the kerb. He looks almost human in jeans and a fleece. "Sherlock wanted his father to suffer for as long as possible. Marina Rudolf's given a full account, including the torture and punishment they inflicted.

"You might also like to know that she's implicated Dr Puncheon," he says. "He helped with the medication and death certificates. He also failed to inform Kim Jaggers she had cancer. She found out when she saw another doctor when Puncheon was on leave. By then it was too late."

Richard looks horrified. "How can people do that?"

"It's nothing compared to the pain Jaggers and Trimble inflicted on those poor children." Briggs takes a deep breath before continuing. "We've recovered the remains of three adults and two children from the cesspit at Collins Farm. I doubt if we'll ever identify them, unlike the people in Trimble's notebooks."

"Who are you talking about?" Richard asks.

I'd like to tell him how the children were groomed to work in all areas of the sex trade, mainly in London and Brighton. I'd like to reveal the names of some of the prominent people Gemma discovered when she read the notebooks, but we can't jeopardise future prosecutions.

I'm simply thankful William Fisher's name didn't appear on any lists.

"Ongoing investigation," Briggs says. He turns to Gemma and me. "Thank you for your help. I also wanted to apologise for giving you a hard time over Miss Watson's death, Kent. I'm sorry for any grief I caused."

"You were doing your job."

"No, I wanted to knock you down a few pegs. You solved cases I dismissed because I was too lazy and too cynical. Well, I've cleared my desk now and I wanted to return these." He reaches into his pocket and pulls out the notes from my windscreen. "You won't be receiving any more now Marina Rudolf's in custody."

I pocket the notes. "When you say you've cleared your desk …"

"I've retired. We're having a few drinks tonight to celebrate my long and chequered career. You're welcome to join us. My replacement, Ash Goodman, can't wait to meet you."

He returns to his car, running his hand along the bonnet. Then he raises a hand like Lieutenant Columbo and strolls back. "I found out why Trimble and Jaggers called the kid, Walter. Ever heard of Walter Mitty?"

"Who's he?" Gemma asks.

"He's a fictional character," Richard replies. "He's an average man with a vivid fantasy life. I think he imagined he was an assassin in one of his fantasies. Ironic, what?"

"Prophetic," Briggs says. "I know how you hate loose ends, Kent."

"Talking of loose ends, why haven't you opened the envelope?" Gemma asks, plucking it from my jacket pocket. "Don't you want to know if Birchill's your father?"

"The result makes no difference to my plans."

"But you must want to know."

I laugh. "You mean you want to know."

"I'm sure he'll tell us in good time," Richard says, guiding her away.

Frances and I walk on to my Ford Fusion, parked near

the entrance. "I'm glad it's all over," she says.

"Me too," I say, opening the passenger door for her. I spot a folded note under the wiper blade and sigh. "Trust Briggs to have a joke at my expense," I say, as he drives past, tooting his horn.

But it's no joke.

Old sins cast long shadows, Mr Fisher.

THE END.

About the author

Robert Crouch spent almost 40 years working in environmental health, mainly as an inspector, checking hygiene and health and safety standards, but latterly as the manager of a team of officers.

While he enjoyed modest success writing articles and columns for national and trade magazines during the 1990s, it wasn't until he turned to writing crime that he found his true niche. He now writes full time from his home on the South Coast of England, drawing inspiration from the beautiful South Downs and his former job.

If you enjoyed *No Remorse*, please consider leaving a review at Amazon UK and Amazon US.

If you would like to learn more about Kent Fisher and the mystery novels, or keep up to date with new releases from Robert Crouch, please visit http://robertcrouch.co.uk, where you can also sign up to his email newsletter.

Other books by Robert Crouch

No Accident – the first Kent Fisher mystery
No Bodies – the second Kent Fisher mystery
Fisher's Fables – the perfect companion to the Kent Fisher mysteries

Author's note

Most people are unaware of the work environmental health officers (EHOs) carry out on a day-to-day basis.

With each Kent Fisher Mystery novel, I hope to explore different areas of environmental health to reveal the depth and breadth of the important work carried out to protect public health.

I should also tell you that the setting, Downland District Council and the events in my novels are fictional. Tollingdon exists only in my imagination, as do many of the pubs, hotels and food businesses. And as the saying goes, all characters appearing in this book are fictitious. Any resemblance to real persons, living or dead, is purely coincidental.

Kent Fisher will return in *No Smoke*.

Printed in Poland
by Amazon Fulfillment
Poland Sp. z o.o., Wrocław